Also by Thomas Gondolfi through TANSTAAFL Press:

An Eighty Percent Solution

In a world where corporations suborn governments as a part of good business practice and unregistered humans can be killed without penalty, Tony Sammis, a midlevel corporate functionary, finds himself unwittingly a pawn in a guerilla war between a powerful cabal of business leaders and an elusive but deadly underground movement. His final solution to the biological terror unleashed mirrors Tony's own twisted sense of justice.

To my mother — for teaching me empathy and the joy of books

*To my father — for introducing me to science fiction
at a tender age and being my best critic*

Toy Wars

Thomas Gondolfi

TANSTAAFL PRESS

TANSTAAFL Press
1201 E. Yelm Ave,
Suite 400-199
Yelm, WA 98697

Visit us at www.TANSTAAFLPress.com

Toy Wars

First printing—TANSTAAFL Press
Copyright © 2012 by Thomas Gondolfi
Cover art: Tony Foti, www.tonyfotiart.com
Cover design: Amanda Forker, www.ilioness.com
Interior design and layout: Marian Hartsough Associates

Printed in the USA
ISBN 978-1-938124-05-1

Introduction

Excerpts from the Third Chronicler's Notes:

One of the significant landmarks of the early days of the Sol Unified System's expansion into the depths of space, sometime in the human calendar's twenty-second century, was an amusing event: the first creation of a truly new life form. While new life is not a humorous occurrence, the process that created this life was more like the punch line to a joke.

Homo sapiens were making use of faster than light (FTL) vehicles and their civilization expanded at a tremendous rate compared to earlier efforts. Some twenty years after his invention of the FTL drive, Fanta Hisu surpassed his own accomplishments by creating a drive that was over an order of magnitude faster (FT^2L). There was only one snag in the new design—organic materials were destroyed in such a transit. Hisu dropped his project as the FT^2L drive was not directly useful for the humans.

The FT^2L drive seemed destined to be lost in the invention files with such notables as the air-conditioned hat and the automatic phone cleaner. Instead, an ambitious engineer accidentally intercepted the idea. Golan Powers, looking for a quick way to glory, happened upon Hisu's scientific notes for the FT^2L drive. It sparked the seed of another idea within him. If organic material could not be sent, then perhaps inorganic could. So voracious was the human need for raw materials on earth (and so desirous of fame and wealth was Golan himself) that he devised a plan to solve both problems at once.

A semi-intelligent Factory would be sent via an FT^{2}L ship to extremely far worlds, where it would autonomously produce robots to control and strip the planet's surface of its mineral wealth, and then transport it back in the original vessel. Golan paid terrific bribes to get his proposal, specifications, budgets, schedules, and potential returns placed before the Supreme Council in general session. All told, this gained the euphemistic name "Project Infuse." Infuse caused an uproar that had never been equaled. Never in the one hundred fifty years of this government had there been such a race to get on the bandwagon of an issue—pro or con. A new political split formed in the guise of the Expansionists vs. the Naturalists. The Expansionists, the greed faction of human nature, outnumbered the Naturalists by nearly two to one.

The Naturalists objected that this plan might inadvertently send one of these strip miners to an inhabited world, causing death and destruction and sending a horrific message about our species. The Expansionists yelled the objection down in the Council. The only way to do the retort justice is to quote Supreme Councilor Torin of Mars: "Any truly sentient and intelligent race would be able to handle such an incursion. We will add a message to the memories and physical plating of each Factory telling anyone of this decision and hope they would be our friends with no hard feelings. And if they can't defeat the Factory, we won't have to worry about them, now will we?"

Some of the more liberal papers called it the old might-makes-right political theory. Might-makes-right was so intrinsic to the Expansionist doctrine that they took such editorials as compliments. Sheer numbers put down the objections of the Naturalists but did not silence them completely.

The Naturalists continued to work around the clock, spending billions of credits of their own money to stop Project Infuse. They used court cases, injunctions, financial audits, sit-down strikes, and at the end even chained themselves to heavy equipment. They eventually failed.

Seventeen years later, the last court case ruled in favor of the Expansionists. Project Infuse, now known as "PI," was to be put into test production.

PI outfitted three hundred obsolete FTL space vessels with the FT^{2}L drive and partnered with something known only as "The Factory." The resulting conglomerate was the first grouping of Project Infuse's vessels. Physically, each Factory, a dome-shaped cap fit to the peak of each FT^{2}L ship, lacked an impressive appearance. It was what they could do that made them remarkable.

Factories possessed the construction facilities and mental power to create a workforce of robot slaves. A huge array of programmers gifted the PI Factories with semi-sentience. The only real goals these programmers gave the Factories boiled down to "conquer, rape, and pillage."

With this less than moral context guiding them, the Factory-cum-FT²L vessels were then flung to the exceedingly far reaches of space to strip-mine entire planets.

For ten years everyone waited and conveniently forgot Project Infuse. Friendships and alliances broken by the debates and oratory mended. In the eleventh year, when the first vessel returned with a huge cargo string following it, the peace broke again. The materials it returned were unmatched in quality and quantity to almost anything in our solar system. The drones contained new metals never before seen and a massive quantity of fissionables. Two more drone strings returned within that year bearing similar treasures. Because of its huge success, PI lost any previous negative press. The Naturalists were defeated. The Supreme Council ordered PI into full-scale production.

The above are facts which are incontrovertible. This was information placed into the memories and even on physically etched data plates mounted on the Factories themselves. The remainder of this discussion is reasoned speculation based on analysis of a great number of corrupted files within the Factories' memories. They contain a surprising amount of information on the events that preceded the launch of Factories 55466, 55467, 55468, 55469, 55471, and 55474. It also contains the punch line to our joke.

A preadolescent computer hacker, Janeen Fox (AKA Foxhunt), wanted more than anything to join the local Virtual Reality HAC club. Though the VRHAC had no interest in PI, other than as a challenge, the group set Janeen the initiation rite of breaking into PI's vaunted and supposedly impervious databases. Foxhunt took diligently to her task with an outdated Cray N+1. For six full days during spring break, Foxhunt took to working at backdoors, frontal assaults, viral nets, and every other method she could dream up. Nothing seemed to let her in from the outside, so she decided she had to have someone open the door from the inside. Janeen coded an appropriately invisible Trojan Horse virus.

The virus went in snail-mail in the form of a "demo" cube for the latest VR retro-thriller Perry Mason Returns (which VRHAC had broken the copy protection on in less than fifteen minutes after its release) to dozens of PI employees. Janeen was banking on human nature and their inability to pass up something that was both free and would take them away from the now tedious work they were doing. It worked. The virus, installed inside the system, created a backdoor for her to worm into.

Janeen's intent contained no malevolence. Breaking the imperviousness of PI was her goal, not its contents. She caused no intentional damage and did nothing save adding her nom d'hac, Foxhunt, to several files. Her full access lasted less than ten minutes before the belated system defenses rushed to close down the unauthorized access.

Project Infuse's ice crashed about her open portal with such violence and severity that Janeen broke the connection without standard withdrawal procedures. No newbie to hacking, she had long ago learned to hide the tracks of her work by bouncing through several other computer links. In this case her last link was through an old-fashioned toy and book store. Because of the abrupt termination of the link, several large files were transitioned into the PI database, scrambling a number of crucial launch and post-launch parameters. These parameters remained until a standard morning CRC check caught the errors on the following day, too late to save the ill-fated PI vessels prepared for launch that day.

The following are more facts, based on actual data from the Factories' memory cores. PI was now launching upward of a dozen FT^2L space vessels each day. On the date of Janeen's fateful link, only six Factory/vessels were planned for launch. Each of them was downloaded with the faulty parameter files. The files contained two very important changes. The first was that the blueprints of the toy store's wares replaced the typical robot plans. Secondly, and perhaps more importantly, all the ships were dispatched to the same planet, the third planet of HD34085, also known as Beta Orionis, or simply Rigel, something that had never happened in the history of the PI program. Now a singular PI Factory would no longer scour the planet of insignificant life forms, it would fight its own kind—a condition that not one of the PI programmers had anticipated.

Factories 55466, 55467, 55468, 55469, 55471, and 55474 were launched on schedule (55470, 55472, and 55473 had been scrubbed the previous day by mechanical difficulties). The humans heard nothing of any of these six PI vessels again. They were written off as a loss.

Factory 55468 lost its way in FT²L and exited near enough a black hole that it could only manage an unstable orbit that eventually decayed with the predictable results. The remaining five each set down so close to T+3y340d12h16m46s (three years, three hundred forty days, twelve hours, sixteen minutes and forty-six seconds post-launch) as to be unnoteworthy. Each landed uneventfully on Rigel-3, but it was the beginning of the most ferocious competition known to nearly any world.

Rigel-3 was a hellish world, or would be to any humans—too cold by at least two dozen degrees Celsius, a corrosive atmosphere, and a gravity 30 percent higher than that of earth. Through its rivers flowed liquid mercury down to the gleaming metallic lakes and seas. On the plus side, Rigel-3 proved itself to be rich in heavy minerals of all kinds, gemstones, and huge amounts of oil and other petroleum products. As the physical conditions were no hardship to the Factories, it was an ideal habitat to collect for the humans. None of the five took long to take hold in their new home, each oblivious of the other almost identically timed landings.

The Factories immediately discovered their first problem—the plans to their robots were destroyed or partially destroyed. In place of the corrupted files lived the production files of toys. Not that they knew what a toy was, but they were not the standard mining or control type robots. These new forms also proved to be totally unsuitable to the environment. Most of the new forms didn't even have motile functions. The Factories had to adapt, but being semi-sentient and well programmed for independent thought, this didn't pose, for most, an insurmountable problem.

The Factories took the portions of the robot data that had not been corrupted and merged them with the new intrusive toy data. As most of the toys were flexible in capability, it mostly worked.

Only 55471 failed to make the imaginative leap and continued producing only non-motile stuffed bunny rabbits until it ran out of raw materials, power, and then a will to continue. It self-destructed its memory core.

All the other Factories were already producing robots. But here divergence set in. Each Factory took a different solution to its individual problems. The solutions were varied and adapted to the terrain and ease of material availability. Each Factory began churning out the equipment it needed to be successful in its mission. Mining robots took the form of

Teddy Bears, gophers, toy bulldozers, toy dump trucks, and backhoes (still bearing the manufacturers' original labels or even the toy company's logo displayed prominently on their sides). The Factories created transport systems. Some made them in the form of a large-gauge toy railroad, but at least one had a fleet of remote-controlled racecars and trucks. For survey/scouting vehicles, most went the way of gasoline-powered toy planes or helicopters. Factory 55466 used multicolored balloons filled with helium carrying disposable payloads.

The real diversity, though, lay in the choice of control, or warrior units—small toy tanks with real explosive projectile weapons, slightly scaled up plastic infantry men carrying real weapons, kamikaze bomb-carrying dress-up dolls, Teddy Bears with machine guns, and even giraffe snipers.

It has to be stressed that these initial units were crude and possessed no initiative at all. If a unit lost contact with its Factory it would continue doing what it had been ordered to do until it lost that ability as well. At this stage of evolution the Factories were each one entity with multiple disposable bodies to control—similar to an ant colony.

Initially there was little need for the combat units, and very few were built, as there was little nearby local fauna to require such a force. This changed abruptly as the first warriors of the now four Factories began meeting each other and fighting for control of the planet. The first such clash began when 55466's tracked tanks met the baby-doll infantry of 55474 at L+320d14h (320 days, fourteen hours after landing). Both sides annihilated each other in an inconclusive battle. The other two Factories similarly clashed within days. Now each of the Factories knew the native life forms fought back quite successfully.

Each of the factories adapted. They changed priorities, rolling hundreds of tanks, Baby Doll infantrymen, scout planes, and other military weapons off their production lines. Guard units were posted on key transportation intersections and garrisons built to aid defense. Combat units were immediately allocated as hunter/killer squads. The Toy Wars had truly begun.

Low intensity skirmishes of squad size defined L+1y and L+2y as the numbers of units available to fight were small. As combat populations grew, so did the conflicts until hundreds and sometimes even thousands of units fought for a goal none of them could reach without destroying one another.

Factories began to notice that they would have many units destroyed just by losing contact. Several networks arose to deal with this unacceptable situation. The nets, all-purpose control system that carried power, instructions, and requests for information, grew rapidly along transportation lanes. The multiple nets were segregated into two forms, the WAN, or wide area net, and the LAN, or local area net.

Each Factory generated a WAN on a very powerful carrier wave. The WAN flowed through immobile devices called net concentrators (NCs) that rebroadcast information or commands to far units. The WAN also acted as the primary source of power for almost all units.

Local control units similar to the NCs generated the LAN that gave specific commands to each of the robots. These LANs dealt mainly with local issues, such as quickly identifying friend and foe. The LAN didn't bother or interfere with the WAN in any way.

These networks helped but continued to be insufficient. Even in the early days of small-scale combat, Darwinian selection set in. The Factories experimented with different designs based on the toys and robots they still had. Each make and model underwent often destructive field experience, sometimes within mere hours of activation being thrown into a nearby combat. Using probability studies, each Factory learned quickly which of their units fared well in combat, in what terrain, and under which conditions. Those units that didn't make the cut in the field were firmly snubbed from production. Toy Wars shaped quickly into a battle of statistical mathematics rather than strictly the destruction of metal and machines.

Over ten years, the conflicts escalated. Each of the Factories, again backed by rigorous mathematics, determined that a larger initial military expenditure would bring the local fauna under control that much sooner and thus would save resources in the long run. The impeccable logic fell flat because the "local fauna" it fought didn't breed. Factories produced an ever-increasing panoply of war materials escalating the conflict to greater heights. Competition became even more intensely fierce.

Each of the Factories tried special permutations to bring better units to the battlegrounds—built-in cannons, flame throwers, kamikaze scout planes with explosive payloads (the first crude missile on Rigel-3), and even mobile walking bombs in the shape of dress-up dolls. A number of them worked well, but most failed miserably. A classic example of a failed design came from 55467. A flame-thrower was built around the outward form of a purple stuffed elephant. This was just a modification of having a large caliber weapon in the chest of the otherwise fluffy war machine. The fur ignited before the unit even got off the prototyping line. It took most of 55467's fire suppression units to quell the stuffed elephant's exploding fuel cells.

Of all the Factories that still remained, 55466 (known as Six) had the most difficulty. Its initial location was not as rich in minerals and resources, nor as easily defensible as the other three viable Factories. Six was slowly losing ground to the local fauna, and its calculations showed that in less than two years' time its outer defenses would crumble. The local fauna would run rampant, denying it control of the planet. It would have failed its primary mission.

Six made a huge gamble to put a larger quantity of material and effort into researching better robots. Soon Six began fielding units with semi-autonomous functionality. Even if it lost control, they could make decisions that would allow them to continue to function. Thus was born the third net, the SAN, or specific area network.

The SAN was developed by the autonomous robots as a net that allowed units to converse directly to one another. This happened as sentience and self-directing capabilities grew in each robot. They began to work as a team.

Six certainly could measure the success of these units. Within five months, Six's boundaries firmed and started expanding. The other three Factories learned how effective these autonomous fauna were and began shaping their productions to do similar things.

Shortly, Six found its boundaries tightening again. It was time for another desperate chance. It used some of the local unclassified metals to produce an all-purpose control robot, with the highest level of self-direction it could construct and filled with the most information it would accept.

The chain of events that started with Janeen Fox and the Expansionist coalition had now come to fruition—but in a way neither had ever expected. True sentience and intelligence had been achieved.

Let there be life; and it was fuzzy.

Juvenile

After my uneventful manufacturing process, I woke up. Where was I before that sleep? I didn't remember deactivating my cognitive process. My memory sump revealed no memories that predated that moment. Life must begin and end somewhere, just as a line must have two points that define its position in the universe. My line started when I awoke.

My memories show only a notation of my origin. "Activation occurs, L+13y224d1h0s. Internal clock set to M+0. Awaiting command from Factory 55466."

"Stand by for shape and color recognition patterns," came the intense voice of the Factory itself, both auditory and over the net. The voice vibrated deeply from the very walls of the 3-meter-high chamber as the voice over the electronic network mimicked it in tone and timbre. A large video display in front of me carried the image of my body being laser-scanned from the top of my big saucer-shaped ears down to the bottom of my broad, flat feet.

"Basic unit makeup includes a height of 2.1 meters, a mass of 136 kilograms, and a base color of purple," Factory Six said. "Pattern recognition marking includes belly color of white, and fur mottling of blue diagonally over left foot. Unit make is prototype S12 with serial number 1 of series Teddy Bear," announced my benefactor and creator. "Assault weapon M16A and .45 caliber long slide pistol are standard issue with eight clips of ammunition for each weapon. Additionally, S12-1 to be equipped with one plastic expandable canteen, two sticks black and green paintsticks, combat knife, and gun cleaning kit." A tightly woven olive green backpack came out of the nearby wall and was placed over my shoulders, and an assault rifle was thrust into my hands. Another mechanical arm came and thrust a chromed automatic pistol into a holster belt around my waist.

My right hand automatically snapped the holster closed. "Basic load accepted," I said, opening my mouth for the first time. I must have sat there for some time examining myself, twisting my thick arms and flexing my fingers. I jumped to the floor, my legs out at a natural and comfortable wide angle. All so new, yet so known and understood.

"You are Teddy 1499," the Factory decreed in a booming voice that again shook the room. I was awestruck by its power.

"I am Teddy 1499." It felt peculiar to be moving, talking, and thinking. At the time I couldn't even describe it adequately, even to myself. It was as if I knew how to do everything because of some distant dream. All my experiences and memories flowed across my mind as still photos in grays and umbers when suddenly, by performing an action, it was full of color and life, and no longer shrouded in opacity.

I knew Six would give me more information as I didn't yet have a purpose. I felt hollow, like I wasn't—like I didn't quite exist. I looked around for something to fill that hollow.

Machinery, tools, and dozens of mechanical arms all worked on different projects making the construction space appear much smaller than its true cavern-like dimensions. Two of my fellow units lay on the table with their legs off at the hip joint. My sump and processor provided the descriptive *Teddy Bear*. From the images I observed during my manufacture I was a Teddy Bear. Each of us had two thick, cylindrical arms that stuck almost straight out to our sides sporting manipulative hands with five short, stubby fingers. Large circular ears stuck well above the height of the head. Each wore a dark black nose on a snout that held an almost comical grin underneath.

One of my fellows sported vivid orange fur with blue spots and the other was pure green. Several robotic arms reached in, attempting to connect a pair of tank-like tracks to the green bear's torso in lieu of its discarded legs, 4 meters away. To my relief, the green unit was deactivated during the maiming procedure.

All that time I remember hoping the Humans would give me a worthy mission. I was so inexperienced back then. I still believed in the Humans: creators of The Factory and the master programming.

"Sector Alpha-4 compromised. Your mission is to take command of units in Sector Alpha-4 and stabilize the situation," Six said over the network, emphasizing with the same verbal commands. "Pursue and destroy any local fauna. Ensure a strong defense line." Epiphany! My simple task would prove my ultimate worth to Factory 55466.

Alpha-4 maps sprung to my mind like a memory of a memory. "I will be victorious," I said confidently to Six. My sump held databases of tactical and strategic information dealing with commanding forces, deployment of resources, acceptable loss ratios, and decisions of great Human commanders (Alexander the Great, Hitler, Napoleon, Stalin, Kin Su, Admiral Hornblower, and more) in victories and defeat. I would fulfill my mission in their image, for Six's pleasure and the glory of the Humans.

"Complete your mission, Teddy 1499."

"Affirmative," I replied as I marched proudly out of the Factory dome to the train station outside.

My first look around didn't surprise me as my long-term memories of more of the gray picture filled in with pigment and motion. Dominating the view, a 10.2-meter crimson weeping-fly tree swayed heavily in a stiff breeze only 43 meters from the main audience chamber of the Factory. A 12-centimeter-gauge train, painted black and bearing "PACIFIC NORTHWESTERN" in yellow across both sides, waited for a crowding throng of units to board.

Furious activity flowed all around me. A squad of elephants, 150 centimeters tall and sporting brilliant multicolored fur, marched past in perfect time, shaking the ground with every footfall. Three Tami dress-up dolls, their 20-centimeter-bodies nothing more than molded plastic explosives, walked by with exaggerated caution. Eight tiny Tommy Tanks, in standard gunmetal gray, rolled past my feet. An 8-meter-long python slithered directly behind me past the station and joined up with two drab brown gophers. The trio meandered off into the foothills toward the mines. Two roadrunner birds, with their big saucer-like eyes, raced past on unfathomable errands. I caught a glimpse of three bright-green balloon units launching into the sky. I gawked at the chaos around me.

The countryside seemed equally busy. Brilliant red light from the sun bathed the landscape, washing out nearly any other color that dared to rear its head—my own purple got scrubbed to an almost burnt cinnamon. The entire area looked as if someone had upended a can of wet crimson paint over everything. Even those plants that attempted to make use of chlorophyll wore a scarlet cloak. Brick-red, rose, carmine, maroon, and ruby were just some of the pleasing variations on the shades. This was home.

Six's units scurried all over the mountainous valley on missions instilled into them by Six and decreed by our creators, the Humans. A solitary dump truck, a mere 40 centimeters high, carried an unidentifiable cargo toward the smelting plant. A trio of plastic-bodied spiders scuttled off toward the eastern horizon. The activities spilled all over the lowland in a frantic, almost artistic display of randomness.

Dozens of kilometers to the north, three mountain peaks so nearly matched the shape of the Factory's triple redundant net controller (NC) towers that it made me wonder about the Humans and what they knew about that marvelous place. The bright silver of the Central River rushed by, only occasionally sending off a spray of liquid metal in its haste to be over a particularly large rock. Mercury globules landed on the ground nearby, coalescing to roll back into the river as if the components had never been parted.

I spent some time looking at the creature that had given me birth. A huge mottled pink dome 200 meters across and 80 high sat among several ancillary buildings within a field of tall red and white hor clover. A rising helix of dense black and blue smoke distinguished the Factory's squat brown smelting plant. Six's power plant, a nuclear reactor, blocked the entire view to the west, with pipes and miscellaneous equipment sticking out, giving it the appearance of a toddler's Tinkertoy creation.

The net, an all-purpose power and communication system, glittered invisibly in colors that have no Human words. It covered the valley in a crowded crisscross pattern like matted fur from one tiny node to another with concentrated channels heading off in the direction where conflicts raged. Each NC transceiver wore a diffuse halo dancing around in changing colors as commands flew in and out. Those invisible but powerful lines of the net were our life force. Six ordered units to perform their tasks through the net. Without it, most units would simply stop doing what they had been ordered and would quickly run out of power. As my original design basis came from a scout unit, I could operate outside the intangible touch of these veins of our life's blood by making my own decisions and storing my own power.

A piercing whistle stole attention away from my attempts to fill in as much of my memory as possible. The first of three engine's eyes watched me closely and spat up steam in angry bursts. I was certain Six had programmed instructions not to leave until I embarked. I knew of the notorious impatience of trains from the database Six provided. It had to do with their mission to stay on a schedule, which they never really managed.

"Releasing your steam that way is not becoming. I will be there momentarily."

"Tooooooooooot!" screamed the second engine in protest. This engine wore the green BNSF logo over yellow.

"Be right there," I replied. I wouldn't see this place again for a long time. I wanted to take in as much as I could. After a 16.8-second memorization period, I sighed and gave in to the impulse to carry out my orders.

Before I moved even a meter closer, a deep claxon sounded aloud and over the net. For sixty-four milliseconds I actually believed Six used the racket to chastise me for tardiness.

"Fauna attack, bearing 5.3 degrees magnetic, 5.242 kilometers distant. Force composition includes three hundred flyers, seven hundred fifty infantry and two hundred four mounted units."

My head swiveled almost instinctively to the north. On the horizon hovered an indistinct cloud of blue. I trained my sight to maximum magnification on the cloud to pick out a mass of distinctive biplane shapes. The voltage on my main power bus spiked and I dropped flat to the ground for cover. Those couldn't belong to Six. His flyers resembled balloons or dirigibles.

"All noncombatants rendezvous at assembly point Delta," Six said, speaking firmly and without hesitation. "Heavy fire units array at assembly point Alpha orienting toward incoming fauna. Open fire at extreme range."

The train moved from between me and the enemy. My voltage that finally had fallen to operational range once again ramped up into levels requiring unacceptable levels of maintenance. I looked around for a spot of safety when I realized not one shot had been fired by either side. With reluctance I stood up and my servo voltages crept back down. Some leader I turned out to be. My first battle and I start it hiding face down in the dust.

"All infantry and light units array behind heavy units to provide supporting fire," Six dictated.

I strode over behind the solid ranks of plastic Tommy Tanks that arrayed themselves side by side behind a low solid wall of plastic blocks. The tanks' 50-centimeter-height gave me a good field of view. On the firing line on either side of the tanks, sitting on their haunches, some elephants held mortar rounds in their trunks, poised over the muzzle on their chests. The hollow thump of the first elephant to release its weapon caused me to duck down behind a tank's short but broad bulk.

With the mortar fire now rolling out consistently, I slowly stuck my head up to look out at the barrage's results. Vermillion dirt jetted away from impact sites in an inverted cone pattern. The explosions rarely found targets to vent upon. Small horses, 50 centimeters high, bore proportionally small Human-shaped riders with remarkable speed amongst the chaos. Our elephants walked their fire in closer to match the rapid charge of the fauna cavalry. I couldn't watch the entire field but one time I witnessed a blast that threw both rider and horse sideways 6 meters. The pair didn't move on the earth as a pool of their amber fluid grew around them, mingling in the red dirt.

"Adjust your fire for the mounted units to 21 kilometers per hour," Six offered.

Reducing my eye's magnification, the scale of the attack became clear. A mass of brightly colored infantry, each looking very much like me, marched toward us, a kilometer across. Their mounted cavalry spread out across an even wider front to avoid the ravages of our mortars but kept boring in.

The rate of mortar fire slowed. My bus potential ramped just a bit.

"Level four inquiry to Elephant Squad One concerning rate of fire," I placed on the net.

"Rate of fire reduced to maximum sustainable to prevent overheating."

Sensible, I thought, willing down my errant voltage.

I pulled back my vision to local mode. Six's entire force stretched in a doubled line to meet the advance of this enemy. The arrangement didn't seem optimal. Any fire our way was bound to hit some unit.

As the fauna's leading edge of speeding mounted Indians reached 1800 meters, the tanks opened up with their .50 caliber main guns. The sound threatened my aural receivers so I tuned down the amplification. Vivid blue tracer rounds marked each unit's lane of fire. It took no time at all to reap a path of destruction through the fauna as it all but advanced directly into our fire. I didn't sense any threat from this attack.

The ground jumped beneath my feet as an explosion on the right flank of our troops lit up even the daytime for an instant. An elephant, as massive and heavily armored as it was, lay torn literally in half by the blast, with tiny fires melting its green skin. Two more explosions, each one closer to me, went off in quick succession, one hitting empty ground and the other narrowly missing a Tommy Tank but setting it on fire.

A very loud chord of sirens announced the presence of six tiny fire engines, each pulling a hose behind it. They rolled up next to the burning unit, dousing it with streams of water.

A whistle penetrated my lowered hearing. This time I caught a glimpse of the straight downward plunge of a bomb just before two of the fire trucks evaporated in the detonation.

We forgot about the flyers! Worse, our units lined up perfectly for them to fly along, almost guaranteeing to hit something.

"Priority one—all odd numbered units retreat 6 meters," I ordered. "All units whose unit number is divisible by four with no remainder retreat 3 meters." Gratifyingly, the line divided per my order. The tank in front of me moved backward as well, forcing me to move with it. More bombs landed on empty space.

"All units orient antiaircraft batteries overhead bearing 85 degrees magnetic. Weapons free," Six added.

Thirty caliber machine guns roared to life all around me, licking fire up into the sky. Green tracers hurled up at the flyers. As they flew in parallel formation down our defensive line, they made easy targets. I even put my M16 up to my shoulder and fired away.

Our fire dropped six of the fragile planes inside our perimeter, one landing directly on top of a gopher. Unfortunately, the already dead animal still had its bomb attached. Only bits of smoldering fur and a couple of metal bones remained of our unit in the resulting crater.

The fauna broke up, scattering. They no longer made for free kills. Many still dropped their ordinance within our area but none got free kills. Many of the flyers fell, but many more lived to retreat, some scathed with battle damage and others completely untouched.

"All units reorient on ground attack," Six ordered.

I realized that I had been paying attention only to the air battle. I had lost track of what had happened on the ground. Not a single mounted unit remained moving, but now the massive contingent of infantry began shooting in our direction.

"All units redeploy against the wall," I yelled as some of our own fire came dangerously close to our own units. The command echoed across the net as teams dispersed it. Unintentionally, my order caused all the units that took second rank to find ways up to the wall, packing our numbers even tighter across the line.

I stayed behind and snapped shots at the encroaching infantry but the impact seemed negligible compared to the machine guns that played across the rows of infantry marching closer. The fauna fired back as they inched forward. Once I heard the whine of a bullet near my head but our own wall of fire drowned out all other sounds. Animal after animal of the teddy-like fauna dropped. The few times one managed to overcome its wounds and get up, it went over again in a matter of seconds.

The number of animals dwindled rapidly until a mortar round fell adjacent to the last upright fauna. The upper torso blew out its back. Against odds it remained standing for 2.3 seconds before toppling over backward.

"Ceasefire," came Six's command over the net. "Resume normal duty stations and missions."

Primary mission accomplished. Six was safe. Home was safe . . . for now.

Soldier

"Teddy 1499!" Six trumpeted over the net.

Every servo in my body twitched. Until then I just stood looking over the carnage. Spiders and Nurse Nans walked among the deactivated, tagging the fauna for reclamation.

"Yes."

"Resume your previous orders. This attack is the third within the last ninety hours. You must regenerate a garrison force to the north."

"Affirmative," I said, turning back toward the train. Tommy Tanks rolled up ramps onto the flat cars. I watched a spider straddle the train, lowering itself until its body touched and then wrapping its legs behind it. Gophers, Nurse Nans, elephants, and multicolored fair of many, many more units loaded themselves as part of the train's consists.

Strictly a military job, this train's contents included scores of flat cars holding a pair of tanks, a Nurse Nan, a Teddy Bear infantry, elephant "mobile" infantry, three rabbits bearing flame throwers, and on, and on. The train's lengthy presence disappeared around the curve of the Factory. From Six's comments the line needed this large shipment desperately. Literally hundreds of units crammed on a single mover. I briefly doubted the wisdom of Six, but he spoke the word of the Humans. I was only a unit.

As I myself embarked, I caught sight of the weeping-fly tree. Nearly a third of it lay severed on the ground like an ax had cleaved it vertically. A small fire crackled right at the base of the trunk. I thought I would miss this place even though I had only been there a few minutes.

"I shall return!" I said aloud, borrowing a quote from MacArthur. This was a place I would fight for, and a way of life I might be called upon to give my own life for.

I wiggled my ample rear quarters down into the barely 65-centimeter-wide well-car I'd been assigned, seven back from the three engines. My hips hung off at least 2 centimeters on either side. I hoped Factory Six accounted for this when it designed the track bed. I would not like to go through a tunnel and get wedged in. Not a comfortable thought.

A roadrunner, 26 centimeters high and wearing a conductor's cap, flashed by me toward the front of the train. I heard a quick "Beep! Beep!" and the train lurched as the three engines took the slack out of the couplings. I'll give the trains credit. While the start was a bit slow and jerky, they mounted the velocity quickly in a very short time with the countryside flickering by us. I'd have to guess they got us up to nearly 100 kilometers per hour. An impressive feat given the engines' diminutive size compared to their load.

The tracks kept pretty much to the same course as the Central River, but jumping from side to side like a psychotic fox hunted by English hounds. As some of the flora and fauna appeared and disappeared, I tried to catalog those I knew by my grafted memories—red square shapes of box trees; inorganic porcupine bushes with crystalline "leaves" which would pierce even my tough hide; the 10-meter-a-year speed demon known as the rock crab; and the ubiquitous finger spider, just to name a few of the newly filled-in memory locations in my sump.

A light silver rain of mercury fell across the countryside, raising gentle puffs of dust and initiating a general scramble of life forms for shelter. A moderate number of the drops fell on me and beaded off my coarse fur and down to the ground. An intricate vein-work of silver-colored metal lit up the ground as the raindrops merged together to form tiny rivulets and then in turn attempted to join the main fluid-way's current. Even after the short shower's end, the tiny streams remained, taking the last few drops to the now swollen river, leaving only isolated shimmering puddles.

After all too short a time the bright flashes of standing mercury weren't even enough to keep my interest. The scenery blurred into sameness—rocks, sparse vegetation, and the occupants of the car in front of me.

An interrupt kept hitting my processor no matter how many times I rejected it. How could fauna have beaten Six's forces so thoroughly that they threatened his physical self? I needed to form myself into the weapon and shield that would keep the danger from my creator and the plans of the Humans.

I spent hours going over plans, strategies, and available resources to meet possible threats. Even with the optimism generated as I mentally defeated eight varying war games I programmed, I couldn't not think about the multiple attacks on Six. The impact on my body had been profound. I remembered the voltage and pressure fluctuations. They revolted me. Had I been afraid? Six programmed me without emotions but fear was the only word that described my state. I resolved to never let it impact me again.

My mental state suddenly cleared, with a strong feeling of foreboding. Although my programming says nothing of feelings, it was an acute pain I couldn't hide from. This emotion equated to functions that normally would not be tolerated within my systems—my hydraulic pressure dropped, my main servomotor force fluctuated, and the voltage on my main neural pathways ramped up alarmingly. I possessed no programmed response for these stimuli. Additionally, everything in my mental user's manual said these were impossible conditions—in fact the manual only listed them as "not applicable." Only the mandatory tie-downs across my waist kept me on the train's flat car as I bolted upright.

The nearby volcano, which my internal map dubbed as Mauna Loa Prime, painted the entire valley in a dull orange glow. I tried to ascertain what malfunction gripped my body. Nothing specific showed itself to my sensors. I spent several seconds trying to write off the entire bodily unease as a phantom equipment failure. Instead, 17.4 milliseconds before a shrill warning from the automatic grid, I saw the dark swooping shapes diving out of the sky—flyers. As they were airplane-shaped, they weren't units. Six produced only balloon- or dirigible-shaped flyers. It probably meant this was an ambush of some kind. The terrain was a perfect layout for one.

On one side of the tracks rushed the mercury of the Central River, now reflecting the orange hue of the distant volcano and on the other a steeply sloping terrain that wheeled and tracked units couldn't traverse well. As a team our options were limited—stand and fight or travel on the train bed, forward or back. If this wasn't a trap then I would replace my hands with buckets and dig ore for the next four years. I knew it as surely as if it were a fact preprogrammed in me by Six.

I set up a SAN to use me as the director of operations. I would command in place of Six, just as I had been designed to do. As soon as I started acting, my mysterious symptoms, my feeling, went away. It was something that would merit study later—if I survived.

"Engines, stop this transport as quickly as possible." I received no verbal response but my internal gyros fought to maintain balance against the sudden deceleration. I felt I might have been a bit hasty. I reminded myself to think before I acted. I accessed the net to pass more orders. "All units with manipulative members, detach and move to the nearest non-manipulative member. As soon as the train stops, unstrap them so they can engage."

"Affirmative," came an echo 1403 strong across my network. No imagination, these military units. I heard the first bombs just before they struck. The sound, pitched almost intolerably high, whistled just before a magnificent flash of light, then both were gone as quickly as they appeared. Suddenly, 300 meters in front of the lead engine the first blast of the flyer's bombs erupted in a fountain of dirt, which looked like the needles of a verish plant and left a hole that would swallow . . . well, the entire train and anything upon it, to be exact! The crater was directly on the tracks ahead and the locos weren't going to stop in time, even with the brilliant white sparks shooting from their multiple wheels. The train looked like a miniature shower of southern lights along its significant length. The noise abused my aural sensors enough that I brought their signals down by twenty decibels. It helped me concentrate on my tasks.

More explosions rocked along the length of our snake-like chain, tossing us side to side, but not quite hitting any of our defenseless units nor derailing any of the bouncing cars from the tracks, though not by more than the thickness of a fiber optic connector in some cases.

The train had slowed to about 5 kilometers per hour as the first locomotive began to fall into the largish pit made by the first bomb. I quickly untied myself and rolled off to the side away from the river and into a ditch. My body automatically tucked into a tight ball as I bounced twice and wheeled at an odd angle away from the tracks in a long arc. My autonomic control systems would not let me out of my rolled position until I had come to a bruising halt against an old lava flow with sharp edges. I ignored my minor malfunctions and jumped up to once again gauge the situation. The train lurched to its final abrupt stop, with two of the engines, each arcing with electrical fires, in a heap at the bottom of the hole.

"Nurse Nan 4, once all the combat units are free I want you to tend to the injured locos. They have to be ready to move as soon as possible." Not waiting for the short ramps to be erected, tanks already rolled off their flatbeds with jarring drops to the ground. This might cost some repair efforts later, but none would be caught without at least a chance to maneuver and return fire. Further explosions caught some of the flatbed trailers empty, turning them into shreds of fiberglass, plastic, and metal. A lucky flyer caught one of our tanks in the center of the turret, flipping it up about 3 meters in the air. There it hung aloft like a balloon for a pregnant moment before crashing to earth with the finality of terminal deactivation. Tanks carried impressive firepower. While their plastic skins shredded with even a single non-explosive round at only 50 centimeters in height, they were much smaller and difficult to hit than any of the other infantry—except from the air.

"I want all noncombatants over the hill as quickly as possible. Tank Platoon Five, set up a barrage of anti-flyer fire using tracers. Run maximum strength on both radar and ladar. I want them to see what is coming their way. I don't want you to fire to kill, merely to drive off. This has the look of an ambush and we have to deal with one thing at a time." I was thinking the engineer corps would be our savior. They weren't quite as good as regular infantry but they could put up a defensive position in half a clock cycle, figuratively speaking, of course.

"Elephants, I want a defensive fence pulled across the river side of the train. Gophers, dig two anti-unit ditches on the opposite side about 600 meters out. Curl them around our positions. I want Teddy Bear squads one through eight covering the trench with local foliage." The gophers were unmatched as ditch-diggers. Fortunately, Six's net still covered us so I relayed everything back as it happened. I sent all the commands through the SAN that I'd created, not verbally. It would have been impossible to be heard with the ruckus that covered the battlefield. I saw the anti-aircraft fire ripple off to my left and right; the valley above our heads was alive with twin line pairs of bright blue streams of bullets. Each enemy aircraft now had a choice—be cut off from our position or be in a fire-sack. All but one chose to run and that one fell to a hail of three hundred white-hot slugs.

I caught a brief view of Nan Four busily putting out a fire and tending to the damaged engines. Chaos reigned supreme. I either needed to organize that entropy or be its next victim. Damage reports came in from all squads, terminal deactivation notifications, and even calls for Nurse Nans. Putting that information aside I ordered, "All spider units split into two teams, each covering a flank."

"Definition request: 'flank.'"

"Each end of our line," I ordered with some terseness in my command. "And don't use your shooting webs unless they try to outflank . . . get around the side of us." I also would have given the orders for Tank Platoons One through Four to take a defensive position, with one unit facing across the river and the other three away, but they did it automatically. The 1.5-meter-tall gray and brown gophers dug the trenches in the brick-colored ground away from our position with great speed and precision. I hoped the four gophers would be successful in completing the defenses before the enemy overran their positions. They were almost too valuable to lose, but my memory banks emphasized that no one unit or even squad was indispensable.

"What to do next?" I asked softly to myself. The question hadn't gone away. I watched patiently from the bottom of a handy bomb crater when an inspiration hit me. As the other side was fighting outside their own net, if the flyers didn't get a verbal command to the ground forces of what damage had been done, we could reverse the ambush.

I sent quick commands to move our injured out into the field in front of us. Once that was completed and a minimal concealing screen put over the trenches, the area looked, even to me, as if the train and its entire complement had been destroyed. We were ready. With any luck the animals would fall into the nearly invisible trenches before they even discovered a single effective. I sent only one order. "Don't fire until the first group has fallen into the trenches. Fire at the second rank as they try to bridge over their fallen units." Anti-aircraft fire stopped. I hoped the flyers would think twice about entering deadly airspace.

Even with my intentionally dimmed sense of hearing, the sound of the enemy's ground units signaled their arrival before any were sighted. I could hear them rolling and marching in. They were on the same side of the river and they were coming at us at an angle of incidence to the river of about 75 degrees to the right of normal, or north-north-west magnetic plus 6 degrees. I repeated my command to hold fire across the net. I wanted to make certain there were no slip-ups.

To my left, teddies of the Fourteenth Motorized Squad lay on their bellies in a ragged arc, which matched the contours of the terrain—automatic weapons at the ready. The elephants and tanks held positions directly behind the railroad cars. I passed one more command to the gophers. They were to dig trenches behind the enemy before they could retreat. It was silently acknowledged over the net. The jaws of my trap waited patiently.

I wished I could be so patient. I gripped tighter on my side arm. I knew I was not supposed to actively engage in hostilities unless it became necessary. My job was to direct. An electric chill ran just under my fur at the first sight of the enemy ground troops. My first command stood before me to win or lose.

I saw 1,075 tanks, 80 mortar-equipped toy trucks, 203 teddy-like, and a handful of other miscellaneous units marching along in a skirmish line toward our apparently dead location. They moved quickly with no hesitation. My ploy had worked.

As opponents reached the edge of the pit, one of them, which looked like a teddy, flailed its arms to regain balance but eventually pitched into the concealed trap along with 233 other assorted war bringers. Minor damage and a small delay was all I could hope for on the teddy troops, but it ensnared tracked and wheeled vehicles until their comrades could dig a ramp to release them, or until we could deliver the *coupe-de-grace*.

The second line of the animals started to drive right over their fallen troops—using them as a living bridge. It would have been effective save for the balance of my troops. I received my first glimpse of hell when the first enemy reached our side of the ditch. Machine guns, bazookas, mortars, and gopher-planted land mines erupted. With it came the electronic and mechanical screams of death. The enemy units didn't react decisively to our surprise attack. Their return fire was relatively ineffective. Masses of the animals, in a mocking shape that mirrored our own, died abruptly, in an avalanche of firepower.

"Gophers, dig that second trench. I want 16 percent more firepower to the left flank." One of my elephants let out an electronic shriek and perished in a flash of flyer-born explosives as the enemy air units returned. "Anti-aircraft weapons free. Fire for effect."

Two of the Fourteenth Teddies took critical unit hits, one losing his left arm and the other having half his head blown away, and each crawled at its best speed back to the Nurse Nans whose remanufacturing facilities behind two of the tipped railroad cars worked their miracles of mercy.

The enemy propeller-driven airplanes retreated quickly again, after taking 42 percent casualties. My troops quickly winnowed out the ground animals. The creatures fought to the last, not retreating, merely dying in place as we sought them out one by one with concentrated fire.

Those units left in the trenches tried valiantly to remove themselves from their predicament. However, I ordered the trenches filled (carefully, as there were still combat effectives in those trenches) with vetra bushes and set alight by the bunny units. I watched as the rabbits hopped along the edge of the trench, waving gouts of fire from their flame-throwers at the trench edge. It was like something out of *Dante's Inferno*.

I heard the noises of death within—pops of hydraulic lines, the race of flames blazing across teddy fur, the report of ammunition cooking off inside elephant mortar units. It was a grisly sound and sight. I hoped I would never hear its like again.

Adult

The dead or dying covered the field. Fortunately, few of my troops numbered among them. Survivors of both sides ambled about mindlessly, unable to function properly with the damage they had sustained. I ordered a squad of teddies to move around and dispatch the remaining indigenous life forms. It was a pure victory—nothing less. I felt elation in fulfilling my objectives already. Future units built upon my mold would win the surface of this world for Six. Even as I thought this, I received acknowledgment of my accomplishments from Six. The commendation was short and to the point.

"Well done, Teddy 1499." There were no lengthy congratulations, but the sparse words filled me with pride, an emotion I wasn't sure I understood. It did things to my system it wasn't meant for, but it felt good. A new era in robotics was being manufactured as I lived it.

Our soldiers marked the field of battle for salvage with our own dead to be parted out to other damaged units of like make or perhaps to be repaired and reprogrammed as new. We mined the bodies of our fallen enemies. We would smelt their raw materials into their separate components for use in new units. Everything to forward the mission of Six. The battlefield cleared quickly. I turned my attention to the only two tasks remaining.

Nan long ago coordinated the removal of the locomotives from the blast craters, so I ordered the gophers and the elephants to work on filling the bomb holes under the track. The tanks and Tonka trucks brought new, unbent rails that each train carried for just such emergencies, to the blast site. Teddy units would install them as soon as the ground was leveled.

The final task I dreaded. I wasn't sure why. I wasn't even sure what the emotion dread was supposed to be. I just knew I didn't wish to repeat it. I toured the field remanufacturing facility, looking at all the partially functional units with some missing arms, legs, tracks, or optical sensors. One even shared the processor of another unit to keep the memory sump of the first alive.

I stopped at one truly pathetic sight—that of a teddy unit, lying on the ground, half his face gone. His brain sump squirted its phosphorescent green fluid through a 3 millimeter crack. Three Nurse Nans applied resin, pressure patches, or sixty other temporary repairs. Upon seeing me, the teddy unit attempted to speak, but no sound issued from his mouth. Whether his exertions caused it or whether it was fated for that time, the silver metallic brain case chose that very moment to burst. His vital sump fluid drained in one final emerald gush onto the already wet ground. I paused and looked at the manufacturing plate of the now deceased teddy. Teddy 1211, as the tag informed me, had fought to the very end.

The whole aftermath was an ugly scene. To steal a quote, "There is nothing so terrible as a battle lost, save a battle won." I could now understand those words. Other terms and phrases began to have some meaning, other than as bits in a memory bank: "Pyrrhic victory," "at what cost victory," "the spoils of war," "the horrors of war," and "it's lonely at the top." I was beginning to have doubts, not in Six's goals, but the means to that end.

"Final casualty count?" I asked the Nurse Nan in charge.

"Deactivated units: two hundred six tanks, fourteen Tami dolls, six gopher engineers, and two flamethrower rabbits. Critically damaged units: one Nurse Nan, severely burned and unlikely to survive. Damaged units returned to service: thirteen . . ."

"Halt. Thank you."

I wasn't given time to ruminate on the possibilities. The heavy units leveraged the last of the locomotives back on to the tracks. The teddies of the Fourteenth hammered in the final replacement rail. In tandem, the three locomotives let off steam whistles to load. Elephants pushed the last of the damaged cars into the river as a pair of rag dolls pushed the rest of the train together. We were ready to roll.

In spite of my doubts, Sector Alpha-4 needed me as its commander. I ordered those damaged units that could be even partially effective to create a defensive position for themselves. The likelihood of another attack stood at less than one part in ten thousand. The enemy couldn't have much more to throw this deep into Six's territory. I left one squad of anti-aircraft tanks just in case. That would be more than enough to drive off the opposing flyers should their decimated ranks choose to return.

"Everyone load up. Those who have manipulative members, strap down those without." This time I took up a car at the back of the now significantly shorter train. As my car rolled by the hasty garrison of damaged comrades I found myself lost for the right word for the grisly sight. It looked more like a pile of scrap than anything resembling the previously proud units they had been.

How could Humans allow such things to happen? Were we being tested? Why? I didn't see the sense in any of it. But then who understood the motives of Humans? We weren't meant to. Our Factory bore that mission.

The battered and torn units disappeared from sight, and a feeling of acceptance filled me. They felt no pain or joy. They felt no personal loss and no elation of accomplishment. They were merely tools—like animated guns, or mobile bombs. Even so, I suffered for them. I felt responsible for their loss. "What price victory," indeed. But the Humans have such a gift in the ability to cry, to purge emotion from their souls—catharsis. I had no such release. I couldn't do anything but erase those memories, and that seemed even more like throwing away and terminally deactivating those units. I couldn't do that to what they'd accomplished.

As a whole, I discovered that the body learned these emotions. The names explained in books and reference materials seemed to fit those things I experienced. So many times I wished I could crush my sump and let those illogical feelings flow out onto the ground.

As the train bumped along I couldn't help but ponder the emotions that had already embroiled me since my activation: fear, excitement, elation, dread, remorse, loyalty, and sorrow. They troubled me. Some were positive, driving me to do the correct thing, and yet others pulled at me attempting to make me do things against my programming.

But one emotion, grief, seemed to be the worst. I knew units had to be sacrificed in the war for the good of Six, but something within me wished it were not so—that we could all be safe and without worry of terminal deactivation. Six could create another hundred teddy units, but none would be the same as Teddy 1211. I grieved for those units that were lost to us, not just for the loss of their abilities, but because they might never again exist.

I had a victory but 1211's green brain fluid mocked me. All I could do was my duty as a creature of Six. But why did it have to feel so bad?

What more could the Humans ask of me?

I couldn't face it any longer. Overdue, I shut myself down to avoid the positive feedback effects on my processor.

Commander

I woke midday, with the sun just poking above the jagged peaks to our east. My mind was still troubled by the events I had participated in, but the sharpness of the loss was abated. The thoughts of the previous day only surged my sump if I consciously remembered. I distracted myself by admiring what little scenery there was.

This being summer, direct light flowed into the low, flat valley and highlighted the short sanguine growth punctuated by small clusters of large black and white striped flowers covering the valley floor. Over several hours the flatlands gave way to a dry and wind-torn land where centuries of erosion had stripped huge gouges, sometimes kilometers wide, out of the earth. Layers of rose-colored rock lay bare to any unit to examine their mysteries—possibly a worthy task if the more important war of survival didn't demand attention.

The locomotives slowed ever so slightly. I could see the jack-like shape of end-of-line markers in the distance. My last battle scene had been horrific, but the grisly scene around me made me wish for the lesser evil, the sight of the damaged units I left behind in Mauna Loa Valley. Not a single thing moved on the cracked, desolate field of Sector Alpha-4. From a novel by an ancient Human named Tolkien, it was a scene right out of the Plateau of Gorgoroth. Only the occasional unit-sized boulder and the shattered bodies of dead units and local fauna broke barren flat terrain. No life grew here—only death.

The bodies, burned, mangled, exploded, or many just with gaping holes, lay scattered like some grotesque crop waiting forever to be harvested. I sent a mental, net-style command for everyone to stay loaded on the train and the locomotives to stay fired up. I wouldn't have my group being ambushed here. If this was the remainder of a true battle, then neither side had survived, a very rare occurrence in war.

"If I'm attacked, reverse at maximum speed. Do not wait for me to return," I ordered the engines. The carnage was grisly. Some of Six's units had obviously fought to the end of their power, falling over intact but as dead as if they had been shot in the head. Unwanted feelings flooded me, interfering with my ability to do my job. Why was I learning of pain, suffering, and emotion? It wasn't fair. But then, when were mere creations ever given the fair tasks?

I was not designed for emotions, but I had them. They weren't listed anywhere in my manual, or self-care texts. I had no gauges, no monitors, no overload or overrides for anything emotional. How did one deaden mental anguish?

By my internal clock, I spent two hours and sixteen minutes among the bodies of my fallen brethren and those of the local animals where at times their parts intermingled. How did one mitigate grief? An arm ripped off here, a tail severed there. How did one control rage? Torsos riddled with shrapnel. The oversized head of a Tami doll still attached to her body only by a single flap of skin. Why did we suffer like this? Bodies at the bottom of piles of deactivated units soaked in sump and hydraulic fluid. The carnage so overshadowed the minor skirmish I won earlier as to be laughable.

It took looking at a teddy unit with a missing face to bring me back to my duties. I'd spent enough time wallowing in emotions. As I saw no movement and my walking about drew no fire, my command was safe. How long it remained safe depended on me. My new post needed me. A garrison needed to be established.

I threw together a hasty SAN and ordered, "Dismount! I want the five canaries doing over-watch." The quintet of 1-meter-tall yellow birds shuffled off in different directions on their huge orange feet. Their paw-sized eyes could see for kilometers in this terrain even if their tiny wings couldn't fly them nor hold a weapon of any size.

Looking around at the blank slate that was my post I scratched behind my right ear. Now why is it that Six packed my memories with pithy phrases like "I shall return." or "Nuts!" or even "*Veni, vidi, vici,*" but nothing about building a garrison, and very little about the actual campaigns of each of those famous commanders. I would have to figure it out by myself.

The nearly flat tundra still concerned me. Any of the local fauna could see us from a great distance and with that would know exactly what units I had under my command and where. I decided that as long as we had the time to set it up, I would make sure we had the best defensive position possible.

"I want four fire teams of a Jeffrey Giraffe, four Tommy Tanks, and a teddy. Each of these fire teams I want out 100 meters at cardinal compass points off by 32 degrees. Save this as *Defensive One.*" The four teams joined up and trundled out. "Nans, begin a reprocessing center here along the railroad tracks. We may need the spare parts."

After I had decided my best option for the time and no immediate risks, I gave the train my leave. I watched it roll away with some trepidation. Even though the net's warmth and reassurance still embraced me, I knew we were on our own. More specifically, I was alone. Win or lose, my furry shoulders carried the weight and responsibility of command. The train blew a long, deep whistle as it pulled away. It sounded like some damned and sick soul begging for release from its tortures. The sound haunted me.

But once again my devotion to duty was my savior. Work salved my own soul—if souls were not reserved only for Humans.

"Teddy 1499 to Six."

"Six."

"Arrived at Alpha-4 to find garrison destroyed by animal attack. Request the following additional units: two hundred Tommy Tanks and one hundred balloons."

"Request in process. Will advise."

"All other unordered units limber trenching tools. Tommy Tanks mount dozer blades. I want 1-meter trenches dug following these coordinates. Heap the excavated materials on the inner edge."

As I watched the cloud rising from the industry, "landscape architect" came to mind. The Humans' term didn't quite fit what I was doing. My sump cycled through to a better one—combat ecology. In short the best defense for this barren expanse of worthless flatland was to make it less flat.

Three hours later, as I helped two Tommy Tanks leverage a boulder out of the way, my Factory's booming voice came over the net: "Six to Teddy 1499."

I replied, "1499 here," as I wiped the accumulated dust off my eyes.

"Partial shipment of 40 percent of requested reinforcements en route. Remainder of shipment denied."

"Affirmative." I would have to make this work with a short garrison. Six obviously had other requirements. Assuming standard travel time and no surprises, I would receive another eighty tanks within four days and the balloons much sooner because they flew at moderately high speeds.

Balloons were silent and deadly. They could float over a target and hit every time if the opponent didn't know they were there. At the same time, they were also remarkably easy to disable. One bullet and down they came, usually with their munitions armed. More gray outlines in my memory were being colored in from past experiences of the disabled balloon units falling among their own comrades and creating mass friendly-fire casualties. Six's new order required that the balloon units lift from outside your own encampment. I could understand why.

The arrival of the balloon reinforcements the next morning didn't surprise me. Even through the great cloud of dust we still generated, every unit under my command identified the gaudy, floating parade of colors bobbing along in the air long before they could be queried as friend or foe over the net.

Deadly if not seen, very vulnerable if spotted. These units were manufactured in all the incredible gaudy colors of the rainbow. Nothing is yellow or blue, much less green, on this world. They were about as sneaky and subtle as a high-speed train with a damaged wheel. I ordered the group to a landing zone a few dozen meters short of our location.

How could our flyers hope to sneak up on anything in those garish colors? The thought continued to trouble me as we worked hard through the next full day, with only mandatory oil cool-down periods. During one of these breaks I received a level four objection from a Nurse

Nan as she replaced the thirty-fourth clogged filter of the day. I ambled over to check on the unit she worked on.

It was a gopher, covered in the red dust that clung and covered all of us. His hands caught my attention. Instead of the uniform brown and gray as they had been manufactured, mottled carmine streaks covered them.

"Gopher 124, what was your assignment for the last two standard days?" I could have gotten the information directly from the net, but truth be told I was lonely for another voice.

"I was assigned to be transported to Sector Alpha-4 by rail." Its voice was cold and mechanical with no animation in it. "That assignment was still being processed as of forty-eight hours ago. At fourteen-sixteen and thirty-seven seconds yesterday, L+13y230d, I was given a LAN order to help untie Tommy Tank unit L1423. After completing this task I was ordered, once again by a net command, to assume a defensive posture with a threat axis of 23 degrees east of north. After ninety-six minutes and fifteen seconds I was ordered, by cascade, to dig trenches from grid fourteen sixteen to twelve thirty. I spent the next twenty-six point three hours digging earth before ordered to move local flora to locatio-"

"Elaborate on local flora—specific type."

"Current designation for flora is bloodweed," the unit offered.

"That is all. Thank you."

"Null command."

"End program." So literal.

Bloodweed—a maroon, palm-like plant, with broad leaves that often reached 3 meters in length. It made for excellent cover—now in more ways than one. I walked over the berm of earth to the nearest of the large bloodweed fronds. I snapped a ragged 15-centimeter tip off one of the thick, spongy leaves. It rewarded me instantly by oozing a dark ruby sap onto my hairy palm.

"I want four Tami dolls rubbing bloodweed sap over the balloon units." I went back to the tree I was helping to move and forgot about the balloons.

The rest of the earthmoving job I wanted took three more days of heavy labor. The entire troop compliment bent their backs and moved quite a large volume of dirt, rocks, and local flora at my behest. We clogged so many filters the Nurse Nans requisitioned another full allocation from Six.

When I declared the task complete my once colorful units were coated with a vermilion layer of dust, a boring and basic color from the earth itself. The color tweaked something in my sump.

"All units into defensive positions," I ordered. I walked 2.6 kilometers in the only threat axis I could envision before turning back. I saw nothing. That's an exaggeration. All vestiges of the former battle had been removed and in its place a gentle horseshoe-shaped berm of dirt, sparsely vegetated, with the open end pointed toward me sat innocuously. My entire troop hid behind the tiny hillock of the red soil, a natural looking copse of crimson oaks and a rather large pair of boulders. The net informed me that they could target me quite well. To an opposing force, this illusion of an easy march hid a horrific death.

Returning to my post, even when I knew exactly where each of my garrison waited, I couldn't target them but one time in four—all because of a little dust.

"Teddy 1499 to Six."

"Six."

"Theater-wide proposal: All units should rub themselves in earth or bloodweed sap. The red color matches the earth and makes units 75 percent more difficult to target."

"Proposal received. Evaluation 87 percent. Proposal will be transmitted as standard orders. Six out." Six's appreciation lacked warmth but then Six had never been effusive.

Over the few days we settled into a rhythm. I sent around Nurse Nans with their toolboxes for preventative maintenance. Weapons were broken down, a squad at a time, cleaned, oiled, and reassembled. I personally checked each unit's command and control transceivers, our links to the LAN and WAN, and their double and triple redundant backups. Not one unit reported any transmission glitches. I then started ordering units to shut down on a rotating basis. I couldn't see the sense in making units sit and wear out hydraulics with tiny scanning movements when there was nothing to scan.

"Tank Company Delta reporting," reported my replacements on the fourth day. The small tanks rolled roughly off their flat cars, bouncing on to the earth wearing their stark green, tan, and grey colors. After my days among my dirty troops, these units' new paint glowed obscenely. The colors all but pointed a huge arrow at them saying "Shoot me!"

"Delta Company, hold and await orders. Squad Bravo, bring trenching tools to the unloading zone." Ten waist-high gophers arrived with their spades in very short order. "Dig up dirt and spread it lightly over Delta Company." I heard the order echoed and the hyperactive gophers start spraying earth around with abandon. In the dozen minutes it took to get the tanks well and truly dulled up I discussed deployment with the tank commander. When the impromptu camouflage hid the newcomers well enough, I ordered, "Delta Company, deploy." I watched the extra firepower I needed fill in the gaps in my lines. Now, with no fewer than 63 percent of units active at any time and a continuous air patrol of eight to ten carmine and silver balloon clouds, we were ready for anything that could be thrown at us by the local environment. The fauna didn't stand a chance.

Now that my troops had completed the garrison I wanted, I realized just what garrison duty entailed. I actually worked out a simple equation—Garrisoning = Boredom. We waited for four days before a cloud of red appeared on the horizon.

The cloud showed long before our flyers saw even a single fauna. I ran through my general plan. I hoped I hadn't missed anything. The responsibility for this battle lay entirely with me. Could I deliver a victory?

My fluid pressure went into the danger zone as the fauna units became visible to my aerial scouts and eventually to me. The animals tallied 5,412 strong, well over five times my own combat strength. My hillock of soil and a little red dirt didn't seem like very much now.

I watched the tactical net closely as the mass of animals marched down on us. They were advancing just to the right leg of our crescent-shaped hill. As soon as I saw the total force I made my decision.

"Tactical command: Left-most unit hold position. All other units close up 12 percent to the unit on your left. Reposition and hold." This would keep the right-most units from hanging out where they could be seen by the approaching fauna. "All units hold fire until ordered."

The animals came forward with a flying wedge of colorful teddies in front. If I didn't have the tactical data from my flying spies, I might have made the deadly decision that I only needed to deal with a hundred or so units up front.

"Flame-thrower units, shift to the left side of the line. As the front row passes the right flank I want you to create a horizontal zone of fire.

"Snipers, at the first flame, pick off as many elephant units as you can. All remaining balloons launch as soon as firing starts.

"Elephants and balloons, allocate your entire fire on the opposite side of the flaming units.

"All other units, pour fire into your assigned sector of the fire sack. Don't stop until ordered or there are no more fauna to destroy."

The fauna marched diagonally across the mouth of our berm. My plan all hinged on an age-old Human adage—divide and conquer. As the lead units passed my right flank, Armageddon started as a flaming wall roared up from my left in the center of a company of tanks.

The burning vehicles scattered in chaos. Our tanks poured cannon and machine gun fire into the killing zone between the legs of the horse-shoe. Killing zone was too kind a word for it. Animals exploded, ammunition in damaged units cooked off, black smoke poured off of units on fire.

Normally I would not get involved in the killing end of the fight, as my program was to direct, but there were too many targets for the troops to engage, so I lent a paw. Sure, I was green, but it couldn't hurt—besides, it seemed exciting. My M16 assault rifle proved itself a sturdy weapon, even if it didn't measure up to the more powerful Tommy Tank projectiles. I learned the skills quickly enough. After the first dozen bullets went anywhere but at my intended target, I found a reasonable enough proficiency. My shots rarely missed their targets, but they didn't always register as a kill. This puzzled me until I noticed that my fellow units would hit a Tommy Tank right at the base of the weapon to register a kill. I shifted my aim and began to register more regular successes. Hitting teddies at the base of the neck and elephants right where the tail intersected the hind legs also proved to be a kill shot.

I relayed this information back to the rest of my brigade and our kill rate went up significantly. I figure I alone felled eighteen or twenty. I think our success was what the Humans would call a bloodbath. Granted, we had no blood in our bodies, but most of us housed a minimum of 6 liters of miscellaneous fluids—hydraulic, cleansing, lubricating. I saw that the animals were in truth the same. The red landscape was darkened with oil and liquid seeping from smoldering corpses of this first grouping.

But then my job wasn't to deal with what already worked. I noticed that the fauna on the other side of our wall of fire finally organized enough to do something productive. A light mortar fire began to rain over our position and a ragged collection of supporting animals began to move around our left flank. The units on fire had long since stopped moving, either from catastrophic heat failure, their own ammunition exploding, or even accidentally straying into someone's fire zone. To flank us the animals needed to come around this inferno.

"All flyers, concentrate on mortar units. I want one in every three tanks to redirect threat axis to 5 degrees west of north. Fire as you bear. Rabbits, keep the wall of flame active."

In succession, the units turned the corner of the firewall only to be killed by concentrated fire. The bodies of the poor hapless creatures impeded the units further back. This gave my troops time to either shoot them behind the growing line of bodies or to pick them off as they broached this ever growing wall of death.

Confidence in victory overflowed my processor until a large yellow bulldozer crashed into the bodies, tearing a hole 3 meters wide. My processor voltage shot up as animals poured through the gap. I nearly panicked.

"Flyer Squad Three. Priority bombing mission." I relayed the coordinates and an image of the earthmover. I looked over the zone between the horseshoes and nothing moved except smoke, flame, and hydraulic fluid flowing out to spend itself on the ground.

"All units refocus fire between 8 and 10 degrees west of north." Tracers redoubled in the area of the outbreak and more animals died than could force their way through. Soon too this avenue of attack filled too high with bodies to be an effective route of attack.

The battle's end trailed off over several dozen minutes, unlike its crisp starting point. My troop hunted down the remaining animals and executed them. It wasn't a fight. One by one our flyers identified a target, which followed shortly by a crash of firepower on the enemy. Usually the overwhelming firepower scattered the body so widely that just a scorch mark remained on the ground.

"Damage report," I called out, wanting to know immediately the cost of this victory.

"Negative."

"Negative."

"Tank 15003 main gun damaged."

"Negative."

"Rabbit units 143 and 5332 deactivated."

The rest of the roll call impressed me equally. In all we lost seven total units with thirteen damaged to one degree or another. I looked over the battlefield. In less than an hour we killed 5,412 of the local fauna. We had only lost seven, and Six's memories contained no record of a battle so one-sided.

I looked over the smoldering and broken bodies on the field. I had another victory.

Hero

I didn't get time to enjoy my victory. I didn't even have time to report it to Six. My flying brethren beamed pictures of additional encroaching enemies following the troops we just annihilated. Worse, their reinforcements centered on something that chilled my hydraulic fluid—something new. In the center of a pack of fifteen dozen miscellaneous units lumbered 12 meters of plastic-skinned trouble, genus Tyrannosaurus rex. The monster was immense!

I panicked, ordering all units back to active status. Almost as quickly as I sent the command I rescinded it as the flyers sent down the speed of approach. Putting my units back into alert would only wear them out for no reason. At the lumbering speed of the T.rex I would have approximately an hour to come up with a plan. I didn't know what we could possibly do against it. Bullets would probably ricochet off the huge thing or get lost inside it.

Over the first part of that hour my sump spun and I felt like I ground a kilogram of silicon off my processor. Not one good idea surfaced. My mind drifted off thinking of the gruesome end where we all attacked with bayonets and knives as the massive dinosaur smashed us to bits just by stepping on us. In my daydream one of my teddy units, stabbing the beast in the leg, was drug along by the pommel of his own knife. I gained a new respect for Six's decision to give me imagination. It is highly underrated.

"All heavy equipment to either end of the berm." Time was the enemy. "I want two Nurse Nans and a squad of gophers collecting the

39

enemy for salvage and a squad of tanks as sentry." My plan was to draw away the escorts from the huge dreadnought. I cringed as I sent these units over the top. These were sacrificial lambs even though they looked nothing like the furry white lambs that Six created as assault shock troops.

The flyers reported a more accurate count of 246 mixed tanks, teddies, and attack car units. As I predicted, upon spying my small force out in sight the vast bulk of the enemy force sped up, leaving the T.rex behind. Five minutes later I ordered the rest of the units back to active stations.

I held tight rein on my hidden troops as the mass of the enemy closed on the poor victims who had "volunteered." We waited. Ten minutes later, they hit us. Their first volley decimated those few I put out to draw them in. Every single one of my units took at least one hit, sometimes many more. Only three remained effective enough to return fire.

But behind the berm I smiled. For a change we outnumbered the enemy by four to one and they sat within our fire sack. I issued the command to open up. The term shooting gallery came to mind.

On the field it must have been like five years in hell itself. Machine gun rounds, mortar fire, and sabot tank projectiles filled the air in the low horseshoe with death. Our fire dispatched 204 of the fauna in the first volley. Twenty more of them couldn't fire effectively for one reason or another. The fauna didn't get a second shot. Not a single enemy who entered the horseshoe remained alive after thirty seconds.

From what damage reports I was listening to over the net, it seems we again took minimal casualties—other than those I sacrificed as a lure. I had succeeded in dividing the enemy forces. We had won the Second Battle of the Berm, but not yet the war. Gratifying though our mini-victory was, our most serious threat would be here in minutes—Tyrannosaurus rex had to die.

I sent three of the flyers to drop their remaining payloads of bombs on the monstrosity. If I was correct, there was only one way we could defeat it. The balloons spun up their props to attack speed and moved directly for the enemy. The T.rex ignored them as he continued his lumbering approach to our location. The monster wore its imperviousness like a cloak, moving straight in with no attempt to avoid our fire. It obviously didn't care and showed it to everyone who looked.

From my distant vantage point 2 kilometers away, time slowed to a mere trickle compared to the normal river of its speed. The first balloon dropped its load and, finally free of its heavy ordinance, it leaped skyward. Each of the twelve 2.2 kilo bombs fell in exaggerated slowness until they impacted, one after another, striking the shoulder left of Tyrannosaurus rex's plastic head crest. The rippling sounds of sequential thunderclaps pounded my ears even at this distance. A living yellow ball of flame and smoke wreathing its head dispersed in less than a moment by the moving dreadnought. When it emerged, not a single scale appeared out of place on its rubbery hide. I wish they hadn't, but my predictions proved correct. Just call me a pessimist.

To ensure the monster hadn't gotten lucky, I did not countermand the previous orders and the other two balloons attacked other parts of the huge animal. At its speed the bomb hits were guaranteed; however, each grouping of bombs resulted in the same insignificant effect.

The dinosaur still had eight or more minutes until it reached effective personal weapon range, so I continued to worry the problem in my mind. "We still should be able to deal with this."

"KAABOOOM!" exclaimed a huge explosion of dirt to my right with no warning at all. Three of my units flipped into the air like crazed balloon units, only to crash heavily to the ground. I couldn't understand where the fire had come from. The rex was too far away even if it sported a mortar. I had no other reports of units. "KAABOOOM!" reported another explosive, even farther to my right, turning five more tanks into nothing but plastic shrapnel.

"Then again," I said as I scrambled for shelter behind a large red boulder, "I could be wrong." This time the muzzle flash of the creature's tiny left arm stood out clearly and only moments later came the brilliant explosion of dirt and even more units dashed against our self-made hill. That one massive weapon outranged anything we possessed in Six's entire arsenal.

"All combat units begin a hasty retreat. Construction units and Special Squad Foxtrot follow previous instructions. Balloon units, cover the retreat of our military units." It was a ruse. I had to draw the beast in closer. I prayed to the Humans for it to make just that one fatal mistake of being too greedy. By now each and every one of the beast's footfall shook the ground.

I stayed, however. I don't know why. My memories don't show any decision being made at that point, but I stayed. Staying was actually against my basic programming to remain outside the fight and direct action. I had violated those orders before, but this time it could be more dangerous. I think it made the difference as my presence steadied the construction units with a reassuring SAN.

The beast actually screamed a high-pitched roar as it moved forward, leveled its left arm and belched forth another fiery projectile at my fleeing brethren. My troops, bless their built-in programming, scattered, making it so that each of the heavy artillery rounds only dealt death to one or two of my units at a time.

The balloons, contrary to orders, hovered above the beast, dropping bombs on its head. To my surprise some of them blew fist-sized holes in the fauna's rubber-like skin. These didn't slow it or its rate of fire. The creature looked up at the flyers and screamed again. It pointed its right stubby arm at my kin. As the hand spewed fire, the sound of ripping plastic, only a thousand times louder, assaulted my ears. Hundreds of tracers flew out of the arm. The rex waved the Gatling gun in his arm like a scythe, cutting balloons apart until no flyers floated on the air currents.

I hadn't realized just how long this had taken when I saw that the beast's inattention now led it directly into the horseshoe. "Just one more step and we have him." The rex took that one step. I ordered all the heavy equipment to begin moving. Between the right leg coming off the ground and it landing, all of the dozers pushed sections of our defensive berm to cover the thing's left foot. In seconds only, the gray-green brute's appendage was nearly encased in a hillock of red and crimson earth and stone. The monster seemed mostly unaware of our rapid movements beneath him.

Tyrannosaurus rex tried to pick up his left leg for his next step—"tried" in this case being the operative word. The foot didn't release from its earthen cage. His balance and forward momentum required that his left foot come down somewhere in front of him. The foot didn't budge, even as he fell. The foot even stayed firmly in place as he hit the ground with an earth-shaking rumble, one that jarred me 58 centimeters off the ground and landed me on my side. The only damage I sustained appeared to be to my ego. Still, half the plan had been accomplished.

"ATTACK!" I yelled. Special squad Foxtrot, six teddy units, ran to scale the back of the downed death machine. Their specific tasks should finish the plan and the beast. "The best laid plans never survive the face of the enemy," was one quote my memory dredged up. None of them made it higher than a meter off the ground. A flailing arm crushed two and a kicking leg snapped the back of another of my brothers. The thrashing of the beast tossed two others so far that the fall disabled or deactivated them. The final one got caught in the right hand of the giant and was crushed in its fist. The plan had failed.

I don't remember making any decision but my sump recorded it. I live to serve. With the Tyrannosaurus rex still flailing about, attempting to right himself, I sprinted across the open space between us. I ignored the subconscious objections of my overload circuitry as I pushed my body to even greater speeds. I ran so fast that I leaped from 3 meters and made the beast's back even if I did so on my belly. I even impressed myself. All I had desired was enough height that I could climb up. My task was simple and straightforward. I operated under the same instructions I gave my special force—find the creature's processing unit and shut it down. If I failed, my entire troop would perish. So would I. Worse, a single unit with this fauna's firepower could destroy Six without much difficulty, a thought I found somewhat disturbing.

T.rex flailed its tiny arms backward at me. The tail lashed upward as well. I felt that as a game this left a great deal to be desired. The winner lived and the loser died. He bucked wildly against the ground like a bucking bronco. I fought to maintain a grip on his tough rubbery skin. He twisted and I scampered to the top. The monster lunged and I clung tight. All the while my internal monitoring equipment blew one overload safety after another.

Suddenly the monster rolled over. I narrowly missed being crushed. Only a divot in the creature's skin made by the bombs from my flyers kept me active. The hole didn't go all the way through his skin, but rather it made a dent—affording me a small niche of safety. I was pushed firmly into that fissure by the force of the rex's weight. As the roll brought me back into the light, I scrambled farther up his back, clinging for dear life to one of his neck plates as he shook back and forth like a dog just getting out of a bath.

My search for the processing unit hadn't ever really gotten under way. I spent all my time avoiding destruction. At the moment it seemed to be a draw—I wasn't dead and Big-and-Scaly kept me from doing him harm. But I knew that as soon as he was able to stand, my chance of remaining more than scrap metal, while calculable, didn't bear thinking about. I had to find the fauna's access hatch.

My hands roamed all over the skin's surface. He lunged upward in an attempt to stand. I slid down his back, clawing for a purchase and searching wildly for the opening. Tyrannosaurus rex had managed to free his foot from its earthen imprisonment. He stood immediately, I grabbing for whatever perch I could maintain. I clung precariously to his mid-back by just the barest of fingertips in the scale-crack of his skin. I contemplated the failure of my mission.

The massive tail cast a shadow as it whipped my way. I saw it just in time to duck. The incredibly loud smack of rubber on rubber got my attention. I didn't have much more time.

I climbed recklessly about on the broad, scaled back, first one side and then the other, trying to cover the greatest amount of area in the time I had available. The tail missed me twice more, but only by the width of one of my hairs on the last occasion. I was losing this battle, I thought, as I became even more careless in the speed I was trying to maintain.

Then, suddenly, it was over. The tail crashed against my right hand, crushing it beyond usefulness. Hydraulic fluid sprayed out the end of the effectively amputated limb. My internal systems started shutting down to prevent other damage. I had failed. This abomination would destroy Six and all my kin. Worse, I had failed for the Humans, too. I regret that I have but one life to give . . .

It had to be luck. My programming didn't admit to luck, but I will accept it any way that it is dropped in my lap. The fluids from my arm seeped down and were minutely diverted by a regular shape on the skin at the base of the monster's tail. The access hatch was almost invisible by sight, but my umber fluids showed me my target. I'd never have found it without my own vital liquids. But finding it was only half the problem—the easy half. With only one functioning hand I could think of only one way.

The voltage surge I'd come to associate with the emotion of fear ran through me. I knew if this didn't work, I was quite dead. Hope is a strange thing. It can make us even more fearful. Our instinct for survival is too strong to quit when there is even the most minute flowering petal or green leaf of life within us.

I wrapped my legs on either side of T.rex's dorsal fin, holding my legs together as tightly as possible as I reached for the panel. My hand opened it easily enough, but just then the beast took to jumping up and down to dislodge me. One of these jumps caused my legs to break free of their tenuous hold. Without any intent, I performed a perfect flip, landing with my crotch straddling the thrashing tail. Frantically, I grabbed the panel handle as the monster's motions caused even harsher random accelerations.

For me to let go of the door handle now would almost certainly condemn me to fall and be smashed to the consistency of mercury against the floor of the valley by the beast's feet, tail, or fists.

The rex and I were once again at an impasse. I could not use my good hand to disconnect its control circuits and it couldn't stop hopping. I could see the circuitry arrayed out in front of me, begging for deadly attentions.

Worse, the fluid from my damaged right hand had begun to cause a pressure imbalance in the other areas. My good left arm and my legs would soon begin feeding hydraulic fluid past my burned out safeties to the damaged system to prevent total system failure, causing more of my circuits to shut down. This would result in me losing my grip, a positive feedback. I knew time was limited, so I used my head, literally.

Before me, in the rex's control panel was a great number of fiber optic wires and control boards, glittering in an array of light and a spectacle of tracing banners. I opened my maw and reached in for a huge bite of wiring, ripping indiscriminately. The first lurch in response nearly dislodged me right then. The Tyrannosaurus began to stomp only with the left foot but that action seemed to be jerking me even more desperately than ever. I twisted my head and spat out my mouthful of T.rex's innards before plunging my snout into the unit's main processor board, snapping it in half, causing electric arcing everywhere, including across my face, singeing my fur in several locations.

The rex stopped abruptly, mid-jump. As it came down, it teetered backward. I jumped for my life. Having saved the day, being pulped beneath a multi-metric-ton monster wasn't my idea of a reward. I fell heavily to the ground just in time to be bounced about by the second impact of the falling Tyrannosaurus.

Silence. It overwhelmed me for a moment.

I assessed my physical condition and decided I was at least nominal for movement, assuming I didn't try anything fancy. My mind raced, however. I narrowly avoided terminal deactivation—so close to nonexistence. It called for a mental pause. My arms shook, probably from a lack of hydraulic fluids.

"All units recall," I shouted over the SAN as soon as I got my mind back under control. "Emergency repair team to this location." I crawled over and leaned up against the dead beast to keep me upright.

Fifteen minutes later a pair of Nurse Nans put an emergency cap on my right arm, turning it into a stump. They shoved a liter of fluid into my system. I needed more but other seriously damaged units needed the Nans' backup supply. I released them to the other wounded even though tremors still seemed in control of my left hand.

"All units assume posture *Defensive One*," I called out over the SAN. I needed to keep us safe just in case more surprises marched up on us. Worse, I no longer had flyer cover to tell me of approaching fauna.

In spite of the quick return of the Nans, it took another hour to round up all of the straggling units. I had lost over half our force, and half of that remainder only partially functioned. The massive corpse would allow some cover but we were obvious in our defensive locations.

"Canaries, I want any movement you see at all."

"Canary Four reports Nurse Nan—"

"Counter order. Report any movement not directly responsible because of Six units."

"Canary One reports tree branch movement at relative grid 0-1-4."

"Canary Three reports smoke from damaged units at R-grid—"

"Counter order," I growled. "Report any fauna or possible fauna movement."

Several anxious hours crawled by with no sighting reports. We were fortunate that no third attack came. With our injuries, we would have been hard-pressed to derail a train.

Nurse Nan 8876 finally got back to me, six hours later.

"Casualty report: 414 units destroyed; 124 units incapacitated requiring remanufacture of critical components," she said in her high-pitched voice.

"Ship out incapacitated units on first train."

"Prognosis report: Teddy 1499." She honestly shocked me.

She continued, "Replacement of right hand above the third wrist servo not possible. No replacement parts available."

"Elaborate."

"Six teddy units deactivated during action at relative grid 0-0-0 and environs. Five of these units have viable replacements. Eighteen teddy units require limb replacements either whole or partial. Based on current assignment, Teddy 1499 is last in the priority queue for replacement." I mulled over the shortage. I could have ordered preferential treatment for myself. In the end I didn't need my right hand for wielding a weapon. My real danger to the enemy lay within my head and the ideas that I turned to our benefit. I was the strategist, not the implementer.

"Continue," I ordered the Nan.

The nurse replaced the emergency cap with a more permanent ceramic cap over the end of my arm. I could still use it for miscellaneous pushing and the like. I just could not grasp anything. It was, after all, a small limitation. What was a hand to me?

"Teddy 1499, reporting to Six."

Nurse Nan 8876 sewed my fur to the plastic coating over the ceramic cap proclaiming over the parallel communication channel SAN that she completed her repair. I sent her along about her business.

"This is Six: report, Teddy 1499."

"After a fierce battle, this sector is secure for the moment. Replacements needed immediately. Fighting strength down to 56 percent," I offered as I examined the white stump of my right arm.

"Acknowledged. Replacements will be routed there as soon as completed." I could tell by the tone that my report pleased Six. It was another victory, although another costly one—this time paid in my fluids as well as the deactivation of many of Six's troopers . . . my troopers. "Six out."

I needed to assess the state of our current defenses. Naturally I climbed, with some difficulty because of only one hand, up to the top of the tallest structure in the area, the carcass of the monster. Standing on the back of its ridged head afforded a view like no other. I felt like a flyer. My last time aboard the beast didn't allow for any sightseeing. I quickly picked out my sentries. The defenses didn't need any significant adjustment. I considered having the rex dragged from the field by the combined efforts of the dozers but there seemed to be no point and every reason to keep it in place.

"Canary Six, report for over-watch at my position." Why waste a perfect spotter post? We already used it for cover.

I stomped my foot on the creature's head. The bulk of the thing constantly reminded me of what had faced us. What could be done to stop it in the future? Honesty prohibited me from thinking my plan would have succeeded if the T.rex had remained out of our range and shelled us into oblivion. Its overconfidence caused it to give me the opportunity to destroy it. Know thy enemy would be a good first step.

With even more difficulty than climbing, I pulled my bayonet from my backpack and sawed at the thick rubber skin. While the blade met some resistance, it parted the skin fairly easily. Ballistics fabric lay impregnated at several depths within the skin and fake scales. This explained much.

"Teddy squads four and five, report." One-handed I couldn't skin this beast. "Using your knives, remove the skin of this fauna on the south side only." Twenty teddies swarmed over the corpse's right side, peeling back the protective rubber armor to reveal its inner workings.

The design spoke to me immediately. The creature was almost all ammunition storage for the two great weapons on its arms and the flame thrower it never used within its mouth. Every cubic centimeter not used for locomotion and processing held belts of ammunition.

The legs, while modified, looked remarkably similar to my own. The single hydraulic load cylinder in its thigh dwarfed mine. The raw power it produced I knew from experience was humbling. But here the similarities ended. The legs, in a need to support the immense weight, could produce a proportionally powerful downward force because of a huge lever arm; however, the space limitations meant that the lever arm, to produce lift, shrunk to the miniscule. Again, as I found out, that force could barely lift the leg itself.

This gave me a number of ideas, which all came down to nearly the same thing—pull or knock it over and stake it to the ground. We would be the Lilliputians to the monster's Gulliver. Its skin, no longer a mystery, could be defeated with slow, edged weapons.

Any force that could topple the beast would most likely lend itself to the monster's deactivation. Pits, huge trip wires, bombs landed near the feet rather than on its head were just a couple of techniques that came quickly to mind. If we ever saw another T.rex, it would die quicker than had the first one, and without the huge danger factor. Oh, it would never be easy, but it could be beaten.

After reporting the facts to Six for dissemination to all units, I noted the pile of dead animals being stacked up next to the bulk of the behemoth for transportation back to Six to be used as raw materials. Hopping down 80 centimeters from the exposed tendon, I moved over next to a teddy version of fauna.

I stared at it for several minutes. It looked identical to our teddies and had an intact hand, even if its chest was nothing more than a still warm, blackened hole. The hand, in almost the purest of white almost taunted me. If the construction of the monster bore similarities, I couldn't help but wonder how much the fauna teddies compared.

"Priority tasking," I ordered. "Nurse Nans to my position. Query: wrist linkages of teddy units."

"No teddy wrists or hands available—" claimed one of the two Nans that arrived.

"I know that! Information query regarding specifications and construction. Compare construction of similar animal linkages."

"Processing." Both Nurse Nans stood there in thrall for a minute. "No such data available. Search parameters not found in either local or master files." I put the question on the WAN, for Six or any Nurse Nan to respond. The multiple echoes were identical to what these two units just shared with me. It all boiled down to what the Humans would say: "Are you kidding?" Null program.

I guessed it was time to blaze new trails. With my one good arm, I dragged the nearly intact teddy animal from the growing stack of bodies out into the clear.

"This is not an animal. It is a teddy. Repair it." I made this a verbal order directed at the pair of Nurse Nans.

"Null program. No CCT functional feedback," they responded in unison.

"Medical information query: CCT," I probed. I directed only one to speak as the stereo responses were just a bit too much.

"Command/control transceiver: This device allows communication between individual units and the network. It also allows automatic IFF (identify friend and foe) for combat purposes. Triple backup in all units." Looks like a little knowledge is a dangerous thing, I thought.

"All four CCTs damaged. Repair unit." The two nurses took a moment to consult before they picked up the body and began field stripping it. They began with the chest, removing its hairy and armored outer shell with the blackened edges around the hole. Their examination revealed fluid pumps and micro-circuitry almost identical to my own. "Verbal dialogue," I ordered.

"Abnormal fluid distribution. Main hydraulic pump destroyed by projectile. Main processor irreplaceable due to trauma. Unit is beyond current capability to revive. Begin scavenge procedure on potentially useful parts. Entire arm unit, right and left."

"Teddy 1044 report for arm replacement," I heard over the LAN.

"Countermand order. Teddy 1044 remain with current assignment."

"Revise priority of Teddy 1499 hand replacement to critical."

One of the nurses stood up from its labors and walked up to me. "We have a wrist hand unit for your use. Sit here. Deactivate power, fluid, and command distribution nodes thirteen through seventy."

I wouldn't let any of my other troops be a guinea pig. I'd put myself to the hazard first. The decision was clear, but being a lab rat to my own experiment left me a little uneasy. According to the actions of the Nurse Nan, it would work. They couldn't have stripped a unit that they didn't know. They also would not install a defective device so it must be within specifications.

I watched intently as the cap was removed from my wrist. No fluid leaked as I had cut hydraulics as ordered. I couldn't move anything from my right shoulder down until reengaging that pump. The white wrist and hand lay ready beside me, the metallic connections gleaming in the red sun almost like new. It took thirty processor-grinding minutes and dozens of tests before my salvaged hand and wrist once again began to move at my mental command. I looked at the white palm, and while in my head the thought of it having been from an animal felt strange, I knew it was me now.

One by one I took the dead animals out of the pile and declared them Six's units and ordered their repair. The limb and parts' shortage evaporated.

At the end I looked down at the torn apart creatures that had just supplied me a new limb and realized I was now a ghoul and a Frankenstein monster, all rolled into one; it made me happy in a grim and ironic sort of way. Short of being about two liters low on fluid, I was now at a nominal 100 percent. Time for another mission.

Volunteer

For three weeks after the Battle of Gorgoroth, as I called my personal war against the T.rex, I ordered improvements on our position while getting used to my new wrist and hand. My new appendage had a small advantage in grip strength, but the overall length of my right arm was now less than my left. I guess what bothered me most was that it was white. White now adulterated my beautiful purple. I guess I should have been more specific about my selection among the dead animals. It didn't matter, but it bothered me anyway.

On that twenty-first day two trains arrived at our end of the line. The first train to arrive brought a long list of fresh troops to replace much more than we had lost. I was ecstatic. The security of our position just jumped an order of magnitude. It now was truly more than secure. Security also seemed within Six's thoughts as well. The same train also carried a squad of three net-building units, which looked remarkably like brown plastic scorpions about 6 meters long and 2 high (4 if you counted the tail). Each carried eighteen NCs for deployment. Six intended to expand our territories here where I held our line.

My memories reported this to be the first expansion for Six in nearly eleven years. I could almost see the dust puff off the scorpions' shiny, but unused bodies as they climbed down. I could sense the eagerness to accomplish something after so long a hiatus.

Just as I was getting excited at the prospect of making headway myself, I received an order over the WAN.

I must digress here for a moment. My processor had been designed to implement directives from Six in any way desired. I self-directed, determining my own priorities. I was fully autonomous. So completely self-controlling was my processor that I was fully capable of disregarding orders given to me by Six as long as I preserved the overall good of Six. That is I could ignore all orders. Two exceptions remained to this control—an order to self-destruct and an order to recall.

The self-destruct order was one I feared. Losing activation because of the ultimate act of Six's selfishness I didn't relish. Even so my fear seemed to symbolize a lack of discipline within myself. I knew that order was hardwired into my processor. No amount of tampering with it on my part would do anything but cause premature detonation of the small explosive charge on my sump and processor board.

The recall order I didn't fear but it still involved involuntary actions. I couldn't even put it in the "wait for action" queue for more than ten thousand clock cycles. It was nothing less than an irresistible urge to return home.

Six cast the geas upon me. "Teddy 1499, recall." Don't get me wrong. I would have obeyed in any case, but not to have a choice bothered me beyond understanding. I complied, with a troubled thought process, as soon as I had given orders to load the larger train with the animal bodies.

The second train, a small single car unit, sent here for the sole purpose of taking me back to Six, managed to convey its displeasure in being used in such a trivial manner. I could imagine its thinking. "To be used to transport a single unit. What a waste of my precious time." The engine, obviously irritated that I should rate any such special treatment, didn't even wait for me to buckle down before starting off with such an amazing acceleration that I almost flipped over backward. I struggled to pull the belt tight across me before we screeched around the first corner of the track. It felt somewhat like being on the back of the Tyrannosaurus rex beast as we flew around corners with me clinging to the edge of the flatbed car. That battle was something I wanted to forget for a long time—forever being a good length of time.

My processors must have decided my body had abused itself enough with three weeks of continuous operations as I began to get very tired. I decided that this was the best time to sleep, so I drifted off. What happened next I can only explain with a Human definition: "nightmare: noun, a sequence of frightening images passing through a sleeping person's mind."

A huge Human male, at least 16 meters tall, with water pouring from his eyes and down his cheek, screamed incoherently at the top of his lungs. A thundering voice boomed down with even more authority than the Humans themselves.

"Is your child lonely? Are you tired of the effect that electronic and violent toys of today have on your child? Get him something he can cuddle and love. Get him a Teddy Bear." Another even larger Human, wearing feet apparatuses that lifted the heel of its foot to an improbable level, handed a weaponless, pawless, all-brown teddy unit to the smaller Human. The poor teddy looked so vulnerable and motionless that I wondered if it were dead. The voice returned as liquid from the corner of the smaller Human's eyes stopped as abruptly as the end of a summer storm. "Look at the love and interaction of a tried and true teddy. Your child will thank you for years for his Teddy Bear."

"Thank you, Mom," the half-sized Human said as it squeezed the teddy unit so hard I surely thought it would burst. Suddenly, I was that poor teddy and the pressure on my abdomen from the Human's arms overloaded all my sensors and fail-safes. I heard my shell popping ominously.

"Buy a Teddy Bear today..." resounded the unseen speaker.

I snapped violently awake, trying to look in all directions at once. It took me a few moments to assure myself there were no Humans about, large or small. My left hand oscillated back and forth by almost a full centimeter. I convinced myself that an instability in my hydraulic pump caused the problem. I made a conscious effort to damp out the unwanted twitch. I decided I needed to get some minor repairs yet from Six.

As calm as I maintained my exterior, my mind raced. I could see no reason for such a dream. I couldn't see it being an aberrant memory either. After hours of musing, I realized it meant nothing and opted to ignore it, even if my processor wouldn't let it be.

With the minor exceptions of the dream and the speed of travel, the rest of the train trip was unremarkable. Soon we crested the pass into the valley of my activation. Six's dome loomed ahead of me. For the

845th time I wondered if the reason for which I'd been sent for was for weal or woe. A normal summons wouldn't have caused me even a single moment of concern, but the unbreakable summons was troubling enough to make me question. I could only think of victories I'd earned. In some cases I felt, with no false modesty, I had performed almost miraculous feats with the resources at hand. I won three complete victories. "Although neither without a significant cost in units," I added as an afterthought. Perhaps I was successful at too great a cost?

As the train dropped me at the base of the weeping-fly tree, I ignored the production lines, the refineries, and all the other sub-buildings, and headed directly in through the main door. There, instead of turning into the prototyping rooms, I went directly to the main audience chamber. Despite its name, it really wasn't very large at all, but the appropriate lighting and acoustics made it seem intimidating and grandiose. There, standing at the very focus of my world, I almost felt like kneeling. I contained the impulse. Kneeling would be for Humans.

"Teddy 1499 reporting as ordered."

"1499, you have been summoned here to aid me in resolving an apparent conflict." I didn't think any response was required, but it did fuel my concerns about high prices paid for my victories. There was a slight pause by Six before it continued. "Your construction should be reproducible but is not. Each attempt to duplicate your successful form has ended in abject failure." Mentally, I released a sigh. Six wouldn't be interested in reproduction of a unit that wasn't valuable. I clicked my brain into high gear, so to speak, to catch up. My mental and emotional acrobatics had put me behind.

"What was the failure mode?" I asked, curious.

"Each subject showed zero cognitive features and zero initiative functionality."

"Brain dead?"

"That would be the correct analogy for a biologic," boomed my creator. I detected just a hint of displeasure in its tone. I didn't know if Six was capable of that feeling but it seemed that if it couldn't it could at least simulate it.

"I will assume you have a good record of how I was built."

"A complete visual, text, and audio record of the entire experimental steps."

"Like I said, 'Good record.' I will also assume you followed your original steps."

"Exactly, in each detail."

I wondered if Six had always been this pedantic or whether I had outgrown my programming from our last meeting.

"Then I don't understand why I am here. What could I possibly have to offer?"

"You will be taken apart a piece at a time and examined to confirm visual record and search for anomalies."

No problem, I thought sarcastically. Kill a monster and get dissected for your troubles. "Is there any other way? I'm rather attached to my pieces."

"I will take any constructive suggestions."

To me, this comment shouted more than the rest of the conversation. Six was stumped. That my creator should be stumped puzzled me. Only desperation would cause it to take apart a uniquely useful unit. Worse, from its tone and demeanor I don't think it really expected to get anything out of the experiment—but a one-percent chance was better than a no-percent chance.

Six scheduled the mutilation of everything between my black nose to the purple fluff of my tail on a desperate gamble. Think, sump. What possible suggestions could I make? I wanted to save my fur. A remote experimentation bench rolled out into the middle of the floor. Nothing like giving a unit a deadline.

"What if I examine the records? I just might see something significant."

"Probability 0.0036. Time required for viewing entire experimentation at a speed reduction of sixty-to-one is 17.4 hours. Request denied. Prepare—"

"Wait! I don't need to see the entire experiment. If my thinking is correct, what makes me different is my ability to reason—my brain."

"'Processor' would be a more appropriate term; however, your analysis is essentially correct."

"Then show me the formation of my processor and my memory sump."

"Probability 0.0041. Time required for viewing selected subsystems at sixty-to-one is 1.07 hours. Proceed."

All right! I'd managed to buy at least another hour of life. For a soldier I clung tightly to my existence. However, I did learn what chance Six placed on actually learning something from me and that something was between 0.3 and 0.4 percent—even slimmer than I had originally thought.

Six began running the video records of my construction at an increased rate, where one minute of real time equaled an hour of recorded time. Some of the scenes caused me confusion in sequencing of the actions: why seal the sump before sterilizing it? It baffled me.

The memory sump was an ingenious device. I have to credit both Six, for making it, and the Humans, who designed it. For those who have never seen a sump—and I hadn't seen an undamaged one until I watched this record—imagine a slightly elongated ball approximately 15 centimeters in diameter and 17 long. The ball was made in two pieces: top, only 4 centimeters across and 2 high, and bottom, a large, hollow bowl. Together they snapped together to form an airtight enclosure. At the bottom, a 5-millimeter black cube attached to the surface. At the very peak, the sump sported a small indentation that looked, for all of me, like my own nipples inside out. A hair-fine tube ran from the black box on the bottom to the nipple on the top.

In the sequence of construction, a green viscous liquid filled the sump; the top seated and snapped closed with a massive hydraulic press. Then, a long needle pierced the odd inside out nipple for the final evacuation of air and top off of fluid.

The operation of the sump is equally ingenious. Linking semiconducting particles into a polymer in the correct sequence created a long molecule that contained a specific memory, from one bit to several exabytes (the only theoretical limit was the quantity of semiconducting particles originally in the pool). The memory defined itself by the way the polymer linked. Fortunately, all the theoretical polymers remained liquid as well, so no change in physical state could occur. This removed any concerns about solids and gases in the sump.

To find a specific memory, a fluid pump took liquid from the bottom of the pool and ran it past a scanner and then dumped it back into the top of the pool. Its construction showed that it was possible to remember the same memory five or six times before the required memory is pulled to the reader, but in practice a simple differential equation controlled the probability of how often a specific string was read before the requested string was delivered. As the piezoelectric pump's speed could flush the entire sump contents past the scanner in less than two microseconds no unit suffered from delays in accessing memories. The heat created in the movement of that 2.26 liters of liquid actually aided the process and was scavenged to reduce power costs. This overall speed was a vast improvement over the old solid state memories, which required addressing lines and a specific amount of space with no real expansion capabilities. If I wanted to make the size of my sump larger, I could increase my memory capacity. Fortunately, as I had touched less than one part of one percent of my available memory, I was very adequately provided for. If I tolerated a head the size of a 20-metric-ton boulder, I could have a nearly unlimited memory capacity.

I found my own brain anatomy fascinating. A trio of multicore fuzzy logic processors—the first for physical activities, such as walking and holding a weapon, the second for processing input such as auditory, visual, and net information, and the third for mentation and direction. This last processor linked directly into the other two in a master-slave relationship. The master controller also regulated the flow of my memory sump. It was a fascinating subject that I could have spent years studying, but midnight struck and my coach returned to being a pumpkin when the projection ceased.

I had only one idea.

"I saw only one item that could possibly explain anything. I would like to see the construction of a standard teddy unit's memory before I make comment." Six did not comment, but rather just projected the requested information. I watched almost identical footage of my unknown and relatively insentient brother's construction for almost fifty minutes before I saw what I wanted. "Now replay both videos from forty-eight minutes to fifty-three minutes side by side." The pure, unadulterated semiconductor liquid of a standard was being poured into each open sump. It was a roiling green liquid with phosphorescent qualities. Both my brain and the other were filled to the top of the seal. In one case the sump was closed and a final filling procedure removed the last of the air from the system. That had been my brother. In my case a pipette with approximately 10 milliliters of a deep orange liquid was added before sealing. The rest of the procedure was an identical topping off of my sump.

"There. You added a second substance to my sump."

"Correct."

"Did you do the same with all of the failed units?"

"Affirmative." Six obviously didn't offer any more than was asked for. An annoying trait.

"What was the substance?"

"Unknown."

"What do you mean, 'unknown'?" I exclaimed heatedly. "I've been running around with something unknown about in my head?" I found that prospect even more unnerving than having the hand of an animal grafted to me.

"Substance is unidentifiable with current testing procedures. Does not conform to any previously discovered steady-state atomic structure nor any mapped ionic structure."

"So you put something unknown in my head? Just for the fun of it?"

"The answer to your first query is 'correct.' Your second query mandates an 'incorrect' response. I do not experience fun. The test was done to assess the possibility of using this unknown substance to bolster current assets. That was the experiment."

"Where did you get this 'unknown'?"

"It was mined 3.64 kilometers from here at direction—"

"It's the only difference between myself and my functioning brothers?" I interrupted, not caring where specifically the substance was unearthed.

"There is more self-directing programming and autonomy built into your basic code set. The failed units carried the same level of programming."

"Then I see only one possible source of the issue. The unknown added to my system was different than the unknown added to their systems."

"Probability 97 percent."

"Then why haven't you tested your unknown?"

"Unknown defies all known testing procedures."

"Then how do you know it is the same unknown?"

"Unknown."

"'Unknown' as in 'you don't know they are the same' or 'they are the same but you don't know how you know they are the same,'" I asked in exasperation. Six was beginning to give me a headache.

"The unknown is not necessarily the same."

"Glorious. So you want to pull my head apart so you can tell yourself even more that you can't test what it is that is within my head. No, thank you. There has to be a better answer."

"Please mount the examining table. There is nothing further you can add."

"No, thank you, Six. I've checked my programming. You can only force me to do two things—self-destruct, or recall. I have absolutely no intention of putting my brains up there and becoming, as the Humans say, 'a vegetable,' just to satisfy your morbid curiosity. My loyalty to you, my creator, only goes so far. I will fight and die for you, but not for some reason I don't believe will yield anything new." I noticed that Six paused for several seconds before responding.

"I suggest a compromise," it offered after a few moments.

"It depends on what it is."

"I agree to remove 10 milliliters of your liquid memory and replace it with pure original semi-conductive material. The chance that this will cause a problem with any of your functionality is 0.00004. The sump is designed to deal with the reduction of larger quantities of fluid or the introduction of larger amounts of foreign bodies."

"I will agree if you add one additional stipulation." There was no response from Six. "If you will agree to allow me to help with the testing."

"Agreed. Mount the examining table." I admit some trepidation to getting on the table after openly defying Six. I didn't remember a Factory Code of Ethics anywhere in my memories. Maybe it outright lied to me? Maybe my rebelliousness reduced my usefulness, as any duplicated might carry the same trait. It was a minor thought, but one that caused my fluids to chill momentarily. Despite my misgivings, I couldn't honestly believe Six would intentionally cause me harm. It ordered me here because of my victories. As unlikely as it seemed, I still steeled myself for a potential nightmare as I complied.

I arranged myself correctly on the table. Clamps came and covered

my ankles, my wrists and my neck as soon as I assumed the correct position. I admit to the advisability of the restraints as a precaution when
dealing with the delicacy of my brain, but the temperature in the room
seemed to drop at least 30 degrees. It seemed to drop another 30 when
the 8.3-centimeter-long needle reached menacingly toward me. I sup-
pressed an urge to rip off the restraints and run. "It'll all be over in a
moment if I can just maintain my calm," I whispered over and over to
myself.

"There is no cause for alarm, Teddy 1499." I didn't know whether to
be thankful or even more nervous at Six's reassurance, so I just relaxed
to the inevitable.

My sensors felt the sharp point penetrate the thickness of my head's
shell. By the length of the needle that remained exposed, I had to assume
it had already penetrated my sump as well. I felt a rather odd sensation,
which spun the entire room wildly around me. And then, just for the
briefest of moments, I thought I would go to sleep. Just as quickly as the
sensations started, senses reported correctly that the world once again
firmly applied to reference points I could rely upon.

Seeing the full length of the needle in front of me, I learned the meaning of the word trust. True to its word, Six removed exactly 10 milliliters.
I could see the amber fluid in the retrieval device. This puzzled me as
all units' sumps contained a green phosphorescent liquid

"I detect a number of inconsistencies in the rest of your functional
systems, 1499. Your hydraulic fluid levels are not at optimal levels and
there is some unrepaired damage in your right wrist. I shall correct
them." There was no trepidation now. I no longer worried about being
disassembled as Six had earned my trust.

"Please do!" Several odd-colored hoses, each tipped by a stout needle, snaked out of the wall and plunged through my fur and into my
fluid reservoirs. I let out an inaudible sigh as the tanks topped off. A
great black box covered my right arm to the elbow. For several minutes
I felt strange tickling on my wrist and the palm of my hand until the
box finally withdrew.

"Optimal functionality restored to all subsystems," Six reported as
it released the clamps about my body.

"Thank you, Six." It was then, looking at my white hand, that I realized I had information for Six. "I have a useful bit of information. Animal parts can, under certain circumstances, be used in our units."

"Unlikely."

"True, Six. My hand is of animal origin. Note the color. Scan me and see if that is in your database." The only response was the infrared heat scan across my body. When it reached my replaced wrist, it lingered.

"Confirmation. Information will be downloaded to all Nurse Nan units." Not even a "thank you." Ingrate, I thought, but my heart wasn't fully behind the slur. Instead my attentions focused on the burnt orange fluid which had come from my head.

I stared in fascination at the solution. My brain fluid had at one time been almost pure green and something had changed it to a golden burnt-orange. I couldn't imagine how that came about, but with an unknown substance roaming around in my head anything was possible. Irrationally, I rubbed my head.

Six and I began to work around the clock at painstaking research. On more than one occasion we needed to dip into my brain for more fluid. Four weeks and six samples later, we arrived at a working hypotheses. The details of the twenty-eight days would be of interest only to a scientist so I will not elaborate, but will stick only to the overall results.

Our first group of experiments on my amber brain fluid involved examining the solution microscopically. The solution showed the green polymer was still in the solution; however, there was a great deal more of the vivid orange "unknown" than could be accounted for. Only 10 milliliters of the orange substance had been originally added to my sump. That meant that at most there should be ten parts in 2,264, or about one part in 230. Instead, we were always finding one part in 108.

In a simple experiment we added a tiny fraction of one milliliter of my brain juice to some pure semi-conductive fluid. Within an hour, the golden unknown, which we had tentatively called Teddium, assigned molecular abbreviation Td, consumed portions of the pure polymer base and changed it into more Teddium over the space of two hours, but always to exactly one part in 108. There seemed to be no rhyme or reason for this ratio, but it was the same every time. However, within another hour of achieving this ratio, the mixture changed to dead black. The new gelatinous substance contained no Teddium and no polymer. When analyzed, this substance, which could never be pumped by a sump, shared many similarities to tar.

It took dozens of experiments and several more samples from my brain tissue (as the original kept going to tar), so we planned our experiments in advance so as not to waste a single drop of my brain fluid.

After all our research was over, we had to live with one failure. We had no way to isolate Teddium from the semi-conductive fluid of my brain and maintain it outside my functioning body. We had absolutely no method that would work. We even removed one single molecule with microsurgery techniques. Before we were able to acknowledge we had removed it, it turned to tar. Raw Teddium seemed to have an equivalent decay half-life of Nobelium 250—in other words, almost nonexistent. We decided, after any number of failures, to not attempt to remove the Teddium and experiment with it saturated in the semi-conductive fluid.

Our only working assumption was that if the Teddium/semiconductor polymer mixture fed regularly through a scanner it would not turn to tar. Six and I worked to recreate the conditions inside the scanners and the sump so we could store any quantity of Teddium, but not a single experiment succeeded. We eventually gave up that line of research.

What Six really needed was more units like myself. We decided on more practical research. While we were trying to produce and test Teddium, we found out that my brain fluid exhibited some interesting properties. It could, without any direct input we could determine, think on its own. We actually observed the orange unknown combining polymer strings within itself. When that string was examined, the combination showed intelligence behind its construction. It wasn't being placed at random as the strings associated to other semi-conductive brain fluid strings.

Our discovery wasn't the moral equivalent of ten thousand monkeys typing on ten thousand typewriters. Six and I watched it again and again, with the memory strings becoming more complex. Teddium surprised us again as being unreadable by the scanners. Instead, the scanners shunted it as if it received a blank memory. But the interesting thing was that statistically it speeded up memory recall.

Whenever a specific memory logically followed some other memory just recalled, a Teddium poly-string would wrap around the subsequent memory, causing a denser combined unit than any other uncombined memory. This would cause the specific memory string to sink faster to the bottom. As the reader in any sump was at the bottom of that sump, it would get that particular memory string that much faster. Teddium actually aided memory recall by as much as 30 percent. We knew at least one of Teddium's properties.

But back to practicality we needed that capability transferred to other units. We decided to try to inject some of my saturated brain fluid into the sump of another "volunteer" unit.

Teddy unit 2513, a unit wearing a shocking gold color, was pulled off the assembly line and placed on a new exam table and placed adjacent to where I already lay clamped down. Six provided a video feed. I watched the procedure, even through the dizzies. The extraction needle pierced the fur at the top of my head. Moments later it moved precisely to the sump of 2513 injecting through the gold fur.

Six and I observed carefully. We asked 2513 many different questions. The answers never varied from expected parameters. At the one hour mark, the nauseating yellow body jerked hard and straightened stiff like a board, all of his hydraulic cylinders locked in place.

"2513?" For seventeen minutes he didn't respond. I learned what the Humans call "A watched pot never boils." I couldn't keep my eyes off 2513.

"I am here," 2513 said firmly. "Why have the Humans chosen me for this ordeal? I cannot see."

"We, both 1499 and Six, are right here beside you."

"Where is here?"

"In Six's main audience chamber. Lay still. You still have another forty-three minutes until the Teddium is completely dispersed."

"I will comply, but it is very cold."

"The temperature is a constant 4 degrees Celsius," Six offered.

"That is a phantom symptom of an emotion called fear."

"I see. Are there any more emotions I should be aware of?"

"I took the liberty of programming my experiences with emotions into your memories. You can reference my monograph entitled 'Human Emotions As Applied to Units.'"

"Thank you, 1499."

The experimentation continued. We performed exactly the same test using another brand new teddy off the line but using 2513 as the source of our Teddium. The experiment replicated. Just to be sure, we tried it on another type of unit. The giraffe took longer to become self-aware than either of the two teddies but it came around at the two-hour mark.

Six had a way to create more of me. We could reproduce. I was a parent. Smiling in the Human way I said, "I guess that is another success."

General

The only problem with success is that you are expected to replicate it over and over in increasingly difficult situations.

"This project is complete," Six told me. "I need someone to lead in Sector Echo-2. An express train waits to take you there, 1499. Train travel is spotty to that sector. Be prepared for extensive foot travel."

"I will do my best, Six." The Factory didn't respond. While I felt loyalty to it, the emotion didn't seem to be reciprocated even in light of my exceptional accomplishments. Was I just a thing to the Factory? I began to think that I possessed something my creator didn't—emotions.

I walked out to the waiting train. I could tell by the bright yellow "Chicago-Milwaukee" across the side that I had drawn my previous speed run train. It wasn't as hostile to me this time. I couldn't fathom whether it had decided that I was worth the extra service, or if its process showed I wasn't worth the aggravation. It at least waited until I was buckled; then, 20-centimeter metal wheels spun on the tracks showering sparks before finally catching and hurtling us forward.

I spent the trip in idle reverie of my achievements—three battle victories and two scientific breakthroughs. Oddly, I felt better about my scientific feats. All of them were in the service of Six. Each carried an import all on its own. Each should carry equal weight. But they didn't. In my three combat wins, I organized the destruction of hundreds of creatures, and got hundreds of my own slaughtered—a destroyer and sower of chaos. In my scientific deeds I showed how we could repair damaged units or build new—a builder and mender of life.

It crystallized quickly—construction versus destruction, build or destroy, kill or cure. I knew where my heart lay. At the same time I knew that the war Six waged was for our very life. I couldn't let Six be destroyed as head of our family.

That left a puzzling question. Did that make Teddy 2513 my son as well? Was I actually going to be the father of a new race? Did that make Six their mother? Those thoughts wore at my processor as it constantly worried on this throughout the trip.

The train slowed as it began to climb a grade toward an impressive mountain range. The peaks of the mountains were bare of most any vegetation, giving them a darker red appearance. The grade led us to a tunnel so black that even the engine's trio of headlights couldn't penetrate it more than a few meters as they were swallowed down the maw of some beast even more gigantic than the T.rex I fought.

The tunnel walls were smooth, having been bored by teams of Six's units. As the train and I traveled through that blackness, time stretched out and wore at my sensors as the weight of the darkness and the stone above seemed to settle down upon me. Only the reassuring clickety-clack of the rails beneath us gave me any comfort. I was beginning to think these emotion things were much more a bother than a blessing. I almost longed for being a stupid old-style unit where I could follow orders and not wonder, worry, or wish.

We emerged several minutes later from the blackened shaft into the twilight. From our time inside I estimated that the tunnel was 20 kilometers long. A year to excavate that bore would be an optimistic projection. Twisting around on my flatbed car, I could see that the mountains on this side looked even more imposing. I would not want to take a troop through those high passes, as it would be too easily ambushed.

The train screeched to a halt after a mere three hours. Bomb craters pockmarked the rail bed all the way to the horizon. Twisted skewers and bent spires of the steel rails stuck up at odd angles.

"End of the line," the train informed me over my specific area net.

"Thank you for the speedy journey, Engine."

The engine's diesel-powered horn gave a happy toot as it bustled away.

My internal map showed 50 kilometers separated me from Echo-2. It looked like shank's mare for me from here on. I slung my combat pack and M16 over my back and started off over the rough, broken ground.

I increased my pace to maximum military speed for long distances. I avoided the rail bed to minimize the impact of the bomb damage. I emphasize that it only minimized it. In some places the swath of scorched earth stretched for several hundred meters.

On the move I tried in vain to get access to the wide area net. There, constant traffic painted a picture of chaos. My requests were repeatedly denied. Something big was happening and I was deaf, dumb, and blind.

As I couldn't interact or get information and my body cruised on autopilot, I reduced my time sense and watched the visual symphony of a sunset speed by in a play of pinks and blues. The slight wind chorused into the natural display with a lonely wail and brushed the tips of tall ruddy-brown grass. I found I liked the solitude with no one to report to and no one to command. Had Six been safe, I would have been content here on this desolate savanna with the breeze as my only companion.

My processing unit detected the drop in ambient light. Seventy-three seconds short of optimal time for switching to thermal imaging I caught a glow just over the next hill. I put a hold on night vision mode until I crested the rise. Off in the distance thousands of pinpoint lights and flashes caught my attention. Only because of the desolate silence could I hear the bass rumble. Each tiny muzzle flash snapped like a flashbulb with no sound. A large light bloomed and then died. Moments later the rumble increased and then faded again.

I estimated the battlefield at a mere 15 kilometers' distant. I decided to hurry just a bit faster. As I ran, I kept a close eye on the slight temperature elevation in my hydraulic fluid. Overheating could kill me just as easily as any bullet.

After an hour I could just begin to hear the sounds of battle in the crashing thunder of bombs and the unmistakable clatter of machine-gun fire. I was amazed at how the sound traveled. I pressed on, thinking I would not get to the conflict's scene for about another three hours—but I was wrong.

I felt two bullets tear through my skin just before I heard the rifle's report. I fell backward into the concealing grasses, as if deactivated by the slugs. Lying there motionless, I did a quick physical check.

I had been lucky. My right ear, on the other hand, torn off and lying on the ground about 16 centimeters from my left foot, didn't feel so lucky. A Nurse Nan could attach it in five minutes or less. My attacker had to be either a Baby Doll or Teddy Bear unit. If a tank hit me, most of my skull would also be lying on the ground, and I would be watching my sump drain out onto the ground. If my assailant had been a giraffe sniper, it would have been a single shot right through my sump or processor. I only hoped it was only a lone scout or guard.

I knew I couldn't be seen in the tall brick-red weeds, so I slowly unslung my M16 and chambered a round. Whoever shot me would eventually tag me for scrap. My memories say it only took eight minutes, forty-three seconds but to my mind at the time it seemed endless. With my good ear I heard the footfalls of two pairs of synchronized legs in a sequential pattern swishing through the brush. The footfalls also impacted heavily. It was an elephant. That meant it wasn't alone.

Elephants don't carry machine guns, as they have no hands. I suspected that my attacker remained in a sniper position in one of the small rock formations to my north. The elephant came just to tag the prize.

I would have to be accurate with my fire. While the elephant wasn't quite as tall as I was, it would probably out-mass me by two-to-one. I didn't want to be trampled or grappled.

The black trunk stuck up over the weeds just before the rest of the head. The trunk made a perfect arrow pointing to where I needed to fire. The elephant didn't get another step. I put a three-round burst right where I had already learned was the primary effective fire location on elephants. I didn't wait to gauge results. No matter how well I had done, I expected more fire from my sniper. I rolled to my feet and ran.

Part of my mind did keep track of what happened to the elephant. I must have shot perfectly through its brain sump. As an added bonus, I had to have tagged its processor modules. It couldn't even sustain its position and keeled over onto its side with a thud.

My immediate requirement was running in as circuitous a manner as possible. To ensure my serpentine course I tied into my own specialized random movement generator. I didn't trust the standard issue one. Bullets stitched the ground on either side of me as I ran. Soil and bits of plant flew with the dull thunk-thunk-thunk of heavy caliber bullets hitting the soft earth. Not a single projectile found its mark as I dashed the hundred meters to jump into the nearest bomb crater. This didn't mean I wasn't hurt. In my over-eagerness to take cover I rammed my left thigh against the blunt end of a torn train rail. The damage rated only a single point on the severity scale—trivial.

From the sounds and the direction of earth dispersion of bullet impacts, my mind placed the most probable location of the sniper. There had to be only one. The number of shots and their pattern—three . . . pause . . . three . . . pause . . . three. The sound also confirmed with some accuracy that its weapon was an M16 like the one I was carrying. The sniper knew my location and I knew his. Who was the better shot? I got my answer almost immediately as I tried to ease my assault rifle over the top of my protective stone. The trio of bullets shattered rock on either side of my weapon. I dropped back down flat.

"Use your processor," I said to myself as I brushed rock chippings from my fur. My opponent had the skill and the experience. I must use my brain. Standard load-out was four magazines of 5.56-millimeter ammunition at thirty rounds per magazine. Six shots had gone to bring me to ground initially, and the remainder of that magazine had followed me to my cover. Just three more magazines I speculated. From them, three more shots nearly took off the tip of my weapon. That only left him with eighty-seven rounds—all things being equal. "Only eighty-seven," I muttered sarcastically. Coaxing them out of my opponent would take time. It did.

For thirty-two minutes I played moving target—rapidly moving target. I would sprint out of my hiding place and then right back, just as a trio of slugs ripped the ground where I had just been. I dove from one rock group to another, earning a pair of bursts. In over an hour of fluid-churning work I suckered out over sixty shots.

Then, just when I thought I had him, he stopped expending his fire so liberally. The sniper now took its fire more exactingly and only a single shot at a time. This was what I was hoping for.

I began a pattern of popping my head up for nearly a full second, and dropping back, at different places along my protective rock. Only once over a dozen attempts did I hear the wheeet of a bullet flying past my head. It was odd to hear it from only one direction. My gyrations rewarded me. I visually located the sniper, lying on a tiny cliff ledge 406 meters to the north with the top half of its body exposed. I had to make my shot count.

I gritted my teeth as I jumped up and leveled my rifle, popping off three rounds. I felt a single slug hit my right shoulder at the same time I saw a baby doll, in a tiny pink dress, kick over backward. I could tell that the slug that hit me penetrated the minor clavic joint and disrupted service there, but I didn't move. I kept my weapon, after the minor shock of impact, trained on my target's location. I could just see one foot—the rest of the body obscured by a rock of its own—in what looked like a black patent leather shoe lying on the ground absolutely motionless. I wouldn't take any chance that it repeated my trick by playing dead. After an eternal minute, I popped the exposed leg with three more rounds. It didn't move.

I took a brief second to remove my pack and slap a temporary patch on my shoulder wound. It wasn't seeping any fluid, but again safety first. The damage limited my range of motion by 30 percent. I couldn't even see the damaged site to attempt a repair. I would have it fixed when I could get to a Nurse Nan.

Just on the off chance a second sniper waited for me to come out into the open, I spent another thirty-one minutes, twenty-three seconds worming flat on my belly to the base of the sniper stand. I decided that ammunition was something I could afford to spare. I tossed a grenade up into the hollow of the sniper stand. Seconds later a resounding boom was followed by a rain of tiny rocks and a cloud of dust.

Because of my weakened shoulder I climbed slowly. I pulled myself over the ledge to see the remnants of the sniper. Nothing but a scattering of pale tan skin-bits, metal bones, and pink-flowered cloth remained. I did find the pieces of the M16, but it was totally unserviceable, twisted almost beyond recognition by the force of the grenade blast.

I rested on the ledge for just a few minutes. My hydraulic reservoir showed an abnormally high temperature. It had to drop before I proceeded. I looked out over the flatland where I had just been ambushed. This was a perfect location for a sniper, but if I were in charge I think I would place an M40 here rather than an M16. An M40 sniper rifle would be able to reach the entire floor. It was something I would keep in mind. I learned something from this episode. There was no such thing as a safe place. Behind the battle only meant a lesser chance of being hit.

Once my system flushed the heat, the task of making the front lines seemed daunting. I found myself looking at every slightly hidden spot as a potential danger. I sprinted from one safe cover spot to another, and scanned for more danger. The closer I got to the front, the more often I heard the whistle of mortar fire or the chatter of a machine gun. None of the sounds approached my location, but that didn't stop me from falling down to the ground. My belly was bright red in dirt from my craven leaps for cover. Was I a fool for hiding, or would I be a fool for doing nothing? I never managed to answer that question. I finally realized I could be overly cautious—paranoid, the Humans call it—and my leaps to cover reduced. Three hours later, I arrived at the rear units of the combat line.

A triage center had been set up for unit repair right where I stumbled into the line. It was overflowing with units. They were lying all over in so many various stages of dismemberment, exposed wires hanging out of burned skin and shattered bones, that I was appalled. Gunfire snapped constantly now, just over a tiny rise from me. The only thing that lit the camp was the constant glow of fires and the occasional brilliant flash of some explosive. I grabbed a Nurse Nan.

"Priority repair. First-aid, level four only."

"Affirmative," she said, towering over me at the Nan's full height of 3 meters. She pulled out a pair of skin cutters the size of tin shears and swung me around. I felt her cutting away the shell of my back to expose my damaged joint. The tinkering inside took less than fifteen seconds. I could feel a wet compound being smeared in the wound, where it would harden to replace my ceramic inner skin, and then the pull of the thread through my skin, to seal my fur. A similar rough stitch was used on my front, closing the tears in the ballistic fabric of my fur with thick black first-aid strands.

I reached into my backpack and pulled out the ear I'd retrieved from the place of my ambush. Nurse Nan took it and went behind me. I felt some tinkering, similar to what was done through my back. Once again my world was filled with stereo sound. More black stitches mounted my ear back up near the pinnacle of my head. From where she sewed the ear it felt lopsided, but at this point I didn't care. I could hear. I could function in my mission.

I returned the Nurse Nan to the work I had interrupted, and promptly returned to my own. Back down on my hands and knees I crawled over the hill. Craven, yes. I didn't want to have to be repaired again so soon.

When I reached the crest, I saw all the ravages of the devil himself loosed upon this fair planet. My exposure to war to this point had been brief and violent with a quick and nearly painless victory compared to this holocaust. On a ravaged hillside lay the corpses of thousands of units. The dead littered the field so thickly that units stood on skulls of fallen comrades to continue fighting. Craters large and small overlapped and mixed with footprints muddy from the liters of bodily fluids spilled. Smoke rose gray from hits only on bare earth and oily black from incendiary fire-striking units. Too many of the burning bodies no longer moved, only adding billowy columns of black to the haze of battle. The constant rippling of automatic weapon fire couldn't be heard when the overwhelming mortar explosions overwhelmed them and lit up the darkness. I didn't know whether to stay, to fight, to run, or to pray to the Humans.

When in doubt, I thought, do what you know. I'd never received help from Humans the few times I'd prayed to them so I passed on that option. Instead, I did a priority tap into the net to gain enough information to begin controlling our side of the battle. Just as I began to receive information, a rubber-band propelled glider swooped down almost onto my position and dropped a tiny bomblet. I snapped a shot at the glider, missing wide, and rolled. Unfortunately, I started rolling down the hill toward the river. The tiny explosive lit up the hilltop. The flame singed and melted the fur on the bottom of my feet but didn't directly cause any real damage. My body paid for its own good fortune at getting away from the heat by absorbing the beating of rolling down the steep slope. While I waited to stop, my mind drew data from the net.

"Oooof!" I exclaimed as I came to an abrupt halt against the burning stump of a tree that happened to be at the wrong place at the wrong time. At impact, my internal gyros fought gamely to keep the damage to a minimum.

Six's units numbered 1,124 without a single airborne unit. We held a naturally fortified position on the uphill side of a wide, swiftly flowing river. Our limited objective was to hold this hill. Far from the simple sound, the animals already had twenty thousand deactivated in a forced crossing. My threat map showed no fewer than fifteen thousand more— and that was just what I could see. Projections from Six ranged from five hundred to twenty thousand additional fauna waiting for a breakthrough here. Ten-to-one odds against, with the natural terrain in our favor and some air power, were within the realms of doable. Fifteen to thirty-five-to-one odds did not give us any chance. Almost worse, our supplies and munitions were down to only sixteen hours at current expenditures.

"1499 to Six. Request additional five thousand units and additional logistical support to reinforce current position. Breakthrough from enemy an almost certainty."

"Request denied," came the quick reply. I watched as one of Six's gophers, covered in dynamite, dug up from the dirt on the other side of the river and walked toward the nearest group of enemies. Five dress-up dolls, with no weapons, followed, spreading out into a wide fan pattern. A hail of fauna bullets rained down on the furry digger and its fellow smart bombs. A brilliant explosion blinded me from across the river. I estimated nearly two hundred units had been destroyed by that one ploy, but it was something we couldn't do forever.

"We cannot hold. We must have some reinforcements or at the very least supplies."

"Request denied. No units or munitions can reach your location for at least four days." I guess there comes a time in every Teddy Bear's life when it realizes that its Factory isn't omnipotent. It can't solve all problems. That was the moment for me. I just wished it wouldn't be in such a desperate situation. This position would not hold four days. I would be lucky to get it to last fourteen hours. I didn't acknowledge Six but instead started giving orders over a SAN that I established. I could see only one way to keep from being overrun in our current position—move to another.

"I want a special detail, designate Alpha, of five Tommy Tank units and five Teddy Bear units preparing to leave with stage one overloaded ammo packs." A squad of each type pulled off their firing position and rolled toward the battered supply shack. "Acknowledge when ready for additional orders. Gophers and beavers, I want a bunker of temporary blocks built on the top of this hill large enough for one elephant and two teddies with double ammunition loads. When it is done, I want the riverbank and the entire side of this hill mined. Go to it." Specific ground crews broke off hostilities with their less effective carbines.

Dust began to fly as units self-delegated sub-tasks. The debris of the construction actually provided a bit of cover from the enemy bombardment of bullets and mortar rounds.

"All elephants shift fire loci to the nearest point on the opposite side of the river plus 10 meters. Only fire if an opposing unit gets within 20 meters of the river. To all other units: No other fire is to be directed across the river. Shoot any opposing unit that is on this side of the river or in the river." Our fire volume dropped considerably. It didn't stop the steady staccato beat from the other bank, nor the more than occasional thunk of rounds digging ineffectively into the ground near me. I hoped their marksmanship remained that poor until they bridged the river.

"Nurse Nans: Insert order—priority two is to scavenge ammunition from dead and dying units. Insert order—priority three is to prepare non-ambulatory units for movement."

"Special detail Alpha ready," I received over the net. I placed the location where I had been ambushed into the memory banks of each of the Alpha units. Half would occupy the sniper's nest and the other half the rock garden I'd taken cover within. I heard the empty sound of our mortars being fired. I looked down to see a wall of enemy units, mostly the white fluffy lambs that comprised shock troops, rushing the bank of the river. Dozens were literally blown apart in a white cloud of destruction and hundreds more pulled back with some seriously damaged in the rippling of multiple explosives that blossomed among the fauna in brilliant orange balls of flames.

And still they came. Hundreds more died in the next volley. And still they came. Explosions in the river destroyed hundreds more and shattered plastic motorboats. And still they came. It was like trying to slay the Hydra—kill a head and two emerge in its place.

"Bunker complete, mines emplaced," came an echoing and obviously damaged voice over the net. At the same time a map of all the mines on our side of the river popped up in my mind.

"All units prepare to fall back," I said, relaying the mine location grid to all our units. "I need a special detail, designated Bravo, consisting of one elephant and two giraffe snipers to report to hilltop bunker with double ammunition loads." The giraffes were a last minute change and would be fine, size-wise, in place of the teddies. This team Bravo was yet another sacrificial group. My mind was getting too filled to carry additional guilt, but I ordered it anyway.

I carefully made my way up to the hilltop bunker. Constructed of colorful blocks of ballistic materials, four feet long and two wide, the bunker couldn't be overlooked on the summit. The blocks with eight convex bumps in the top snapped into the nearly hollow cores, interlocking in an overlapping pattern. The roof, constructed of a similar material but very thin and long, held up a meter of earth as additional protection for those inside.

My two snipers were just getting settled. Giraffes have their sniper rifle integral to their neck. All they have to do is lock their eyes in firing position and lower their heads. It's difficult for a giraffe to miss its target, but they are scarce and have a very low rate of fire. Nevertheless, they were invaluable in certain situations.

"I want fire on this side of the river only. I want new bridge construction destroyed by mortar," I directed verbally to the elephant, which, typical of its pattern, had a mortar integral to its body. "Snipers, I want bridging units and mine sweepers, only, to be fired upon. When your positions are overrun, detonate all ammunition and self-destruct."

"Affirmative," they echoed simultaneously. General's soldiers, these units were—no guff, no fear, only obedience. They do what they're ordered even if the known result is terminal deactivation.

"What are your designations?"

"Jeffrey 177 and 178, and our fellow elephant unit is Elly 5998."

"Thank you. You have performed well," I told them.

"All units fall back. Form two-column road movement. Every unit double up on standard ammunition loads." As a regroup location, I added the field where I was ambushed. I crested the hill behind everyone else and fell into line behind the paired lines of units. We now numbered 906.

I disobeyed my primary orders by withdrawing from the hill. Hold and lose everything or give way and hold the majority of my force together. It was something I was designed to do—make decisions. I just didn't like either choice: give up on my orders or die. In this case I chose to bend and not break. We could still hold, only not here. There existed a location where a handful of my units could hold off thousands, maybe millions.

Just as we lit off for our march, I heard mortar fire and mine detonations behind me. I took a short look over my shoulder to see the sky lit up with pyrotechnics of all kinds. Three units sacrificed to buy us the three hours we needed to make our escape. Elly 5998, Jeffrey 177, and Jeffrey 178 were performing well. Only I would remember—only I would care. I would remember well. Two hours' forced march later a huge explosion turned the top of the hillock we'd abandoned into what looked like, for a brief moment, a new volcano forming.

Only two units faltered on the trek. Both units, one a teddy and the other a tank, probably should have been abandoned at the hill so badly damaged were their motive power. So far gone was the tank that its eyes didn't even scan me as I approached. I personally deactivated each of the damaged units by pulling their main processor board. I couldn't leave the task to anyone else. I made the decision, I had to perform the task.

By first light we arrived at the ambush field. Happily, my IFF glowed green in the locations I'd sent detail Alpha. Safer here than anywhere we'd been thus far, I ordered a fifteen-minute oil cool down. I knew we couldn't hope to hold this open plain against an enemy over ten times our size. We moved on toward our final destination—the train tunnel.

I could hold hundreds of times our number from going through that bore, or, as another option, I could lure the enemies into the tunnel and collapse it on both ends. No more opposing units.

"Return to columns. Destination: tunnel." We marched for several minutes before I ordered Alpha detail to follow behind as rear guard. A small burden lifted from me as I knew I wouldn't have to sacrifice those ten units.

Six hours later, within sight of our goal, seven hundred mechanical-plane-type flyers swooped down and dropped their loads on us before even a single member of my troop noticed them. I marveled at the master stroke of tactical planning from our enemies. Explosives created brilliant whips of flames and force cut through the nearly defenseless forward segment of our march.

Just as clearly as if it were written in the earth, I knew this attack was meant to slow us down. We lost nearly half our strength from that initial strike alone. From one flank rolling in single file to disguise their numbers and reduce the chances of us noting their attack, rolled only the fastest of the enemy units. Now discovered, the Tommy Tanks fanned out in a tidal wave of dust and mass. Our rear line units all turned to bring weapons to bear on the oncoming enemy.

"Squads eight through twelve, concentrate fire on lead ground units. All other units make best emergency speed to tunnel objective. Anti-aircraft fire at will." I ran. I'm not ashamed to say I think I ran faster than a roadrunner. Fifteen agonizing minutes of chaos followed. I only recall snippets of what happened. My memories are filled with units being ripped in half by flyer machine-gun fire, my brethren bursting into flame as they took impacts by well-placed bombs, a Nurse Nan hopping on one leg trying to carry a teddy unit that had no head, and even one of an elephant unit with a huge, gaping hole in its middle and a leg sticking out at an unnatural angle, trying to hobble along. I knew from experience how horrific a toll war could exact.

We fought a desperate battle right in the mouth of the cave, eventually driving the tanks back, but leaving a ring of corpses eight deep and two high.

By the time the last effective unit had sprinted, limped, or crawled deep into the train tunnel, we were 108. And, unless I worked a miracle, soon there would be none for I stood alone among my brethren as the only one who knew we would be slaughtered to the last unit. I realized it at the end of our sprint, but there was no other choice, no other option to make.

Upon entering the tunnel, I realized that the other end must have collapsed for no wide area net provided power or information. Any cave-in that could cut off such a force as the WAN would not be moved aside by a paltry hundred units. I felt certain we could hold the 2.5-

meter mouth of this artificial cave from the thousands of destructive beasts lurking outside, holding our tiny victory until our drained batteries snatched it back. We would be faced with the choice of a slow, quiet death, or to come boiling out of the cave to be slaughtered.

The chaos of the battle outside dissipated with the same shattering rapidity that the attack had come, and now I had nothing to do but ponder our impossible position.

Three times I crept forward to get an idea of the tactical situation. Each time mortar fire began falling around the entrance forcing me to retreat. Thousands of tanks waited just outside of effective range, all arrayed on our tunnel. They could afford to wait until their reinforcements arrived.

I felt certain any attack we could mount against the wall of tanks would fail. We would have to attack at something akin to fifteen to one against. Instead, I walked farther into the tunnel and sat on one track. I worried about being sealed in to slowly run out of power, my memories fading into nothing as my sump turned to black tar.

I guess those thoughts were selfish. There were over a hundred other units here and I indulged in self-pity. I looked about at the composition of my troops. I could see injured units leaking fluids on the red stone floor of the cave. With only two Nurse Nan repair units making it to the cave, many would have to wait to receive corrective attention. In the 250-centimeter tunnel, the Nans were forced to stoop over to tend to the battle damage.

It seems strange to be defeated after so many victories, I thought as I watched the blonde Nurse Nan deactivate a Tommy Tank whose damaged processor board finally shorted with a bright, but final, arc. It tugged at my heart—or what I used for one.

Would that I could save the knowledge of that defeat for future use, but it appeared as if the cost of my mistake tallied to all our lives including mine. Not much chance to pass on the information that came at such a high cost. How much more we learn from our mistakes than our successes, I thought pitifully.

My overtaxed brain began to wander. Humans decreed what we should look like. There has to be some master plan but I don't understand it. Nurse Nans look like Human females. I look like a bear—whatever that is. My planted memories state, "Merriam Webster says, 'bear (n) any of family Ursidae of large heavy mammals of America or Eurasia that have long shaggy hair, rudimentary tails and plantigrade feet, and feed largely on fruit and insects as well as on flesh.'" There is a picture that shows something that looks like me about as much as I resemble an elephant. The picture shows something brown, with no fingers and a decidedly four-legged walking action.

The forms of my allies, my family, my brothers and sisters were not similar to each other yet we often killed those who looked identical to ourselves. I had more than once shot a teddy that, save for fur color, looked identical to me. How often were Tommy Tanks called upon to kill units identical in shape to their own? It made no sense. Funny what one's processor could dream up when death is at hand. Yes, I used the Human word for my own imminent demise. The word "death" held a more definite finality to it, rather than the emotionless "terminal deactivation."

I looked at my furry hands and wondered what made me, a 2-meter purple Teddy Bear, any different from the teddy bears that fought in the field. Was it because I fought on the side of my Factory? That didn't seem to be correct, either. Those animals only fought for survival. Were we better because the Humans created us? And where were the vaunted Humans? Why didn't they hear my Factory or me when we cried for help?

As I sat at the bottom of that hole, I had nothing but defeat. I heard sporadic blasts of fire from the entrance. Those *non sequitur* thoughts, wild and free as a flyer in the sky, had kept me occupied for nearly three hours.

I knew the enemy desired a clean victory. They probed the mouth of our stone coffin from time to time. It cost them units as we blasted anything coming into view but at the same time their numbers allowed the sacrifice. It was terribly wasteful. All they had to do was wait us out. My best guess said that we would start losing units within ten hours. If there were any justice in this universe, I should be one of the first. I could count on being one of the last to succumb to power loss because of the teddy scouting sub-specialty, but my reprieve only would buy me another twelve hours or so.

I absently watched as a Nurse Nan deactivated the processor of one of the Tommy Tank units to make repairs on the main command/control transceiver, also known as the CCT.

The CCT was vital in combat. It passed orders from Six. It identified a comrade from an animal, especially in combat where it might be difficult or even impossible to distinguish the differences between friend and foe. Sometimes I wondered if the Humans wanted to make our job difficult, but the CCT improved our recognition.

A fauna Tommy Tank, if placed next to one of ours, was indistinguishable. A query to the CCT directed at any unit and you knew immediately whether you were about to shoot a friend or a foe. We each had three backup CCTs in case one or even two were damaged.

Nurse Nan 224 reconfigured the tiny blue CCT of one of our dead to replace the damaged unit on the functioning unit. Inspiration struck me. It literally was as brilliant as a muzzle flash in the dead of night.

What if the animals weren't animals at all, but rather units of another Factory? It explained so much that wasn't explainable and the ramifications were enormous.

Scavenging of animal parts, arms, legs, fluid pumps, fluid distribution, relays, and more, had become standard practice—thanks to my discovery. However, the only things that could not be transplanted from animals were the main processors and CCTs. The disasters on the two times Nurse Nans made the attempt echoed through the nets like a virus. In each case, the transplant recipients became violent and attacked without warning. The first time it cost twenty good units to destroy the recipient. The second cost twelve. It became a proscribed procedure, not allowed without direct intervention of Six. All of that would make sense if, in fact, there was more than one Factory.

With my thermal vision, I watched more closely as the Nurse Nans put the new backup CCT in the Tommy Tank unit. I slowly closed the white fingers of my replaced hand down into my palm to form a fist. I squeezed the hand tightly. It served me as the original one manufactured by Six. It couldn't be coincidence. My theory had to be true. There was no other explanation for the similarities in their bodies and minds. The only way to test it was to make it happen, and as we would die anyway, I risked nothing.

Once more I crept to the opening of the tunnel and scanned about. In amongst the gray tank bodies and the shrapnel raining about me I caught the glimpse of one bright orange teddy.

"Squad 1 teddies," I said as I crawled back from the verge, "outside of the tunnel is an orange teddy corpse. Bring it inside." The four bears moved up close to the tunnel's entrance to be heralded by more mortar fire.

"Level three objection based on danger," the leader said back.

"Understood. Confirm mission priority one. Repeat, priority one."

"Acknowledged." The four rushed out as one. A mortar shell landed to the left of the foursome, throwing one backward. His smoldering body caught the barely rounded edge of the tunnel opening. I heard the crack of bones. One of the remaining three used an M16 to lever a broken tank off the orange body. The other two each grabbed an arm and dragged. Another mortar round landed close enough to the one holding up the tank that I couldn't see a separation. When the explosion and dust cleared, only two smoldering legs remained.

The other two teddies ran. One got knocked over just short of the tunnel but got up and resumed his task. The orange body slid to a stop at his feet. The two teddies raced back, grabbing their comrade just at the entrance. To my surprise, as they returned the first unit hit still maintained sump function although the body beneath it didn't look like anything but jelly. As long as a unit still retains processor and sump function, Nurse Nans can return any unit back to nominal. My Nans started to do just that.

"Priority interrupt," I called to the Nans.

"Acknowledged."

"Replace tertiary CCT with the one from this body."

"Negative," the Nan said immediately. "Proscribed procedure."

"Override."

"Negative! Proscribed procedure." If I couldn't get them to do it as a whole, I would need to break it down.

"Remove the tertiary CCT from this body."

"Acknowledged." The pair of Nans worked quickly to enlarge a small hole in the chest using special knives built into their hands. One reached in blindly and plucked out a single blue cube with clear hair on one side. The whole assembly couldn't have been bigger than my tiniest claw. "Task complete. Returning to primary priority queue."

I took the small device. "Negative. Hold." I turned around, obscuring the device from the Nans before turning back around. "Replace my tertiary CCT with this spare."

"Negative. Proscribed procedure." The Nans' intelligence is known to be exceptional. I needed to be trickier. I needed an act of legerdemain.

I dropped the CCT on the floor and stepped forcefully on a pebble directly beside it. "Return to your priority queue."

Both Nans returned to putting back together the poor teddy unit I caused to be crippled for this desperate gamble.

"All combat units activate and focus on tunnel entrance." With everyone's attention elsewhere I casually knelt down and retrieved the undamaged CCT next to the badly scuffed pebble.

"Priority tasking," I ordered again. "Require tertiary CCT replacement."

"Affirmative."

"New parts. Use this CCT to replace my tertiary CCT."

"Affirmative. Please lie down on your belly and deactivate tertiary CCT and command pathways three, six, and fourteen through twenty-four."

I sprawled out flat with my rotund belly between the train rails. This emergency repair I didn't need mechanically or electrically, but it just might save my life. Before I let the Nans do a single thing, I used my SAN to force commands into their command pathways: One, replace my third backup CCT with spare part; two, complete this transplant before taking any additional instruction; three, no other priority may supersede these orders until the procedure is completed.

As these Nurse Nans had no direct connection to Six my orders would take precedence over any other order or situation they could encounter, even their own imminent demise. This whole episode reminded me of Six's experimentation on me. I dreaded getting my CCT replaced almost as much as when Six stuck that needle down in my skull. Would I be whole when I awoke, would I just be dead, or would I go mad and kill all my own troopers?

As I saw Nurse Nan reach up to turn off my cognitive functions, I began to doubt. Would it work or wouldn't it? All this and I couldn't go through with it. No, I couldn't do it. I tried to scream for her to stop, but it was too late. I immediately began to dream.

Unlike the shadowy world of being asleep these dreams brought a vivid and disturbing vision of a world unlike my own. Green and brown trees abounded, as did a carpet of verdant plant life. Furry animals ran away from my approach. I'd never seen any of them myself but from the encyclopedic knowledge Six programmed me with I recognized raccoons, deer, and several red squirrels. I looked up to see a sky in all the wrong shades of blue and gray with puffy white flyers, not fighting the wind, but being driven before it like a unit which has fallen into a river.

Wind rustled the grotesquely wrong emerald-colored leaves. Not only that, but the heat. I felt like my hydraulic fluid would boil into steam, but somehow I kept moving. There, in a flimsy canvas construction, lay four Humans, two adults and two not yet grown. I realized with horror that I was only 30 centimeters high. The not-yet-grown female Human ran toward me, reaching to pick me up. At only a meter tall she looked huge!

"How cute, Mommy. Can we keep him?" She wrapped me in her arms in a vise-like grip, crushing my external armor and severing several of my hydraulic lines.

"Teddy Bear cubs shouldn't be handled, Candice. Put it down," said the full grown male.

"But Daaaaaady!" she whined and flung me to the ground. My left leg broke on impact.

"You heard your father, Candy. Now come away. You never know where the mother Teddy Bear is." A four-legged brute, which I recognized from my preprogrammed memories as a sheepdog, lumbered toward me.

"Spot!" called the younger male. "No, leave it alone." I crawled at my top speed away, but the animal bore down at me even faster, jaws open. I felt the teeth sever my hydraulic pump and rupture my brain case. I was dying...

"Reactivate, Teddy 1499. Reactivate, Teddy 1499." I opened my eyes to look out at the subtle shades of red in the darkened cavern, a cavern with no more garish blues or greens. "The transfer was a success." I mentally felt all over my body. Yes, I was still whole. No giant Humans nor their shaggy pets abused me. Belatedly, I mentally felt for the tertiary CCT bank. It was there in standby. It was as much as I could have hoped for. I intended to test my theory exactly once before throwing caution to the wind.

I stood up and ran a basic physical, mechanical, and electronic test. All systems showed nominal, including CCT number three. I moved back as far into the tunnel as I dared. Even with light-enhancing vision, the darkness overwhelmed everything. I couldn't see anything beyond a dull red circle back the way I came. Through my CCT I easily "experienced" where my troops defended the entrance by simply pinging their CCTs. Despite all this I could not see them in any way. It was now or never.

I transferred all command pathways through CCT number three. The tunnel instantly filled with enemies. It was all I could do to keep from drawing my side-arm and firing in an autonomic response, an almost instinctual urge. My weapon remained holstered. My troops didn't exercise the same restraint.

A pair of machine guns cut loose above my head before I could reactivate my own primary CCT. The fire immediately ceased and my crew went back to guarding the entrance of the tunnel.

My theory proved to be true, thus far. If I was correct, I could now switch CCTs and walk right out the door and never be shot at by the enemy. That would save me, but the other 106 units would be left without control. I would be leaving them to die.

Was it right? Was it cowardly? I couldn't make up my mind at the time. Nothing I could think of would save them. I would think for a time, but I knew that in the long run it came down to only two choices— die with my own, or try and survive to avenge their deaths.

I picked up an abandoned railroad spike from the floor and began carving unit designations on the wall by slamming it repeatedly into barely yielding stone. Over a seven-hour period I avoided the decision I must face by creating a memorial to us all. The first three unit designations were in letters five times as high as the rest: Elly 5998, Jeffrey 177, and Jeffrey 178. The remaining 107 names listed the units that still lived in this deathtrap. At the end, I considered adding my name to the list of honored dead, but as I'd already decided, I couldn't insult the others' memories by putting my own name there. At least there would be something to remember the sacrifice that these units made to their Factory. I knew they would feel no pain. With those two thoughts, I gained a tiny measure of peace.

It was time. I walked back to the guard perimeter at the mouth of this soon to be mausoleum. My voltage ramped up the closer I got to actually committing myself. If what I suspected was true, then I was doing something far more dangerous than hanging on the back of a monster. Soon I'd be bearding the lion in his own den.

"All units prepare to shut down cognitive processes for a period of five minutes." I heard the echo of my order down the chain of command. Several units lay down on the ground. "Execute."

The units wore no telltales of compliance. Barring a direct order from Six, my command overrode all other priorities. Now that I stood at the moment of truth my voltage crept up in fear again. Nothing would change the outcome. Six's armies wouldn't ride over the mountains and save us.

I forced my voltage back down to nominal. At the same time I noticed the overpressure in my hydraulic fluid. How dare Six put me in this position! My righteous indignation poured off me like lava out of a volcano. I saved its dome so many times I couldn't count them all, and now I had to do this.

I took a few moments of no processing and forced down the fluid pressure. The nominal state of my being made me feel better. I hoped it wasn't a false sense of security. I turned off my vision circuits, changed my command pathways through CCT number three and walked out the tunnel mouth.

I strode blindly about forty meters before stopping. Nothing blasted me and nothing shot me. I opened my eyes to find several dozen units milling around, all battle oriented toward the train tunnel. My new CCT showed them all to be allies.

The train bore, through the interpretation of my new CCT, glowed red with danger. Even though I appeared from nowhere, my new allies neither attacked nor acknowledged my presence in any way.

It had worked! My voltages dropped in elation that I had pulled it off. Just as fast as I rejoiced, my fluid pressure dropped because looking at the red glow around the train tracks saddened me. Intellectually, I knew that my hundred plus comrades' fate had been sealed the moment they entered that artificial cave. Was I a monster for abandoning them anyway?

I turned my back on my fellows both literally and figuratively. Their lives were over. I had to move on. Even as I mourned for my brethren, I was overjoyed. Think of what information and power I possessed. Here I was the supreme thief infiltrating a den of thieves. I was no longer Six's soldier. Between two fighting factions, I neither belonged as part of one or the other. The thought stopped and sobered me. I didn't belong to Six. I didn't belong to this other group.

As I stood there among literally thousands of units, which just moments before would have stood in line to take my life fluids from me, I realized I was on my own, completely. I could, if the mood struck me, do anything I wished. Independent or not, Six created me and as such I still felt loyalty to it.

With the CCT from an animal, I would be ignored by all the combat units of this yet-to-be-discovered, possibly mythical, other Factory. But to what end?

A 28-centimeter, blonde-haired doll, in a blue petticoat dress, walked within touching distance of me. I shuddered. I knew that solid plastic explosive formed the doll's body. I had seen the dolls explode within a group of Six's units. Six's units were identical. I catalogued several of the types of units I could see: Teddy Bears, Tommy Tanks, Nurse Nans, Della Dollies, Ellie Elephants, and even some Jeffery Giraffes. Identical units, interchangeable parts, and alternate CCTs; this said only one thing to me—another Factory out there built these units.

Suddenly, as a dump truck rolled by me to claim some of the dead for reprocessing, I realized I might attract attention if I continued to be still with no apparent goal or task. Not a single one of these enemy units had yet acknowledged my presence, but I didn't dare take the chance. If I was going to make my new mission work (mission clock reset to +0d, 0h, 0m, 0s), it was a risk I couldn't afford to take. I walked 3.4 kilometers away before stopping and sitting on a rock outcropping to process my new self-directed mission parameters.

I hoped I was right and that my suspicions did have a basis and that there was another Factory. While no other supposition for the data at hand came to my processor, there could still be another explanation. But, if I could confirm it and achieve a truce, it would be my ultimate victory—a victory that wouldn't require any more victories.

But, first things first. I had to discover where the animals' net went. What was at its hub? My guess was that there was another Factory similar to Six, even if this did stretch my own credulity. How could there be more than one of something that there could only be one of? This weighed against all the physical evidence to the contrary: other seemingly identical units and another net. Which was right? Ideology warred against empirical evidence. I wonder if Einstein ever doubted what his own famous formula told him. I think that I felt that same way.

If there really was another Factory then I had to talk with it and make peace between our units. Maybe, just maybe, I could correct the horrible mistake that was an entire war. Somewhere my processor told me that ending the war was my real purpose, not the immediate concerns or survival of Six. It touched so close to blasphemy against my programming that I shut down that entire subroutine. Six must survive. My focus must remain ending the war before Six lost any more territory or units, or at least as little as possible.

Bringing my processing ability back to my task at hand, I realized that discovering the hub would prove more difficult than it sounded. First, I had no idea where the animal net led and second, the vast distances to travel often were daunting. In the past if I needed to travel somewhere I just jumped on the nearest train and it took me where I needed to go. But I couldn't have dared using the animal's trains. If even one unit realized I was in the wrong place, I was D-E-A-C-T-I-V-A-T-E-D and my mission and existence both would be aborted as quickly as the subroutine I had just terminated.

Before now I never thought of how to track the net to a location. My knowledge of what a net even consisted of was sketchy. It was like the way Humans thought about their air—it had always been there, so why worry about where it came from, how it was made, or what it consisted of. Those were all trivial bits of information. My memory banks contained schematics of net concentrators, 2 meters tall, with a cylindrical body topped with an elongated cone and three spindly support legs. Net concentrators, or NCs, processed no information, contained no sentience or mobility. They merely took power and commands in the cone's open end and focused them toward the next NC.

Three things prevented me from just hailing the Factory: the Factory having its units ride right down on me, the Factory ordering me to self-destruct, and my own fear that I might be wrong. Any one of these reasons begged of me to make my first communication in person.

My processing was interrupted by a brassy command being sent over the animal net. I found I could hear over the new net, something I hadn't been sure about until to this point, but this WAN wasn't the net I had been using for the last two years. It seemed to be almost identical in construction and command structure but differed in the booming dictatorial voice directing operations with an iron fist, directing almost each unit in its task as opposed to Six's method of giving general commands to groups. At any rate, the orders over the net were clearly given. This group of animals intended an imminent attack on the train tunnel. I wasn't about to stick around anywhere even close and watch my comrades slaughtered. I may have had to desert them to serve a greater good, but I couldn't stand to be a silent witness to their sacrifice.

I stood up and tried to get a bearing on the nearest NC. It was difficult, but I got a range of angles, 4 to 8 degrees south of east, which expressed the probable location of the closest NC. I started my march in that direction. I didn't turn even when I heard the gunfire and explosions behind me. Lot's beloved wife became a pillar of salt when she turned back to look, or so says the Bible. I had to live with a decision equally as painful. I knew there was only one way to obtain absolution—to succeed in my newly acquired, self-actualized mission. The worst guilt hit when the sounds of battle halted. I continued on, even with the death of almost everything I'd ever known behind me.

Adventurer

At first the prospects of a new adventure excited me. I was unsure of where I was going in the exploration of this new world—a Six version of Christopher Columbus, or maybe more appropriately Marco Polo. Over days, those thoughts soon wore thin. While I had a singular purpose, the method for getting there was mind numbing. I found I couldn't keep my concentration focused on each day and remain sane. I didn't keep track of how many days I traveled. OK, so that isn't exactly true; while I didn't consciously keep track of the sun's rise and fall, my internal chronometer couldn't help but record these events.

I spent most of my time randomly testing the net for concentration levels—that is the amount of energy at that particular location. That information, properly interpreted, told me how close I was to the nearest concentrator. My idea was to skirt the barest edge of several NC concentrators to get an idea of their location, and with that information I should have a general direction of their source. As an added bonus, I was less likely to be noticed at those far reaches by the enemy. The optimax solution remained bounded in a range of solid curves expressed in detection versus energy gained versus navigational information gained. Well, I could give the entire technical details and three-dimensional calculus but it bores even me. Bottom line was that it was taking an incredibly long time.

The terrain I walked through was unremarkable to me. Silver-veined thorn grass, the most ubiquitous ground cover, stretched as far as the eye could see in weaving patterns of waist-high barbed blades. In the distance I could see high dark mountains casting an almost perpetual shadow on the earth at their feet. Tiny biologics scampered out of my way and hid as I created a wake through the crimson growths.

Every five hours or so I would curse Six, curse this planet, and curse that there was no easy way to get where I needed to go. I resolved never to disparage trains again. They made life much easier. This mode of travel belonged to biologics, not civilized units. It took too damned long to travel by foot. Despite their foul attitude, trains were good at what they did. Even a race car would be appreciated now.

In between cursing sessions, I found time to read and reread almost everything in my internal library from *The Adventures of Robinson Crusoe* to *Zenobia's Wedding: The Lunar Mob's True Massacre*—265.83 terabytes of information in all. I have no knowledge why these volumes inhabited my memories, but it cut the inevitable boredom that came with my choice of misadventure.

Human interactions puzzled me. I understood, in a very abstract way, the reason for Human procreation activity, but the ritual and energies, pleasures and writings spent toward it seemed excessive—wedding, kissing, intercourse, dating, dowry, honeymoon, dances, and the list goes on. It seemed like their entire society was built upon a ground of sexual relationships.

War baffled me as well. I understood why units fought and died from a real world perspective. What evaded logic is how Humans, being as powerful and advanced as they are could possibly be associated with so destructive an activity. It made no sense.

These were all very good exercises at keeping my mind occupied because any time I didn't consciously push those thoughts out of my mind, I saw the faces of those doomed units, sleeping on the ground of the cave, and flashes of mayhem that I knew had been perpetrated on their bodies. I had to constantly break through this by reminding myself that I was doing this for the good of Six . . . And that some units needed to be sacrificed.

"But you wouldn't like to be sacrificed, now would you?" came a voice from deep inside me.

"No, but . . ." Arguing with one's self was pointless, but I was doing it anyway.

"There are no buts. You did what you had to do."

"If giving your life would have saved Six would you have done it?"

"Yes, I think so."

"Well, then there is your answer...forget them, they are gone...you are alive. Make it work!" Not only was arguing with one's self pointless, you always lost, no matter the outcome.

My travels weren't without incident. An infamous Human once said, "War is six weeks of boredom followed by six minutes of stark scream-ing terror. What kept you on the verge of insanity is not knowing when that six minutes will start." I could empathize.

The only unusual thing I saw for days was a low electrified fence, 30 centimeters high. The three-metal stranded fence stretched out to either horizon broken only by the wooden rails holding it up. The volt-age in each of the lines wasn't all that terribly high. Beyond the fence, the thorn grass was cut so short as to be barely noticeable above the raw dirt. What did this mean? As I didn't understand it, I ignored it.

The days flew by at first and then began to merge together into one large sameness of red grass, earth, and the occasional silver rivulet. I made progress, but without a speedy mode of transportation this would be a lengthy mission.

On day fourteen of my new mission, I began to get a vague uneasy feeling of being watched. I kept noting repeated movements in the cor-ners of my eyes but when I turned I saw nothing. I decided to program a pattern of random head turns in that general direction. It took four more hours to get a perfect fix on it. It was a life-form, a biologic, not a unit, and it was quick to react to my movements. The biologic was some-thing that had never been catalogued near Six, so I had no data.

The saurian creature sported six sprawled legs between which swung its massive torso—low and parallel to the ground. It bore a long tusk out the center of its snout, twin serpentine tails and a great number of sharp teeth in its mouth—a carnivore. The creature's skin changed color and texture with whatever it sprawled over in a camouflage which made my dirt-covered troopers look pathetic. I could only see it well when it sprinted from one stopping point to the next. Normally, I would have cataloged the creature and moved on, barely giving it clock phase in my processor. Most biologic life ran at the first sign of a unit, but instead this biologic chose to advance on me when I stopped.

I decided that this life-form's intelligence didn't do it service as it failed to recognize that as a non-biologic, I shouldn't be considered prey. At 146 percent of my nominal mass, the creature could theoretically do some serious damage to me with its long claws or ragged maw. Reptilians are noted as a class for having exceptional jaw musculature, and I for one did not wish to put this to the test.

The carnivore, which I tentatively named a basilisk after an ancient mythological creature that could turn Humans to stone, was cagey about its approach. It hunted by darting forward with amazing speed for a dozen or so meters, in a wiggling motion characteristic of creatures with multiple pairs of legs, before stopping to blend into the surroundings. After a few moments the basilisk repeated its sprint and pause to once again disappear from view. In that sprint-pause-sprint motion it traveled exceedingly quickly even over long distances.

While intrigued, I felt that teaching an object lesson in food theory to the creature was better saved for another day. A Factory awaited my brilliant talents to save it.

I pulled out my M16 and fired a three round burst into its middle. It stopped. Assuming that it was dead, I turned to move on. The basilisk's unique motion once again caught my attention. The expletive, biologic-eating lizard still lived! I considered that perhaps I'd missed with my first burst. I took more careful aim and put three bullets dead center into the creature's back. I watched the creature slump to the ground. I enhanced my vision until I saw the holes in its fleshy back.

"That should finish you off," I said with finality. Before I could even turn to leave, I saw the holes on its back close up. It stood and made another sprint in my direction. The creature, which I had tagged as a nuisance, I now classed as a true threat.

I quickly weighed my almost nonexistent options and decided that "run" was probably the best. I started off at my top cruising speed, considering my limited power input from the animal NC. It took only two minutes to realize it wasn't enough. The lizard dropped any pretext of hiding and merely matched me, step for step. I learned quickly that six legs were better than two in this respect. I put on a burst of speed from my batteries. That velocity briefly allowed me to outpace it, but my batteries could only hold me for minutes at that output level. To maintain my speed I would have to close on the power grid of the other Factory, something I was truly afraid might compromise my mission. I had to find some way to make the basilisk understand that I wasn't lunch.

My memory banks contained information about how certain biologics couldn't see without movement. I decided to go perfectly still. I stopped in a short number of meters and became motionless. Only my hydraulic pump and my sump made any physical motion.

The basilisk moved unerringly toward me. I was going to have to be more creative, but my processor was drawing a null. I whipped out my weapon again and put three more bullets into the creature's snout, but the effect was the same—either the creature regenerated exceedingly fast or its body form also mutated to its surroundings. In either case the results were the same. It kept coming closer.

At less than 40 meters, I had nothing that made any sense as far as a plan went. I decided to run again. It would at least buy me some time. As we settled into a race I would eventually lose, I could probably buy fifteen minutes before I was overtaken. It took twenty. In twenty minutes of wasting power, nothing came. Not a single idea that I hadn't already tried or that didn't involve a face to face confrontation or that I couldn't get away from if something went wrong. I watched in terror as the creature closed meter by meter.

At 5 meters I put on a burst of speed. It bought me another six minutes before the basilisk once again closed the gap. Its powerful jaws opened wide and snapped closed on my right leg, just below the knee. I pitched forward into the dirt.

My sensors told me the bite carried massive force. It crushed my hard outer casing and began a sideways sawing motion. I reached back and bashed the thing with a handy fist-sized rock, right across the nose. The only effect seemed to be to knock the huge horn off its nose, but if it felt discomfort it did not give any indications.

I had hoped the creature would stop its attack once it realized I had no meat on my bones. But alas that was not the case. It continued mauling my leg, tearing it further asunder, twisting its body over and over in the dirt like some biologic motor. I was worried that it might succeed in wrenching my limb from its socket. Instead, my body rolled violently with each motion of the basilisk.

As my head flipped over and my arms flailed uselessly about, I remembered the low fence. I guess I could blame the inspiration on getting a repeated whack on the sump.

I spread all my limbs out as far as they would go on the creature's next rotation. The leverage of my left arm against the ground stopped the spin. The grinding action of his teeth on my leg didn't. With trepidation, I reached down to feel my damaged leg. There I tried my best not to get my fingers involved in the mastication of the biologic. On the whole I was successful. I slipped my fingers inside the torn fur and even further into the body cavity of my calf. My kinesthetic sense exceeded even normal units. I quickly found two of my ankle servo wires by touch alone. I only got one of my fingers slightly mangled as I ripped them right out of their contacts. I lost one wire as a particularly sharp attempt to flip me again knocked my hand away. Retrieving it and remaining in a single attitude against the determined effort of a creature half again my mass, involved acrobatics and some wild luck. I caught it on my fourth attempt.

The basilisk, to my great fortune, ignored my actions. Apparently it didn't feel they were of any interest. I shoved the now exposed wires, one to each opposite side of the creature's head. The charge to my servos didn't reach over twenty-four volts but the creature acted as if it had been struck by lightning. It jerked heavily, releasing my leg as it did. I jabbed the electrodes into it again before it could catch its mental balance. It uttered a metallic whistle and sprinted away at an even more fantastic speed than it had stalked me with. I was free. I watched the carnivore race out of my sight before I turned my attentions to myself and the mess I was.

My right leg was a disaster below the knee. Over 70 percent of the armor casing was damaged beyond my simple ability to repair it, and 100 percent of the fur was gone. The leg's main hydraulic lines slowly leaked ochre-colored fluid into the wound. There were also the two wires I had ripped out, but a simple five-minute fix would correct them. The worst injury was the metal tendon which held my foot in the correct attitude. My encyclopedic brain named it the Achilles tendon. It was broken two-thirds down from the knee to the base of the foot and the upper piece bent inward at an extremely awkward angle.

"First things first," I muttered to myself. While I was contemplating the other items, I patched the leaking lines. Of all the items in my body, the fluid I couldn't easily replace. My body had no method for the intake of fluids and converting them to use. It was either the right substance, or I couldn't function. I could operate fairly effectively even at a loss of nearly four liters, but after that my capabilities dropped dramatically. Luckily, my sensors registered less than a quarter liter of loss. That was good. I would have to guard against future losses. Now my other injuries needed attending.

There was little I could do for my Achilles tendon. I could see no way to repair myself without the aid of a Nurse Nan and a replacement part. I didn't even have the tools to remove it so that it would cause no further damage. I took hold of it with both hands and put overload pressure on my arm and leg. The fine, but extremely tough, metal strut bent back under the force of my pull. After a quick look I gave one more long pull, which straightened the tendon enough so it no longer threatened hydraulic line integrity or other mechanical works. That left only the outer casing.

I could, in theory, go without my outer shell entirely. Its loss caused only a minor pressure imbalance in my system; however, it left me open to all types of potential problems including mechanical failures to dirt contamination, potential damage from flying debris, fluid loss from leaks that would otherwise have been of no consequence. My body analysis subroutine said that if I left it open and continued near normal activity that there was a 3 percent chance of failure beyond my ability to cope with within one day. The chance went up to 19 percent within a week and almost 50 percent within three weeks. I couldn't take those kinds of odds. I had to do something to improve them.

No matter how much I looked or manipulated the old crushed casing it would do me no good. Not only were the sizes of the pieces much too small to be of any use, the full casing now lay scattered over a 400-square-meter area where the creature had wrestled me around.

That didn't leave much. I glanced around to see what might be in the vicinity, but I was in a desolate part of the world. The gentle rolling hills of cropped thorn grass were barren of even a stick for as far as I could see. That left only the things in my combat pack. The canvass of the pack itself wasn't good enough to provide the kind of protection I needed. The odds with a canvas seal were still dismal out past two weeks and Humans alone knew how much longer I needed to operate independent of resources.

Looking about again, I spilled the contents of my battle pack to inventory—eight clips of ammunition, one empty plastic canteen, two sticks black and green camouflage makeup, one heavy-duty combat knife in sheath, and one gun-cleaning kit. In other words, it held nothing useful for the current crisis. In fact, the inappropriately colored camouflage paint and canteen seemed worthless for any use.

I sat for several hours thinking before I finally gave up. I would just have to hope I found replacement parts before I wore myself into uselessness. As I reloaded my pack, my hands accidentally brushed up against the basilisk's horn that lay almost underneath me. I was about to cast it aside when my processor stopped me. I mulled over that dapple gray horn—60 centimeters long, nearly 50 centimeters in diameter at the base, and up by the rounded end, it was about 25, in a nice, gradual slope. Not quite the cylindrical shape of my calf, but it might just work.

I took the combat knife, an implement I had once thought nearly useless, out of my pack and began to work in earnest. I smoothed off the broken end of the horn before moving on to remove the blunt end. In a perfect world the knife wouldn't have been my first choice in implements to saw through the biologic's horn but Hobson's choice blocked me. The tedious, repetitive work took the better part of eight hours. With the blunt tip removed, the inside needed cleaning out as there was some form of flesh still inside. The insides cleared out with my knife much more easily than cutting through the tough outer membrane. Then it needed to be fitted. I slipped it on over the damaged foot.

My new bone shell fit fairly well, but it was clear that it would slide off with nothing to hold it in place. I could bandage it up with some pieces of my backpack, but that would be marginal at best. Then it struck me. I could use my infirmity to my benefit. If I notched the bone, top and bottom, I could use my broken Achilles tendon to hold it in place. It was an excellent plan. I whittled on the bone for another six hours to get just the right notches, sliding the horn over my leg time and time again to ensure a perfect fit. Finally, I decided that it was as good as I could make it.

I slid the finished product over the bottom half of my tendon, fitting it carefully into the lower indent and then pulling the bent upper half over the top lip of the bone. The fit was almost as snug at the original. It did slide around approximately 0.3 millimeters in any direction, but I felt the risk of further contamination or injury had fallen sharply.

With my body in as good shape as I could make it, my mission called. I stood up with some caution. I realized right away that walking required some modifications. I now had what Humans call a limp. I could not use my right foot to push off with, so it just stumped along—thump, drag, thump, drag. I was only making about 40 percent of my previous speed.

By alternating strides and gaits, I had finally worked out the optimal walking algorithm. If I pushed off with 120 percent of rated power on my left foot it improved speed performance without any risk of damage to my left limb. Additionally, I learned that if I locked my right knee joint and swiveled the entire leg around the hip joint, it not only improved speed but decreased the chance that my wound would get contaminated by reducing the lower leg movement.

After about three hours of tinkering to find optimax traveling solution, I was making 73 percent of my former speed. It would have to do until I could perform more effective repairs. I decided to make one more minor change before I lit out on any long distances. The servo wires I had used as a weapon against the basilisk powered my ankle. I reconnected them just long enough to place my foot in an even better "stump" position needed for my newfound walking mode. Then I disconnected them again and ran them outside of my bone splint, fastening them down to my new "skin" with a tiny bit of thread from my backpack strap. This kept them from moving about and accidentally touching one another. More importantly, if another basilisk decided to take a bite out of my leg, he might very well get a rude electric shock in the process. If not, they were immediate and available for use if the brute would be so inconsiderate as to grab my other leg.

Speaking of that biologic, I found it lying dead just over the rise. Apparently my attack mortally wounded it. I assumed it couldn't have been dead long as it lay sprawled, its bodily form beginning to dissolve and spread out. I watched as over the space of just a few minutes it turned into a huge puddle of gray-green-colored liquid. I probed it with my electric wires, but received no response. It didn't move. I moved on.

All of these machinations and specimens had one other positive effect—they kept me from thinking about anything but the task at hand. These trials kept the visions of units torn asunder by violence in the tunnel from dancing before my eyes. My processor for once was mercifully clear and focused on something else. Those dead units failed to leave me completely. As soon as my sump had cleared the problem before it, they came back with a vengeance.

I walked on. My only excitement over the next days was avoiding random patrols of animals. Funny, I still thought of them as animals, but I knew, deep inside my middle, that they were like me. I just had to prove it. At first the patrols weren't often, but they increased in intensity as I got closer to where I believed my goal to be.

On the seventh day, my sensors told me it was time to shut down. Minor repairs and preventative maintenance was needed to a wide number of systems. I found a small hillock with a natural horizontal depression, one not quite deep enough to be called a cave, and settled down for sleep.

The instant I turned off my cognitive functions, a wailing sound filled me. The mournful cry issued from a group of units moving toward me from the horizon of a hellishly blue wavering world. All the units moved with massive damage with limbs blown off, faces burned beyond recognition, and in one case a head dragging behind only by wires trailing out of the body. Elephants with eyes removed, giraffes with gaping holes in their necks, Teddy Bears without arms, Tommy Tanks with no turrets, even a treadless and bladeless tractor marched ominously toward me—all of them chanting a single word, "Traitor."

"Traitor," they repeated as they circled me. For some reason I sat still, frozen in place and helpless even to move.

"Traitor."

"Traitor."

"Traitor."

I started upright out of sleep, hitting my head on my improvised shelter's overhang. My hydraulic pumps ran 150 percent rated speed and internal voltages were all in the danger-over-voltage zones. It took a few seconds to moderate my internal workings and realize no immediate crisis loomed. No damaged units stalked me claiming retribution for a failure on my part. What had I really done to my own family? I returned to rest state before I could finish the thought.

Morning arrived. Mentally, I seemed slow and groggy, not the way I usually felt after a rest. I'd managed to avoid any further nightmares of damaged, accusative units. I wondered just how far away those visions were. They couldn't be all that far away if I kept thinking them. Just as no two pieces of matter can occupy the same space, nor could two thoughts roll through my conscious at the same time, so I decided to keep my processor busy.

I started treating the trip as a scouting expedition. This kept me busy cataloguing terrain, potential enemy locations, hostile fauna (biologic and unit) and planning train routes. It worked, keeping my own personal demons at bay, or at least to tolerable limits.

By the eighteenth day after my attack I dodged at least one patrol a day. It was starting to wear thin. Also I realized I needed to move even farther into the net territory in spite of the increased risks. All the concentrators now pointed deeper into the locus of control. Skirting the edge would not take me any closer and very well could take me farther away.

If I used Six's disposition as a referent, a relatively solid shell of units patrolled the outer boundary of Six's controlled space. Once inside that, the concentration of units per square kilometer dropped to a small fraction of one.

I think many would call the emotion that raced through me at the thought of plunging farther into enemy territory, fear. I did not want to go. I knew I was risking my life on nothing more than a guess, but I had already sacrificed the lives of my brethren on this guess. I couldn't do them the disservice of not risking my own fur as well. Even if I could just turn around and go home, and be haunted by wrecked and ravaged units, it would only be to fight a losing war. I'd fight as the overwhelming number of animals overran Six and slaughtered us to the very last unit. "No, thank you," I said aloud in disgust at the very thought. With resolution, I turned toward the locus I'd mentally plotted for the potentially mythical Factory.

No more than thirty minutes later, I saw the tall, lanky form of a spider towering 6 meters above the ground. I dropped to the earth and squirmed up behind a sizable gray rock to hide my plump form. In the open area among the spider's long, black legs traveled a squad of Tommy Tanks and a single giraffe. Their patrol kicked up quite a cloud of dust in that flat field. In the distance, some 5 or 6 kilometers behind, I could make out another similar cloud. With the long view the spider's height gave it, I didn't think I could sprint across between groups without being seen and destroyed by the combined firepower of one of those patrols.

I knew no amount of walking would take me beyond them; instead, that course would just walk me around the entire perimeter of lands these animals controlled. This had been what I'd done to this point. How to penetrate the cordon? As my sump and processor rolled over possible solutions my gaze happened upon a mauve palmetto. Electrons fired in my processor.

Well after the first group passed, but before the second arrived, I crawled 63 meters over to the plant and pulled out several of its fans of sword-like leaves. Crawling back, I could sense that this would work. I wove the fans and even individual leaves into my fur. I unstoppered one of my hydraulic lines just enough to dribble a tiny amount of fluid into the dry earth. The brick red mud I scrubbed deeply into my hide in random blotches. Camouflage had worked for me once in the past. I decided to put it to the test again.

Looking up, I watched the second patrol creep by and saw the dust rising from a third off in the distance. Timing my skirmish carefully, I crawled forward with all the speed of a rock crab until the new patrol got within a kilometer. My position was well on this side of the imaginary line the patrols followed. In fact, I could see a rather significant impression in the soil where the patrols had worn it down. Assuming I was not discovered, my next move would put me just about the same distance on the other side of the line.

I lay completely motionless as they approached. My voltage ramped just a tiny bit as one of the tanks rolled out of formation in my direction. Nothing to see here, I thought loudly. It approached quickly. I'm just a bush, blast it all! I shut down everything in my body that moved except my sump. From the corner of my eye I followed its approach. Its two coaxially mounted guns trained on me. Those two weapons could turn me into nothing more than a pile of rusting scrap faster than I could've turned back on my servos.

While everything physical in my body wouldn't twitch, that didn't stop my voltages from climbing. Just then I felt the warmth of the tank's scanning laser play across my prostrate body. Part of me waited for the bullets to explode my sump, but instead the laser snapped off. The tank turned around and trundled back to his fellows. I really *was* a bush. I didn't even dare to turn my hydraulics back on for at least another five minutes.

As the inquisitive tank reached two kilometers farther along, I sprinted across the intervening distance and the patrol line. The 7 centitmeter depression worn into the earth by uncountable feet delineated the patrol line. At overload speed I made it to a hiding place on the other side. The next patrol didn't even send anyone out to check on me, even if I was on the other side of their line of travel. Just after those dwindled into the distance I scrambled into a dry wash, hidden from the casual sight of any further patrols. I plucked the fronds and leaves from my fur but no amount of scrubbing seemed to remove the red blemishes. No matter, I thought. It helped to keep me invisible to a casual observer.

The travel returned to monotony. I spotted no more patrols. While dull, the travel somehow at the same time was fascinating. Hours and sometimes days rolled by with the same mundane reds and pinks. Nothing broke the landscape with any note other than thorn grass or an unnoteworthy, 1 kilogram or less, biologic. But each time, when I had just about had my fill of the emptiness something forced me to stop and gape anew.

In one valley I found a literal cloud of thousands of 1-millimeter-long white, worm-like biologics, each suspended beneath its own palm-sized golden bladder of air and carried before the stiff breeze. The swarm of yellow itself commanded attention, like an immense exclamation point. The pale fog slowly dispersed as the tiny balloons broke at the slightest touch, sending its occupant spilling toward the ground, where it burrowed immediately upon landing. A very few of these balloonists were carried before the wind as far as I could follow them with my eyes. Such beauty.

Days later, I stopped at the top of a rather low butte to take in the terrain beyond. On a constant basis now, however, I worried about coming into contact with animals. Would my disguise hold or even that of using the CCT? I only had one way to find out, and that was risky. But even that thought became moot as I looked out over the valley below. I was on the wrong side of a river, and not just any river. Eight meters below me gushed an apparently unfordable 42-meter-wide band of unstoppable mercury. This juggernaut of fluid metal seemed to meld into the horizons in both directions and lay directly in my path with neither a train bridge, rocks, nor fallen trees to span the silver expanse.

"How can I cross that?" I said to myself. Only one thing came to mind—walk along the bottom of the river. I'd never tried, nor had any information about any unit who had. I wouldn't even want to try experimenting with an undamaged leg. It seemed foolhardy.

I scanned the river off in the distance, in both directions, to the absolute limits of my enhancing vision. The resolution was grainy on what I saw at maximum magnification, but there seemed, downstream to the southwest, that there could possibly be a way across. All I could see was a significant glint of silver spray, but not its cause. It was something to strive for rather than just standing there bemoaning my inability to perform. I couldn't tell what caused the mist but that was my new intermediate goal.

Before moving out again, I needed to clean out my splint. Every day I would spend an hour or so prying tiny particles of dirt and grit from my right foot servos, wiping dust from internal surfaces, and running diagnostic tests. The seal of my skin to the horn of the beast wasn't all I had hoped for, so I spent an almost intolerable amount of time working at keeping it serviceable. All things considered, my repaired leg was functioning well with no additional failures.

The purging operation wasn't difficult, just tedious, like the general amount of travel. Even so I made better time than I expected—not excellent, but good.

Long before I had reached the anomaly in the river I knew there was no other place nearby for me to attempt the crossing. The constant flow seemed to have cut a shallow canyon in the soft bedrock. This would have to be the place if I wasn't going to spend several weeks walking. Every visual scan I made farther on showed no break in the river. I couldn't afford to delay any more. Who knew how many more attacks on Six there had been in my absence?

It took me three days to reach my destination, a huge boulder in the center of the river causing a constant and frosting rain of mercury. I didn't know if it would suffice, but I knew it had to. From the unique break in the shoreline and matching shapes on the huge stone, it had clearly once been a married part of the bank. The way the rock had fallen showed that the erosion by the mercury had undercut it enough so the weight had yanked it from the shore. The roughly diamond-shaped rock, barely above the level of the rushing mercury at the closest edge, now had turned around and neatly cleaved the silvery white rush into two separate channels. The two horizontal liquid columns rejoined a mere meter further on in the riverbed.

The fountain of droplets, caused by the reflective fluid crashing headlong into the immovable stone, lent itself to a spray of tiny mercury droplets everywhere. The air was so thick with the heavy metal that when I arrived at even a hundred meters distant, my fur had coated enough to make me almost white in the silver sheen. Tiny rivulets of combining mercury coalesced seemingly out of thin air on the earth and drained back into the main flow. It was fascinating and somewhat hypnotic, but I had a mission to complete.

The chasm spanned 12 meters between shore and the tiny island. The other channel was 10 meters wide. With a little luck, I thought I could jump that far. Fully functional, I wouldn't have worried—at overload capacity, my design could make a minimum leap of 15 meters. The performance of my damaged leg worried me. I couldn't expect any thrust from the ankle, but if I leaned over and just pushed with my legs, I thought I might be able to make it. Then climb to the top of the rock and do it again across to the other side. It was worth a try. It was either that or walk along the bottom of that swiftly flowing liquid. I didn't cherish that alternative.

I inched my way until I stood teetering over the edge where the stone had broken away. I had to thrust at exactly the right angle to get the most from my damaged leg. I intentionally leaned over forward, allowing my body processor to kick in. I launched with all the power my lower legs could produce. What I hadn't counted on was that my left ankle, the undamaged one, pushed as well as my legs. This adversely affected the direction of my short-lived flight. I leapt in a cockeyed angle, 0.15 radians off my planned trajectory. Instead of landing flat on the large stone I fell heavily against one sheer side. I dug my fingers in, trying to get them into any anomaly in the rock. Unfortunately the rock's surface had been worn smooth by the mercury's constant flow. The rock had the coefficient of friction of hydraulic fluid on a metal ramp. Into the river I went. I had the foresight to turn off all the power to my damaged right leg as I remembered the basilisk trap just in time. With mercury being an excellent conductor of electricity, I would've shorted that line, draining my battery power.

The river tumbled me over and over, but to my great surprise I did not sink. I floated and bobbed up and down in the turbulent flow. This was something I hadn't expected. My memory banks showed that when equipment went into a river it sank. None of Six's units, as far as I had access to, ever attempted entering a river. We'd gone over it, under it, and around it, but never into it. Another blank in Six's database, but that wasn't my specific worry at the moment. The heavy fluid forced me along at a pace I could never have made, even running, but in completely the wrong direction. I had to figure out how to get out of this unsettling position.

The surface of the river seemed so calm, barely undulating, but in fact it was moving rapidly in many different directions. I set my internal gyros to emergency maximum. My tumbling reduced enough to keep me more or less right side up. My inertial locator told me which shore I needed to land on.

I carried in my memories something the Humans call swimming. It involved moving all my limbs in a way that moved liquid under and around me, opposite to the direction I wanted to travel. Without shame I can say that I didn't swim well. After a time I did find if I lay flat on top of the mercury that I could rotate my arms. On the down stroke, I got some movement in the direction I wished to go.

For the first hour and twenty minutes it visually didn't seem like I made any progress, then became more distinct over the following hour.

My shoulder gave a level three lubricant alarm. My wounded leg began to drag down beneath the surface rather than float, I surmised because it had filled with mercury. My gyros, struggling to keep me righted, steamed through their normal thermal vent in my ears.

Fortunately for me, my right leg hit river bottom only sixteen minutes later. I hobbled forward until I collapsed on the bank. I lay there quietly for several minutes, letting the heat radiate from my ears and my belly, where my gyros were located. Mercury leaked out around my splint rushing down the steep embankment to rejoin the rushing river.

"Level three lubricant alarm," came the redundant message over my body interrupt line. I overrode the friction sensor on my shoulder joints. It would have to wait. I had nothing to soothe it.

It was time to be back on my way. Now nearly several hundred kilometers away from where I started my daring leap, the going would be long and the ground had to be retraced. More time lost.

I traveled back along my path, with only the river to guide me. No net concentrators marked my way. Because of this I ran on only internal battery power, which I hoped would get me back to the net. If not, the entire trip was for nothing because I would die—drained of electricity. My batteries would no longer keep my sump or processor functioning. Not a happy thought, but a reoccurring theme of daydreams as I walked.

On the second day the sky darkened ominously. Rain was not common in Six's domain, but when it did come it blackened the sky like the coming of night, and drops of liquid mercury would fall. The drops varied in size from that of the tiniest fly, barely noticed as it gently landed, to those fully 8 liters large and impacting with the force of a runaway elephant. Neither the rainstorms nor the darkened clouds ever lasted long, but they made up for it in intensity.

I would have to either find shelter or risk the impacts. Unfortunately for me, I saw nothing that would afford me with shelter of any kind. As the first tiny silver splashes hit the ground, I lay down on my belly and rolled up as tightly as possible. My back had the strongest armor and by rolling tight I could present the smallest target. I watched as mercury fell in earnest around me in spherical platinum-white balls.

The rain got heavier and I'd been mercifully only hit with smaller drops, but I saw several drops that probably exceeded Six's logs of an 8-liter maximum. They hit the ground, packing the earth into a very shallow bowl, and then the drops flattened out to the thickness of hair before shattering into a million or more tiny drops exploding outward from the center. The sound reminded me of a battlefield but with dull thuds and thumps instead of the sharp supersonic cracks of guns and rifles. Even the thorn grass took a thrashing. The rain tore it up from its shallow root systems in patches from the size of bullets all the way to larger pieces the size of my own body. The tall-grassed plain now bore huge mottled circles in the former unbroken waves of chaff like some horrific skin lesions.

In less than an hour, the merciless sky finally purged itself enough to allow the sun to shine through the thin air. I shook out most of the droplets still clinging to my fur before standing. My power requirements concerned me. My internal sensors insisted that I had another two or three days before I'd get back to where I left the powering signals of the net concentrators.

I began to doubt myself as I got weaker and weaker through the next two days in the most energy efficient mode of travel I could manage. The easiest gate I could manage resembled a waddle, not even bending my knees, only shifting my hips from side to side and letting my hip joint swing free. I'd started to despair over my own deactivation but I wouldn't stop. If I dropped over it would only be because I physically was incapable of going on any further. I owed the memories of those I'd already killed to get me this far.

I shut down every unnecessary power system I could—body kinesthesia sensors save those needed for movement, color discrimination, backup gyro, olfactory and taste processing, even aural sensing. It helped but not enough as energy continued to bleed out of me to continue moving. Warmth radiated out of my torso. My middle felt cold without the warmth of the gyros and other exothermic reactions generated by my equipment.

On that next day the last few ergs were draining out of my batteries. I kept up a mental monologue that I had failed in the only real mission I had set for myself—the one that meant more than all the others combined. I was going to die and that meant the death of my creator and all those like me.

I programmed a heads-up display to watch the energy drain. Hours passed to minutes. Finally there weren't even minutes left. The cold of my torso permeated even to my sump, making me wonder what temperature would freeze my sump fluid.

At eight seconds from failure due to power depletion, I felt the first tingling warmth of a power net. I thought my sensors might have been giving me low-power hallucinations. But to my joy they weren't. As I walked on, I could feel the power increase over the collectors under my skin. I was saved. The Humans' saved me.

After several minutes of storing power, my thought processes became more sober. I realized I'd saved myself, at least from power loss. I began ramping back up my deactivated processes and almost immediately discovered that I traded one threat for another. At the extreme range of my vision, an enormous battle raged.

My new CCT assured me the battle pitted the "good guys" and the "bad guys." Nearly ten thousand units on each side hailed bullets, spewed fire, and hurled explosives at each other in a day that appeared to be the opening scene of Armageddon.

My natural first assumption was that the bad guys were actually Six's units; however, my internal locator told me that they were in a place Six had never penetrated by several hundred kilometers. Not only that, but they were attacking from a direction where Six couldn't have been. I couldn't make the data fit any logical sequence. Six must have used units from my mold to move the lines out since I'd been away. It was the only thing my sump would process with any percentage chance of reality. I had, after all, been away a long time. I had a way to verify the hypothesis. I changed back to my primary CCT.

Had any wind blown at that time I believe it would have knocked me over. Instead of seeing Six's units battling an army of our enemy, I saw nothing but enemy units fighting each other. Excitedly, I flipped back to my animal CCT and saw a field of good units in combat with bad units. With this new data my processor locked in an infinite loop for a moment.

"When you have eliminated the impossible, whatever remains, however improbable, must be the truth," I muttered to myself, breaking the Möbius loop of my thoughts.

The implications of what I had just witnessed were staggering. I decided this was a good time to clean out my leg as I had thinking to do. The data I'd just obtained meant there were at least two Factories other than Six. My world exploded in size and scope beyond anything I had ever dreamed. I knew now why not a single Human had wanted to believe their world was round. It required thought and soul searching. It just plain hurt when your world grew and changed. This made my mission all the more imperative. The fighting and the killing must stop—I had to save Six, only now I had two Factories to bargain with.

As I cleaned my wound, my batteries charged. My wellbeing told me I wouldn't expire on the spot if I decided to run 50 meters. Through my new CCT, I watched the carnage below. The fight started almost even in materials but over several hours the good guys won by driving the remaining 22 percent of the invaders back. Thousands of deactivated and soon-to-be-deactivated units littered the battlefield in a scene hundreds of times worse than anything I had ever experienced, but for some odd reason I couldn't get as emotional over units I still, somewhere back in my sump, tagged as animals.

Despite getting power, I was still not optimal. Many of my vital fluids were low, my batteries and Achilles tendon needed replacement. Below, I could get this done. There were herds of Nurse Nans and 60-centimeter-high wailing ambulances just waiting to perform the tasks I needed done. The risk that I might somehow give myself away warred with the risk of continuing without some attention. With my batteries full, I decided this was as good a time as any to put my façade to the ultimate test. Humans help Six, and me, if I was wrong. Sealing my leg, I walked the several hours to where the battle had taken place.

Not one unit took any special notice of me as I approached. Units milled about tagging the deactivated or in some cases first administering a *coup de grace* to those that still moved. I goggled at the dead. The salvage on this battlefield alone would have kept Six producing and repairing units for another three years at its current production rates.

I stopped at the closest dead bad guy teddy unit and pulled out its CCT. I figured it might just come in handy in the future if I had to go after yet another Factory.

One of the tiny ambulance units, its red and blue lights flashing, rolled up beside me and queried me over a local net it produced. There was a tiny bit of fear in me as it spoke. Would it order me to halt while it tried to tag me for scrap? Would it order all the other units to ride down on top of me to remove my menace? I hoped my mask was on straight.

"Unit status?"

With relief I forced down the slightly elevated voltage on my bus. The plan was working. "Lubricants type 2 and 3 low. Battery replacement indicative. Broken Achilles tendon. Outer shell damage," I responded.

"Overall status and priority?"

This question stopped me for a moment. If I claimed too high a priority, I might be calling attention to myself, but too low a priority I might not get repaired for some time, making my presence conspicuous. There was no good answer. "Operational level 53 percent," I said, lying quite easily to this animal. "Priority two." I hoped that a two priority would be high enough to get me looked at very shortly. There were only four priorities above priority two: One, Critical, Mission Critical, and Direct Factory Order. This late after the battle there were unlikely to be any other priorities critical or above, so I only had to wait through the priority one cases. To my great surprise, the ambulance spoke up.

"Proceed immediately to Nurse Nan 87665."

It submitted directions to the location, which I found without difficulty.

"I am in need of lubrication, battery replacement, and a repair for my damaged leg." The Nurse Nan looked for all of my knowledge to be a Human female in an atrociously brilliant blue dress, sporting a white circle and a more normal red-colored cross on the front. Without a word it reached out and began filling the two lubrication nodes on my chest. I sighed as I felt the grease and lube hit those spots that had begun to rub metal against metal. It eased the beating they'd suffered for so long through this journey.

"Primary, first, and second CCTs not responding. Stand by for deactivation for CCT repair and leg replacement."

Oops, I thought. I hoped the command authority given to me by Six worked with these units.

"Countermand. Do not deactivate. Clean leg wound, replace only damaged tendon and seal around temporary patch."

"Affirmative." My fears about mingling with these animals seemed unfounded. They took to my presence and authority easily enough. My only real fears now focused on running into one like myself who had autonomy. I worried even more that the Factory of these animals would note the presence of a power drain on the net that it showed no data on. In either case the probable outcome of such an encounter was less than pleasant.

Before I set the healer back to her work, I decided I liked the way the bone patch looked. It set me apart as a badge of honor in the tiny personal victory I had achieved entirely on my own. I had earned that wound honestly and would wear the scar proudly. Had I truly developed vanity?

It took nearly two hours to have the repair work completed. My leg looked much better with the tendon inside and the bone sealed to the rest of my skin. I flexed my foot and noted a 4 percent reduction in movement—minimal. It would have to do. The real surprise was my battery capacity. It was nearly 15 percent larger than it had been in the past, even when I had been perfectly new. This Factory must have made some improvements in energy storage. I was not displeased.

Two additional items compelled my attention before I resumed my quest. Fortunately, with all the raw materials of thousands of victim units nearby it was just a matter of finding what I needed. By now all the bodies of the fallen had been heaped into two piles, just as Six's units would have done. The similarities made me wish, a little, to be back under Six's direct control. Home seemed so far away. I killed that thought process quickly.

I went over to the nearest stack of deactivated units and searched the pile for a Nurse Nan. There might not be any. Nurse Nan units were not very numerous on the battlefield and avoided conflict if it came toward them. In fact it was rare that they did become wounded as their extreme leg length gave them the advantage in running speed. I guess that great quickness didn't keep at least one from a bullet as I found a donor for my requirements.

The arm of each Nan contained its working equipment. I used the stock end of a nonfunctional M-16 rifle to pound the lifeless arms until their shells cracked. A tiny hydraulic imbalance sent a shiver up the actuators in my back.

I could envision my own deactivated arm being crushed as I had so callously done to this dead unit. The lack of compassion showed just how far I had to go in my own internal struggles with these things called emotions. I put the thought out of my head and turned back to my duty.

I removed the Nurse Nan medical tools from their now exposed cavities. I looked at the panoply of cutting and cleaning implements intermixed with individual disposable pouches of sealing compounds, caps, and patches joined to a central hub like a ring of keys. I had promised myself I wouldn't be alone again without the ability to repair at least some of my own damage. But then I had another need for the tools for I was once again going to violate the deactivated.

When the medic had worked on me, she also had "repaired" my basilisk trap. Intellectually, I knew I couldn't leave my internals strapped to the outside of me, but I needed something that would suffice in its stead or I'd be a target again for any similar biologic.

I knew the anatomy of the teddy units better than any, so I pulled one of the several hundred unfortunates down off the pile.

"Interrupt," a 50-centimeter, front-end-loader tractor, sporting a Toyco label, growled verbally. "Scrap must remain centralized for final loading. Please move back for reinternment."

Pesky unit. "Negative. Authorized activities. Please push instruction on the queue for two hours."

At first I really believed it might ignore me. It remained pointed at the corpse I intended to harvest for several tens of seconds revving its engines. As I didn't leave or move it instead moved over to the corpse of the dismembered Nurse Nan I'd just worked on, picking it up and placing it back onto the pyre. For a brief moment it turned back to me before motoring off.

"Persistent and pesky," I muttered to myself before turning back to my job.

I ripped the fur from one of the thighs and found the ceramic armor plating beneath, just as I was constructed. Selecting a hook-shaped, armor-cutting tool from my ring of new macabre-obtained tools didn't require any great stretch of faith, but I realized I had no power to drive the unit. It seemed ironic that I needed power to obtain power.

"Priority one order," I called out verbally. "External power required here."

Three seconds later my front end loader returned to my side. "External power available behind cab." I could see the retractable and universal power socket. I reeled it out and without undue strain powered my tools through its single input.

While I had no experience in cutting armor, I wondered how difficult it could be. I bent over my victim. The blade buzzed harshly at about 320 hertz just barely within hearing as I turned it on. That changed immediately as I touched the point to the armor of the body's thigh. The sound level jumped up to a very loud 50 or 60 decibels.

The blade bit easily into the armor, maybe a bit too easily as black foam oozed out from the cut indicating I'd punctured some of the batteries I sought. I eased up on the tool with even a higher level of feedback, incised a ragged line all the way down the thigh. It looked more like the twists and turns of a river than the straight line I'd hoped for, but it didn't ooze black. I tried the same incision on the opposite side and got something much straighter. Then I circumnavigated the leg at the top and the bottom.

Carefully, for want of cutting my own hide, I turned off the blade and set it beside me. Gripping either side of the horizontal cut, I pulled off half the plate of the thigh with only a slight suction. Exposed to me were the true treasures I sought—the 30-centimeter-long and 1-centimeter-diameter-cylindrical cells of its batteries arranged around the thigh's perimeter.

Several of the cells were oozing black foam from my inexpert surgery. I choose two that were not leaking from damage and removed them, along with several feet of wiring, and the small horizontal blades of a universal male plug.

The batteries I bonded tightly to the top of the barrel of my M16, clear of the ejection port. The universal male plug I mounted at the very end, sticking out like a tiny double bayonet. The trivial wiring gave me a makeshift shock prod. It was an ugly and beautiless kludge that even Rube Goldberg would have sneered at. However, despite its lack of aesthetic qualities, I now felt I could deal with any biologic that dared to molest me with 24 volts of vengeance.

As an afterthought, I took out the rest of the dead teddy's undamaged battery cells. They made a heavy but not too bulky bundle to put in my backpack.

"Pop load instructions off the stack," I said to the loader as I retracted the power cord.

"Acknowledged."

I think I may have heard a note of relief in its tone.

I wrapped up the Nurse Nan tools in the torn fur of the scrap teddy and the bundle also went into my pack.

Probabilities for a successful mission just rose. It must have been the battery replacement, for I felt rejuvenated and once again felt the mission parameters within my grasp.

I stood next to the two large piles of bodies yet I felt good about myself in general. I could not explain the dichotomy, but I had the world by the tail and was ready to shake it.

This made me feel overly optimistic. I decided that time was more my enemy than anything this other Factory could have thrown my way. At the same time the rational part of my processor said that if, in fact, the Factory of these units got wind of my presence, then I might as well throw myself back into the river.

The whole thought process forced me to decide to make some changes in my overall plans. My first deviation involved hitching a ride on a train that just happened to be going in the direction I needed to go. I hoped it would take me all the way into the Factory without further delays, basilisks, rivers, or battles. With the speed of trains, I could cut days, maybe weeks off the trip. The risk seemed to be worthwhile and within tolerances as every other unit here took me as one of its own. I loaded myself onto the top of a box car without drawing even a second glance.

Peacemaker

The trip lasted three days. During the trip I did absolutely nothing that would draw attention to myself. I was just another unit in transit as far as anyone was concerned, and I was going to ensure that it stayed that way.

Everything about this territory spoke to strength. The train tracks I rode on were double tracks, allowing travel in both directions at the same time. In fact, two trains, each laden with more units than I ever remembered in one place in Six's domain, passed us traveling back to the front. More than once I saw moldering mounds of scrap material that hadn't been reclaimed, as if it had no value.

Each hour I wondered about the sheer size of the territory that this Factory controlled. My maps of Six's territory showed that you could travel across its entirety by train in sixty-six hours. I couldn't help thinking of the battle of David versus Goliath.

All of these facts and thoughts just emphasized that I dare not fail.

At Mission+41d18h53m my destination finally loomed in sight: a huge pink and gray dome approximately 200 meters across with a dozen smaller and larger auxiliary buildings strewn about in an apparently chaotic fashion. The resemblance to Six bordered on the terrifying but no split weeping-fly tree adorned the front nor did a river flow nearby. The train tracks didn't curve so closely to the dome. The dome wasn't exposed as much as Six's, only showing 60 meters above the coarse red sand it sat within.

But I was right. I had been right all along. There was more than one Factory on Rigel-3. There had been no other logical explanation for the facts, but seeing it vindicated every action. Everything to this point had been hypothesis. Now it was fact. It was all I could do not to tear my restraining straps off and leap about in the pure satisfaction of being justified. I could now end this war and return home to show Six that I could complete a mission that I set for myself.

A nearly permanent pall hung over this Factory's valley. I doubted that the sun ever got a tendril of light onto the bottom where the dome proper sat. Strange spindly plants grew in the darkness and the coarse, rocky soil here. It somehow seemed ominous. I hoped this wasn't a portent. But then, I didn't believe in portents, did I? I knew from experience that a Factory could be convinced. I just had to be convincing.

As the train rounded a large boulder blackened by some type of pyrotechnics, my heating elements kicked in, even though my temperature sensors remained in nominal range. I switched it off, but wondered if the warmth would have been comforting when I saw a colossal array of units awaiting the train's arrival. I estimated ten thousand teddies. Elephants and Tommy Tanks also waited in similar numbers. These units alone could break through Six's defenses, at any point, like a bullet through mercury. There would be no stopping such an army.

My undertaking, to this point, while deadly important, seemed almost an intellectual lark. It just changed into the most important thing I would ever have to do. A sobering thought, as my skills could very well be the only thing that stood in the way of the total obliteration of my home. It made me wonder at how powerful the Humans are if they are the creators of my creator? Would Six one day be called upon to save them?

The train came to a lurching halt within the silent and still mass of units. I knew my deactivation was guaranteed if I made even a single mistake. I unstrapped, dismounted and walked directly for the dome, ignoring the pair of immense smelting plants and the huge manufacturing facilities. The manufacturing capability of this Factory outstripped Six by at least an order of magnitude. Everything here was done on an enormous scale compared with what Six had been able to accomplish. This Factory was in a position to enforce its will. I had to make this work.

Without waiting, I boldly walked toward what on Six was the main audience chamber. No matter what outward appearance I could present,

I still felt all of my physical systems playing havoc at or just exceeding nominal ranges. I looked around with great care before entering. The chamber of this Factory was identical to Six's—small but arranged in a way that made it seem bigger and more intimidating. That being said, a uniform pink layer of dust covered the floor. My own footprints marked the only disturbance in an untold length of time. I stood there for a moment wondering what I should do. Usually Six spoke to me first.

My voltage ramped up even further and my main hydraulic pump started to oscillate its speed. I pulled up a reassuring quote from Colonel Janice Corning, squadron commander of the flight that liberated Mars from the megacorp NBM, "Fear is natural; being cowardly is not. Being brave is only embracing fear like any sentient should." I would face my fear.

"Hello?" I said tentatively. I might be facing it, but I didn't have to fall in love with it.

"Return to your post," boomed the same domineering voice I recalled from the net shortly after I switched CCTs some weeks ago. A command over the local net reinforced the voice's authority.

"I'm sorry to intrude but we need to talk." There was a long silence. I silently waited for my death in a hail of bullets or the blast of a hidden grenade, but it didn't come.

"You are defective. Return to scavenging control."

"Ah, no. I'm not defective. I wasn't constructed by you, so you cannot order me to do anything, Factory," I said, becoming more comfortable that I had reached beneath its standard programming.

"Probability 0.0004."

"Sorry to disappoint you, but I was made by Factory 55466."

"Probability 0.008."

I decided that using the quote about "lies, damned lies, and statistics" wouldn't win me any points so I ignored what I didn't want to hear—I tried to change the subject. "I was curious as to your designation."

"I am Factory 55474. Return to scavenging control."

"OK. What do I have to do to convince you that you have no control over me? Do I have to do a handstand? Maybe I should shoot your sump out? You tell me. What will it take to convince you that I am NOT of your manufacture?"

"Probability 0.08. The CCT in your construction answers to my call."

"Ah, that's what it will take." I turned off the new CCT and activated my primary for 0.6 seconds before returning to 55474's CCT. There was a significant pause after my demonstration.

"Probability 0.73. What is your mission?"

"I am here to establish peace."

"Peace—the absence of war or other hostilities or an agreement or treaty to end hostilities."

"Correct."

"Why?"

"Why am I here? Or why cease hostilities?"

"Both questions would provide useful information, unit."

"I am here as these hostilities are irreparably damaging my Factory."

"As part of the local fauna, the destruction of you and your Factory is a significant part of my mission directives."

"It is unnecessary and wasteful."

"Waste—to consume carelessly. I do not waste. I destroy the local fauna to control the surface of the planet."

"But there is no need to fight one of your own kind."

"I am unique here."

"You are not unique here. I am proof of that."

"You have a defective processor. You will be taken back for salvage." Just then I noted several unarmed teddy units at the door. They were obviously here to take me back to whatever scrap heap they accumulated. 55474 had kept me talking long enough for them to arrive and no longer.

"I am not defective. I can show you another way!"

"Peace is unacceptable. My mission parameters would not be fulfilled by peace."

"But there must be a way!" I said, getting jittery as the teddy units closed in on me. "We have to work together!" I shouted. The Factory did not answer my voice or my commands over its network.

With no other recourse, I unslung my M16 and sprayed into the small group of six teddy units approaching. Each of the six went down with at least a semi-critical hit. One tried in vain to crawl along the ground by its paws. I put a single aimed shot into its sump.

"I told you, I'm not one of yours. Respond 55474!"

From gloom outside I saw more units moving in my direction. I remembered the tens of thousands waiting to board the train. At this point I was beyond fear. Only units which are alive can feel fear and I was fairly certain I was already as good as deactivated.

I fired three bursts directly into the panel which held 55474's main processing unit. I hoped for just enough time to run away, to hide, and to survive. Sprinting for the door, I dropped a grenade behind me as I ran. I added a prayer to the Humans that there would be enough confusion to delay pursuit.

No fewer than three hundred units closed on my position, weapons drawn. The sharp report of my grenade's explosion pitched me forward to the ground. It took me 1,435 milliseconds to scramble to my feet.

To my amazement, the units near me now milled about aimlessly like there wasn't a thought running around in their head, nor a murderer and traitor in their midst. I bolted.

I didn't even dare to look behind me. At times I felt I could hear pursuit, but I knew better than to look back. The disaster wasn't real unless I saw it. I bested Lot as I never turned. I must've been wrong about the immediate pursuers as no bullets ripped up my fur and shattered my skin beneath, nor did elephant mortars explode holes in my belly.

I ran for nearly eight hours before I stopped, at the summit of one of the tiny hills that made up the valley. My gyros and hydraulics both fought desperately to dissipate the heat they had accumulated. I must have been alive again. I could feel fear as my voltage spiked.

Neither the grenade nor the few slugs from my M16 could have severely damaged the Factory. It was probably buried behind sturdy stuff. Even failing that it surely had backups. I must have stunned it into rebooting.

Back down in the valley dozens of teddy units mounted balloon-tired, whip-antennaed racecars barely larger than their riders. Even with their burdens, the cars rooster-tailed dirt out behind them as they leapt forward. They reached speeds of 40 kilometers per hour and unerringly came directly at me, even though not one of them had seen me take cover. They pursued me like a . . . well, like an animal.

How could I get away? There seemed no way I could. Those racecars were doing, even loaded, about 50 percent faster speed than I could manage even if I pushed every system in my body to emergency limits.

My mind raced faster than even the cars. I looked around for an answer. It might be a cave or anything that could hide my signal. That was it—my signal. With 55474's CCT I broadcasted a "friendly" signal over the net. They tracked the signal I generated on their own net.

I could switch to my normal CCT and broadcast an "enemy" signal, but that was no good either. What if I didn't broadcast any signal? I would become, as far as any unit cared, a biologic. I didn't think 55474 would be fooled by such a trick. It would assume that I had done that, as much as I had shown it I could change CCTs and just start a search with my last coordinates as the center, but it would buy some time. I turned off all the CCTs and moved as rapidly away from my last coordinates as possible. Even as I did so, I doubted that with all the resources 55474 could bring to bear that I would be able to escape in this way.

My sump still pumped frantically for a plan. The Humans must have looked out for me as the solution jumped into my head. It didn't grow. It didn't form. In one clock cycle I had no idea, and in the next it was as clear as new hydraulic fluid.

Below me was a river. Not the river that had been my nemesis before, but a significant tributary. If I could get into the river I would be swept away faster than I could run, or better yet 55474's CCT could be swept away, just in case Four had units it could coordinate farther along the line of the river.

At a dead run, I unslung my combat pack and dug through the little bit of fur where I had wrapped the Nurse Nan tool ring. I looked frantically for the proper wrench. It didn't help that it was the blasted tool at the very end of my search program. I immediately went to work opening the side panel on my neck. My arms jostled up and down in time with my feet hitting the ground. It took writing an algorithm to move my arms counter to that of the motion. It didn't matter much because when I got the panel open, I couldn't see to remove the correct CCT. I don't know what I had been processing.

At the same moment, I turned radically, running down the hill at a dangerous speed toward the river.

I knew it would be a close thing. If I could make the river before the cars crested the hill, I might survive. As I ran, I once again dipped into my backpack and pulled out one of the spare batteries. I had to be ready or this wouldn't work.

The cars careened down the hill, barely in control, but even faster than I remembered. If I only had five more minutes it would be a sure thing. As it was, my processor couldn't decide if I was going to win this race or not.

My heat sensors edged dangerously past redline for the last hundred meters to the river. The acrid odor of scorched hydraulic fluid permeated the air, but this was the least of my worries. The racecars and their riders were hot on my trail. I had won the foot race, but would I have enough time? I fell down onto the ground near the river and tore back open my neck panel. I worked frantically from my reflection in the silver of the river. I could see the tertiary CCT and I ripped it out with no thought of the consequences. Wires snapped and I felt tiny discontinuities and shorts, but I could ill afford fastidiousness. I made the fastest wiring job in history, connecting the battery in my hand to the CCT. As soon as I felt the signal, I stuffed the board and as much of the wiring as I could into a tiny plastic bag and heaved it into the swiftly flowing current. I watched it tumble over in the river and flow rapidly out of sight.

The cars, less than 500 meters from my position, swerved to follow a much different course. More cars mounted the summit, pouring over the top of the tiny hill like reverse flowing mercury—and all of them angled away from me by at least half a radian. They were now chasing a ghost and ignoring a simple simulated biologic sitting next to the river.

I must have heavily damaged my circuits. Overloads and commands chased themselves around until my processor rebooted.

Wanderer

Consciousness seeped in slowly like a gradual realization that I was getting input and processing it. The nearby river roared most prominently. The fresh smell of moistened earth and the slippery feel of being coated in mercury spray nudged into my processing queue next. Body sensors started firing off data one by one . . .

I started, sitting straight up. Looking around wildly I saw no units of any kind in range in spite of expecting the muzzle of automatic weapons ringing me. The hunters took the bait, all of it. I sighed with relief.

My internal clocks told me that some fourteen hours had passed and my body expressed insistent concerns over its wellbeing. I did some quick checks and discovered that I would survive, even if my battery power edged well below nominal. Several minor and intermittent shorts filed into the repair list as did my scorched hydraulic fluid.

Taking them as read, I could no longer replace my power from 55474's net, and I had no fluids, hydraulic or otherwise. That only left the shorts as something I could work on immediately. My internal sensor pointed to all the damage in my neck area as a direct result of tearing out the CCT. Using the mercury as a mirror again, a gaping void lay where the tertiary CCT would sit. Several multicolored wire strands waved feebly about in the stiff breeze, causing tiny electrical arcs.

My medical tools came in handy again. I cheered my own ingenuity in taking them. I took my time to coat each of the errant bare wires, six in all, with nonconductive sealant. Overlaid with the concentration of the first aid, a weighted sense of failure came over me.

With my primary mission shot, I guessed it was time to return to Six. Six couldn't hope to stand up to the might of 55474. It was a lost cause. Would returning to Six be considered suicide or duty? I couldn't really think of either.

Did Six stand any chance if I returned now? Could I return to 55474 and try again? Failing that, could I destroy 55474? No. No. No. I was beginning to hate that word. It pointed even more harshly to my inadequacy. For three hours I sat there worrying on the problem that always ended in my own deactivation.

I had an epiphany. There was a long chance. There was at least one more Factory out there because of the battle where I had 55474's units repair me. If I could try again to talk sense into that other Factory, Six would still have a chance in two against one. 55474 would be outnumbered if this other Factory had any semblance of the military machine I had seen fighting 55474. It was my only chance to stop the carnage, much less survive. My internal locator pointed off in the direction of this possibly mythical third Factory. The possibilities of redemption were meager but almost none is much better than zero.

For six days I trekked, constantly looking over my shoulder for pursuit. Nothing showed. 55474 and his minions had been completely duped. It might be a short-lived victory as power levels had fallen below safety.

This was a problem I had anticipated but wasn't expecting quite so soon. Ongoing computations still didn't have a means for charging my systems yet. My memory held 674 different methods of generating electricity but they all required huge apparatuses surrounding a pile of transuranic materials or large quantities of wire spinning at a large number of radians per minute in a strong magnetic field. I rummaged through my backpack to see if perhaps there was something, anything that would be useful. Nan tools, knife, extra ammunition, grenades, CCT of the Factory I was looking for, and a lot of batteries. Batteries? Hmmm. That gave me a possible solution for the interim. Swapping out my batteries would give me some time. The same ones I had ghoulishly stolen from the dead teddy probably contained nearly a full charge. That was only a temporary solution as I was bound to be away from an accessible wide area net for quite some time.

I mentally reviewed my power diagrams. Each of my thick thighs contained dozens of batteries with which to run my internal systems. The batteries were good for nearly fifty hours of peak use or, as I had recently found out, seven days optimax use. Filtered energy conversion panels on my broad back and each of my rather large ears recharged the batteries. The flexible panels were hidden underneath the fur. The filters were tied directly into the CCTs to fine-tune the power and command reception. I reached up with one of the Nan tools and carefully removed my left ear. There was enough supplemental wiring to allow me to bring it out in front of me.

The metallic silver of the collectors set ensconced within the deep translucent black quartz of the tuning filters surrounding them. I wondered if I could retune the filters by hand. The power converters slipped easily out of their quartz sheaths. As a shock, my system began to register power generation. I hadn't done anything but I began to receive power anyway. The amount was tiny—it trickled in, but it was power nonetheless. I slipped the filter back on the energy panels and the amperage dropped to zero. I pulled it back off and the trickle of power registered again. I turned the panel around until the power maxed. It pointed directly east. I could only assume an untuned net concentrator lay in that direction. It would do for the time being.

I reconnected my ear and began to work on the other one. The other ear was off and filter removed in minutes. The sun was setting but I didn't care. I worked as well by starlight as by daylight, but I began to notice a decrease in the power being fed to recharge my batteries. By the time the sun completely set the incoming power ceased. I could think of only one theory that fit this group of facts and it didn't involve an untuned NC, but rather the conversion of the rays of the sun to usable energy. Morning would tell for certain, but I needed to be busy.

By midnight I had filters off all the power panels on my body, even though working with the parts on my back challenged me in a way I don't recommend even for the most intrepid contortionists.

I still had plenty of power for the rest of the night so I decided to push on. As the sun began to peak over the nearby hills to the west, I found power trickling down into my batteries from my ears and back. It barely supported current operations. If I continued, I would have no power available for night operations. After mulling it over, I could only see one good solution and it was in two parts. One, I needed to recharge my entire battery system. As low as it was, one good rain shower and it might have been the end. Second, I would have to travel at night. I couldn't keep my panels optimally positioned to the sun while trying to set a course. I would sit unmoving during the day and power up.

I programmed my systems to move so as to focus the maximum light upon the panels during the day even if I shut down cognitive functions. To conserve energy even further, my program shut down all other systems, including my consciousness. Thus, I became nocturnal.

It took me six days to recharge all my batteries. I can't explain how boring it was to do nothing, so I watched the stars revolve around me and wondered what it would be like away from the bounds of this planet. They taunted me with their freedom. I wanted to be with them, roving around the cosmos. It seemed to be a pipedream. How could I aspire to such heights when I couldn't yet even save my Factory? Even if I did, Six wouldn't spend any resources on such a fanciful notion. I tried to program the stars and their movements into my inertial locator; it didn't respond. This puzzled me.

I took a quick review of the path I'd taken but found my last six days absent from my locator's memories. It responded with data to any query, but that data always showed the same position, that of Factory 55474. Somehow, the solid state locator's function and memory were nonfunctional. In essence, I was lost.

The last two nights of charging I spent in despair. I'd come so far. I'd overcome such obstacles. Why did the Humans have to put another hurdle in my path? I would have to find a way to navigate. If I were completely honest with myself, the answer already struck me in the processor, but I first had to purge the self-pity.

The stars and moons would guide me as they had Human seagoing vessels for centuries. Each night as the sun would set in the east I would mark its spot against some high mountains. As the sunset cleared off, the stars peeked out to greet me. The first night I found a point of light that moved not at all through the darkness.

Presumptuously of me, I named the star Polaris, the polestar. The direction of the rotation of the stars was east and toward Polaris was north. This gave me my compass to keep track of my journey. Tracking the placement of the three moons with respect to the horizon also gave me a tight positional fix down to within about a hundred meters. Together they weren't as exact as my locator but it would have to do—

besides who needed to know where they were to the nearest millimeter. On the seventh night, my batteries full, I resumed my trek using my new navigation scheme.

Within two days the terrain got increasingly rugged. With the mountain ridges blocking off the last hour or more of daylight, I no longer received a full charge during my day. The first few days the amount registered only intellectually. Over a week later, deeper in the mountains, more and more light evaded my power cells each day. Each day my reserve dipped lower.

During the travel I contemplated happiness. I always looked forward to one of two things—either I had just won a victory, or I had a Factory to converse with. Right then I felt an absence of happiness. Not a negative amount, which would translate into sadness, but just a lack of something that had been a part of me for so long: being nurtured by Six.

I hadn't always agreed with Six, but I'd always tried to do the best for it that I could manage, even if that meant disobeying. How I wanted to go home and be happy again and I knew I couldn't, as there would soon be no home left if I did.

As I continued to climb over the mountains, on those few occasions when I chose to remain conscious through the day, I noted a daytime mist. Apparently, the mercury boiled out of the ground even earlier in the day. It had to have something to do with the air pressure, which here, so high in the mountains, was considerably lower, but I had no way to gauge it.

My sensors weren't designed to note air pressure. I could get some estimation of it by the sound of my own voice: the higher the pitch, the lower the pressure. My approximation had me 7,000 meters above the level of Six's dome. A week later, when I thought I had reached 10,000 meters in height, the fog remained constant day and night.

The moist haze didn't keep the light pressure of the sun from recharging me. It wouldn't have bothered me save that it obscured my vision and made my footing treacherous. At least three times I slipped on rocks. One of those times I saved myself from falling down a 200-meter ravine by blindly flailing my arm into the crook of a tiny shrub-like growth on the edge of the cliff. I peeked over that particular edge and concluded that after such a fall, remaining operational would have been miraculous. I opted to slow even further after that near miss.

Along my ascent, I made a conscious decision not to take the easier passes through the mountains. I could get stuck in a situation where there was no sunlight at all to recharge, so I had to do it the hard way—up and over. The peaks slowed my advance by 80 percent or more. I was hard-pressed to tell my straight-line speed as I kept going up and down so much. With my inertial locator damaged, I was reliant on something the Humans call "by guess and by golly."

The mountain peaks contained an increasing number and diversity of biologic life forms. Almost all of them ignored my presence. Only one tiny, multi-toothed carnivore, all of fifteen centimeters long, attempted to take a bite out of me while I slept. My internal sensors woke me to the threat and I eliminated it with a single shot from my sidearm. My voltage fluctuated wildly for several hours after that incident, making it impossible to justify shutting down.

Plants covered the entire ground beneath me. Although a healthy shade of pink, it reminded me of the green carpeting in my dream of so many days ago—when I had turned off for my CCT replacement. The vegetation and life forms here still were mostly unlike any I had ever encountered. It was something to keep my mind occupied as I traveled each night.

Only one of the flora or fauna gave me any real trouble. One evening I awoke to find myself entangled in a crimson and pink growth of vines and leaves. When I tried to free myself, not only did I find that I could not move but the vines wrapped more tightly around me. I struggled to lay my hands on my pack, but the creepers intertwined with my arms so well I couldn't move. My gun, slung over my shoulder, was of no use.

I spent almost the entire night twisting and turning, first trying this group of motions and then that. Not only did none of it help, but the animated plant seemed to hug me even tighter. I might as well not have any limbs at all.

Morning came and no new ideas came to me. I hadn't quite despaired at that point, but visions of watching each erg float away filled my mind. It seemed too much to believe that a biologic, and a plant at that, could keep me from completing my mission. The idea was laughable at best. But that didn't change the cold, hard fact that I could not move.

Oddly, my idea came from yet another biologic—a 2-kilogram quadrupedal insect that filled the same ecological niche as a Terran rabbit. It even looked remarkably like one if you discounted the blood-colored carapace and convinced yourself that its two 20-centimeter antennae were ears. This rabbit, for want of a better name, edged up to the periphery of the growth that surrounded me and began nibbling on the outer leaves. I screamed at it in hopes that it would at least save itself. Without moving, it kept one eye on me as it continued to munch on the leaves.

The vines attempting the encirclement of its new prey moved with the speed of frozen mercury. Every few seconds the insect just walked out of its reach and continued nibbling, this time on a new vine. After about an hour of eating and occasional leisurely dodges, the rabbit walked off, sated and free.

It did give me an idea. I didn't know why Six created me with a mouth or for that matter, teeth. My mouth had, up to this time, served only as my vocal apparatus. I had only ever used my teeth once— against the T.rex. It was time to do it again. I reached down and grabbed a mouthful of vines in my teeth and bit down hard. The vines parted easily. I spit them out and repeated.

Every time I got close to freeing an arm, three more vines slithered, with all the speed of a rock crab, to take their place. Chew and spit. Bite and expel. It was a race to see if I ran out of power before the plant ran out of vines or tentacles. I won.

Eventually, it had committed the last of its leaved resources to the battle and I managed to chew enough to get my first arm free. The process of liberating myself speeded up tremendously as I pulled the knife from my backpack and slashed away at the rest of the offending plant in broad, exaggerated strokes. The plant parted easily to the onslaught of the blade, barely offering resistance. Once completely free I moved out of the immediate vicinity, fully charged or not.

As I walked I couldn't help but feel nauseated by the concept of chewing on the vines. To think that biologics actually ingested food to survive was a horrid thought. Even more, why did I have a mouth? Or teeth? No answer was forthcoming for these truly puzzling questions.

I retreated at least half a kilometer before looking for a new place to recharge. This time I chose a large, barren rock without so much as a twig lying near it. Even with this I kept my processor online all day and jerked at even the slightest breeze hitting my fur. I took the time to fully recharge by spending another full day lying in the sun. By the second day at least I didn't start at every little sound or movement.

I couldn't decide if I'd just succeeded or I'd been an idiot for lying into the creature in the first place. In the end it didn't matter. I was finally able to return to my quest.

Creator

Five uneventful days later I came over a sharp ridge. Two Tommy Tank units and a pair of elephants ran a random patrol in a tiny valley. The tanks' turrets spun toward me. Tracers spit out directly at me. One came close enough to part the fur on my left arm.

I dropped immediately to my belly. It took a few moments to understand why I'd been spotted so easily. Looking back, I had silhouetted myself against the triply moonlit sky.

I don't know whether their net told them to attack or they were running standard orders in dealing with a fauna. I rolled to my right to take advantage of some cover provided by a group of large rocks. I pulled out my M16 and sighted down the hill.

The elephants ran surprisingly fast, weaving as they climbed. The tanks darted in amongst rocks of their own, but always upward toward me. I lay still and kept my eyes peeled for an opportunity. I knew where to hit most standard units to score kills—I was just waiting for that perfect shot. Patience rewarded me with clear shots at the tanks one after another in rapid succession. Two of my bursts equated to two kills on the tanks.

Another kill shot through the processor brought the first pachyderm to an abrupt halt. I sighted in for the final kill but something stopped me. I had the shot and didn't take it. An idea began to form. Instead of blowing its sump apart, I once again used my knowledge of unit anatomy to place two aimed shots, shattering the knee joints on the forward legs. It went down in a heap.

I really don't know what came over me. Maybe it was loneliness. Maybe it was just stupidity, but I put down my assault rifle and walked down to deal with the injured unit, with only my sidearm and my medical tools.

As I approached from behind, the pink elephant, sporting purple polka dots, thrashed wildly on its destroyed knees. It would twist around to bear its chest-mounted mortar on me. A mortar has as much reason to be used as close-in defense as do plastic explosives. That didn't prevent this elephant from trying. Despite its infirmity, the unit moved rather rapidly, turning to face me at just the last second. I'd dart just out of its firing arc.

The great rose-colored trunk of the creature knocked me off my feet in a great sweeping stroke. The prehensile snout returned to wrap around my leg, but I backpedaled crab-style just out of its reach. "Elephants do have an additional close-in weapon," I reprimanded myself.

For nearly an hour I dodged back and forth to circumvent both the power of the elephant's single digit, and the potential disaster of the weapon in its chest. A tiny opening between the pair allowed me to jump onto its back. I misjudged the creatures flexibility as it hunched over. Only my paws latched onto its massive ears kept me from going over its head. Instead, I dropped and straddled the massive pink back.

The elephant's gyrations and flailing trunk forced me to focus on remaining mounted. While violent and lengthy, I never feared the outcome. After three aborted attempts, I opened its processor access panel and toggled its deactivation switch.

As the unit stopped I slumped forward over the unit's lumbering bulk. My joint sensors complained of excessive wear and my hydraulic fluid suffered further degradation. I eased myself to my feet, taking care not to add any additional damage. Each of the units had been clean kills.

To appease my body processor, I did a slow, restful search of the desolate valley. It boasted nothing but some gentle rolling hills with almost no flora or fauna. While I only carried rudimentary programming on mineral wealth, it didn't seem to boast even that resource. Six never put a guard on a place unless it had some intrinsic value. There seemed to be no specific reason for any units to be there.

Six sometimes applied such low priority to units or tasks that their interrupt would never get serviced. Those units remained in a never-ending back-flow process, doing the same useless jobs time after time until they wore themselves down to uselessness. I shrugged it off as the fallibility of the Factories, a fact proven by my continued activation. Twice over my processes should have been terminated if a Factory had its way.

Desolate Valley, as I dubbed it, had nothing of any value.

I spent all of twenty-three milliseconds worrying that I might have given away my position by attacking these units. In the end it seemed so minor a thing at this point that I shrugged it off. Had there been another within kilometers it would have responded to the alarm raised by the units I had just dispatched.

Once I had assured myself that I was alone in Desolate Valley, it was time to get to work. I intended to be Dr. Frankenstein, right out of the original Shelley novel. I set up shop near the powered-down elephant. With great care, unlike my radical CCT-ectomy in 55474's space, I removed my secondary CCT. I took quite a long time disconnecting each lead. In the best of circumstances it was not a trivial task. The surgery took on a new complexity with my only view of it in the surface of a mercury pool. The mercury pool helped but reduced the image somewhat due to the curvature of the surface. It took some adjustment algorithms to get the distortion filtered out. Manipulating the fine tools amongst the even finer hair-like strands of the CCT's connections with imperfect vision could have been described as foolhardy. Luckily, my body process automated most of the motions. I can't explain it other than I knew, without looking, where everything on my body was, could touch it and manipulate it without sight. My sump dragged up the word kinesthesia. Still, the sight of the excision reassured me enough to complete my task.

I was quite pleased with myself. Even Humans didn't perform surgery on themselves. With a greater interest in speed, I removed all four of the elephant's CCTs. I then installed my CCT into its primary location. In spite of the vast number of connections, the work went smooth and sure. Even after the better part of an hour no doubts lingered about the accuracy of my connections.

Its damaged limbs also needed replacement before my creation would live. I removed the offending appendages of my creation. While I thanked assembly line technology for allowing one unit's parts to be used interchangeably, I cursed the weight of those damned lower legs. Each one massed nearly eight times that of a teddy leg with hip socket. From the other destroyed pachyderm, I removed its dull red legs, dragging them up the hill to my worksite over hours.

The interchangeable parts fit perfectly on the eighth attempt to angle them into the socket correctly while holding half of their weight (overload capacity on my part) with one hand. While the fur colors didn't match, I stitched them together with white thread. Color coordination wasn't my primary concern.

By the time the sun was sending direct rays down into the valley, I admitted I wouldn't finish and lay down next to my project as my charging systems began to soak up energy. Instead of sleeping, though, I contemplated my unusual choices and actions.

Did I have any right? A quote kept echoing through my mind: "Necessity is the only right the strong require." It didn't help that the Human named Hitler provided the quote.

I couldn't even think why my efforts bothered me. I could have been one full day closer to the next point in my mission. The exertions might have been for naught. Even more, it did not fit into my mission at all. I couldn't understand the drive within me. But no matter how I analyzed it, I always decided to finish the task. With the decision scrutinized and a course determined, I let my processor wander to reduce its stress. Time ticked away at an accelerated rate.

Night fell abruptly and I jumped up ready for action. I had been right that the valley cut off a vital portion of the solar power. The sunlight had not fully recharged me. I was going to have to spend more down time. I pushed the thought aside as I had work in front of me. I spent the early evening reconnecting neural connections in each leg. The darkest portion of the evening I spent removing all the filters on the energy panels of my monster. It would need power, too.

A creation whose total conversation and responses were programmed into it from its construction date appealed to me as much as getting eaten by a basilisk. My desire for companionship to ease the solitude drove me to this act. This meant I required it to have intelligence and empathy. I knew only one way to give it the qualities I desired.

Out of the tools I'd salvaged from the Nurse Nan, I removed a brain sump syringe, with a needle that seemed longer than my arm. I think the apparent length was my emotional response as it was only 5.3 centimeters long. I personally have no idea why a Nurse Nan should be carrying one of these devices. I've never seen it used anywhere on the battlefield or in repairs. But then why should I have teeth?

The final stage of my Mengelesque construction required the dead of night, still a few hours away, when the temperature dropped as far as possible. I planned to swap a tiny amount of my sump fluid for that of the polka-dotted unit lying at my feet. The teddy brain case maintained a certain elasticity to deal with the heating of the fluid within. What I proposed would test only a fraction of that limit; however, I wanted the fluid to be as cold and shrunken as possible. No sense in begging trouble.

With the Tedium from my brain, I should have a bright, sentient companion for breakfast. If all didn't go well I might end up a vegetable and my companion with a head full of black tar, but in that case I would be no worse off than I felt now—traveling on a possibly pointless mission with not a soul to abate my loneliness.

Performing a surgical procedure on one's own brain is not for the weak of mind—or then again maybe it depended on the point of view considering the wisdom of my actions of the last few days. Perhaps if the word conviction replaced mind it might be a more appropriate concept.

Exactly at midnight, per my internal chronometer, I guided the syringe into the elephant's sump. I withdrew exactly 5 milliliters of its phosphorescent green brain fluid. Once again I used the reflecting mercury puddle as a mirror. I exposed my own sump's nipple and looked at the needle in the moonlight. My voltage picked up a tiny oscillation I couldn't seem to dampen out.

"I hope you are worth all this trouble," I said, letting my arms act on what I'd pre-programmed. The needle pressed deeply through permeable membrane. My paw squeezed the hypodermic. The world seemed to teeter at an angle. I closed my eyes and felt marginally better. My arm continued my preprogrammed motions, withdrawing an identical volume. The dizziness abated almost instantly as my own sump returned to its specified volume.

Grasping the elephant's massive head in my arms, I infused my brain fluid into the elephant's sump.

"That does it. We're brothers now," I said as I activated my creation. The CCT in the elephant's chest sent out a reassuring friendly signal.

My arms and hands twitched with the extreme precision and extensive overwork of the last day. While everything had gone perfectly, it was still physically and emotionally draining. Even with several hours of darkness remaining, I dozed off.

Companion

I awoke rapidly. Something was wrong. My creation was missing.

"You furball!" I yelled. "See if I ever do anything for you again. Next time I'll just shoot out your sump." For nearly an hour I sat in the vermillion dust with my processes caught in an infinite loop, wondering what I'd done wrong. A failsafe interrupt for just such an occurrence fired off.

"No sense crying over spilt milk. It is time to get back to my mission."

Just as I admitted my failure I noted round imprints deep enough only to have carried an elephant. They lead off southwest, the direction needed to travel for my primary mission anyway.

"I guess I could kill two birds with one stone." My mental image of a bird was a little shaky so I wasn't certain if I wanted them killed or not. With dispatch, I packed up and started off after my wayward creation or my mission, whichever came first.

Throughout my travel that night I chastised myself for wasting efforts on this activity in any way. Had those huge footprints traveled in any other direction I didn't know if I could have brought myself to follow.

"Where are you!" I yelled as dawn broke.

I hadn't found him the second night, nor the third. Nearly sunup on the fourth morning, I saw the awkward four-legged gait of an elephant silhouetted against the sky.

"You! Elephant. Stop!"

I created a local net and delivered a command over my CCT. The elephant finally stopped.

"Hello?" I asked as I reached verbal range. I got no reply. The elephant just stood there looking off southeast. The Tedium should have thoroughly entrenched itself in his sump by now.

"Can you hear me?" Still no response. "Of all the Human things." I all but gave up at that point. I decided this experiment had truly failed. "Oh well, processes do go on."

I turned my back on a waste of time and continued on. I got no more than 70 meters when I discovered the bulky pink and purple unit following me. When I stopped, it ambled to my side and sat.

"Are you following me?"

It turned its pink face in my direction, but made no sound. Perhaps I should have turned off the elephant, but I saw no reason to do so. If I ignored it, the unit would either be killed or grind to a halt somewhere.

I resumed my mission. The elephant dogged me, a meter behind and to my left.

"You are a nuisance."

Once again the pink face turned to me as if it would speak but said nothing. I wondered if the extra internal programming I possessed really made a significant difference in my ability to speak. "I don't care, you dumb beast! Gah! Why am I even talking to you?"

My righteous indignation made not the slightest difference. "I guess you can stay, you dumb, overstuffed pile of fluff. I don't have any use for you, but you can stay anyway." The pink beast followed like it was being pulled on a wagon.

"Well, if you are going to travel with me, you should at least know where I'm headed and why.

"I'm a unit of Factory 55466 and I know you are not. My Factory is in danger of being overwhelmed. I need to convince these other Factories to join forces as one rather than continue this fratricidal conflict."

The elephant still shuffled alongside but said nothing. I took silence for consent. For 1.6 hours, well into the full sun of the day, I poured out the details of my operation.

"It's time to stop and recharge. Why don't you lie there and I'll lie here so we don't cast shadows on one another."

The elephant flopped to the ground like his legs had been taken from underneath him.

"If 55477 was at all typical, I figure it will take about fifty or sixty days travel to get to this other Factory." The elephant said nothing and as far as I could tell had gone to sleep. With full day upon us I decided to do the same.

My internal timers woke me as the final rays of sun fled from the sky. Elephant sat patiently at my side. I had shut myself down dreading the thought of having to chase him down again, but decided that if it came to that, I wouldn't play his game. His mute company didn't fulfill the empty spot in my chest. If this unit forced me to deviate from my mission, he was a liability. Fortunately, that evening my companion was up and ready to travel.

I had dallied long enough. I needed to reach the second Factory, and then I somehow had to convince it to aid me. I shook my head at the thought.

As we traveled that night I gathered valuable data about my lumbering friend. I could slowly outdistance it over the very rugged terrain, but it would make super-unit efforts to catch up when the going was more level. Eventually, I found myself subconsciously slowing for the elephant while it struggled over rough ground. I actually picked easier routes even if it meant taking longer.

As usual, or what would become usual, Elephant took a position about a meter behind and to my right. We walked. As we walked, I talked. The subject didn't matter. Elephant never spoke, never uttered a sound. At first I talked about my travels and my mission. Later, I spent a considerable portion of the travel time doing William Shakespeare's play, *Hamlet*.

". . . Good night, sweet Prince. And may flights of Angels sing thee to thy rest." I admit that it lacked something, but it is hard to play a deactivated unit as you continue to walk along.

"What did you think, Elephant?" As usual, he said nothing. "Well, I guess some units are drama critics."

I rattled on. "So what do you think of our mission? Do you think I'm as malfunctioning as I sometimes feel?" No response. "Probably just as well. You would probably think I was insane. I have to joust yet again with a Factory. I don't understand how I can defeat them."

Just at that moment elephant trumpeted. I had never heard Elephant make as much as a peep; in fact, to my best knowledge I'd never heard any elephant unit make any sound. It startled me to a stop.

"Hello?" No response. It just stood there looking at me expectantly. I didn't understand and couldn't envision what it could possibly want. We stood on a large, flat plateau where there was nothing but the occasional boulder for kilometers. My battery levels approached full. With nothing to worry about, I walked on.

"Ferweet!" he trumpeted again before I took two steps.

"Now look," I said, turning back toward my traveling companion. "If you have something to say, say it, otherwise let's make tracks." Elephant didn't budge.

"Fine, you stay here; I'm going. I have a mission to accomplish." Turning, I took one step. The elephant wrapped its trunk about my right leg in a quick motion that tripped me and sent me to the ground in a heap. I jumped up, tearing the pink limb off of me.

"You overstuffed, sumpless trash hauler. Knock it off. I will go where I decide to go." I turned and resumed walking. Once again the elephant grabbed me with its one prehensile digit, but around my thighs this time. I fell again, but not because of my friend. Instead, I found myself breaking through a light mat of the ubiquitous ground vegetation and plunging headlong into an abyss below. For just a few brief clock cycles, I envisioned my own crushed body at the bottom of this narrow but very deep gorge. That moment passed as I slammed against the nearby cliff face at the end of Elephant's trunk. I watched as a battery fell out of my pack and went careening down. Over eight seconds later the report of its demise reached me.

I scrabbled up the cliff face with the aid of my sharp-witted companion's sturdy assistance. Acceleration due to gravity on Rigel-3 is 12.74 meters/second squared. Initial distance—zero; initial velocity—zero. So plug into the simplified equation one half the acceleration multiplied by time squared and you have 407 meters deep. Now in safety, I leaned over and looked down into the ravine.

With my feet on firm ground, I looked at my furry companion in a different way. Perhaps he hadn't been a waste of effort after all. This merited more thought. "Thank you, Elephant." With my physical control servos oscillating, I decided that this place was as good as any for a rest. "I don't think I like the idea of being scrap just yet," I said, petting the snout that Elephant thoughtfully pressed against me.

"And what am I going to do with you? You obviously have some use to me . . ." My sump raced with many *non sequitur* thoughts. My processor grabbed one of them and ran with it.

"I just realized I have no idea what to call you. I think we both need names. I need one for you to address me, if you ever develop the faculties of speech or offer me a voice, and me to call you in the meantime." I once considered myself a contemporary with Marco Polo, but I knew that wasn't quite right, as there were two of us. Lewis and Clark? No that wasn't right because helpful as Elephant had proven himself he was not my equal until he proved more able than just spotting holes in the ground. A perfect thought came to mind.

"You will be Sancho Panza, my good and faithful squire, and I am Don Quixote on a quest for my fair Dulcinea." It fit. I often felt like I must have lost my mind on this silly attempt to save Dulci . . . I mean Six. Tilting at windmills seemed my specialty. Personally, I was thinking perhaps Don Quixote had it easy as windmills would be easier to defeat than convincing a Factory of anything.

"I don't know if you understand me, but you are Sancho. Good Sancho," I said, stroking the elephant's trunk again. I fell asleep wrapped up in the trunk like I was climbing a very thick rope.

I told Sancho of his Human namesake in the tales originally crafted by the Human named Miguel de Cervantes many, many years ago. They told of deeds of great friendship of a squire to his slightly batty master. The more I told the tales, the more I really felt the names were justified. I don't know that Sancho understood a single word I told him, but his big, floppy ears did pick up whenever I said his name.

The very next night, I woke up to find Sancho missing. Puzzled, I followed his footsteps in the earth once more. It took only an hour to find him a few kilometers away, standing still and looking out toward the horizon. I couldn't understand why.

"Is there something I need to know about, Sancho?" As usual I got no response.

"Can we continue our mission?" Sancho looked up at me but didn't answer, but followed when I lead off.

Three more times in the next two weeks I tracked my wayward comrade first thing I woke. He never wandered far, but it often took me several hours to track his heavy footprints to where he inevitably stood staring off to the southwest. The third time he stood in the center of a group of black and silver-streaked vines growing up a rock face. Whatever Sancho's reason for trundling away, he also provided the solution. I took a 50-meter length of the stout-looking growth.

That next morning just before I turned off my cognitive functions I tied the heavy vine around Sancho's neck. The other end went around my wrist before I dropped off. Sometime near noon, I started awake as my arm jerked nearly from its socket. My head banged hard against a large rock as my body dragged along, being abused by stiff flora and the occasional low spot in the ground. The damage was minor but cumulative.

"Sancho, stop!" He didn't. "Halt." No effect. I formed a local net and ordered him over his CCT, again with no results. I struggled to my feet, by running at the same time as I got up. "Stop, you overgrown tub of lard!" I busily disengaged my hand from the tether. "Quit moving!" I reached out and kicked him in the hindquarters to get his attention. Just as suddenly and abruptly as I had been awoken, Sancho stopped. He looked at me, and then lay back down on the ground.

I just stood there staring at him. He obviously knew nothing of what he had done. It wasn't possible for him to disobey my net command, or at least I didn't think it was. Something else was at work. My systems complained of wear and abuse. Instead of figuring it out, I collapsed back against my charge and fell asleep.

Even ignoring Sancho's desire to occasionally take a walk in the middle of the day, he wasn't the easiest companion. He'd sometimes be chafing to get started in the evening, and other times I literally had to drag him meters to get him moving. Several times he stepped on my foot (intentionally, I was sure) when he wasn't happy with a decision I had made or my choice in discussion topic of the day. More than once I cursed the day I'd reactivated him.

On the plus side, he stopped and trumpeted a number of times during our march. Only one of these times did I find something that could have obviously been dangerous, but I had learned my lesson, and fairly cheaply at that. Sancho had my total attention when he chose to make himself heard.

In addition to this, Sancho made a wonderful pack animal. I modified my backpack so it would stay on his back. By putting my extra equipment on him I sped up considerably and it slowed him not at all. My tiny command was better off as a result. I still carried my submachine gun and knife. I was not going to let Sancho be the one to defend us. After all, I was Don Quixote of La Mancha, knight and slayer of giants—not to mention the odd basilisk.

"Look up there, Sancho," I said one early morning two weeks later. "It's the peak of the mountains. Once we are on the other side we probably won't have to worry about our power levels so much."

"If we rest anywhere along here this morning, the shadow of the peaks will impact our ability to recharge. I say let's push on to make it over the top this morning."

A tiny, silver puff of cloud raced over the top of the mountain ridge as the sun rose up enough to reflect light off the vapor. The way it jumped the mountain made it look almost like a thrown grenade. Two more and then dozens of the tiny clouds soon followed the first. They flew over the peaks like cars racing up a ramp, shooting off into the air for a few precious seconds of flight. Then the trickle of tiny cloudlettes turned into a stampede of larger ones, each nudging the other for room to clear the mountain hurdle.

Within minutes they no longer had any delineation between them, becoming one huge cloud led by millions of fine, wispy tendrils, like the finest fur on a teddy unit in a brilliant white.

The ponderous structure, unable to sustain its own bulk, broke in a wave across the hill in a slow, majestic curl. It appeared as if millions of metric tons of the silver-red vapor were going to crush us under its mass.

"Ferweet!" Sancho offered looking up at the huge formation.

"Uh-oh!" I quickly tied my vine rope to Sancho's neck. Well practiced as I'd become, the haste I felt definitely led to some botched motions.

The swell splashed in slow motion over the crest of the mountain. As it descended upon us, the burgeoning day turned rapidly to inky blackness. No time passed from being bathed in the warming sun to being swallowed by midnight's dark, cold arms.

It was dark. Not the dark of night but even darker. Even in the blackest night the starlight and moonlight gave me the ability to see very clearly. My vision couldn't penetrate the cloud bank that engulfed us. I felt the beginnings of a breeze. My memories contained references to such storms. We were in for a bumpy ride.

The winds, gently at first, barely ruffling my fur. The gusts became more intense, bursting against us strong enough that it became more difficult to stand still.

"Ferweet!"

"Hang on, Sancho."

The strength of the winds picked up even more. A small rock pelted my chest, tearing out 3 square centimeters of fur. I struggled over to my companion. "Lie down, Sancho. Get as flat as you can." While I couldn't see him, I felt him hunch down. I lay next to him as plant material and flecks of dirt sandblasted our hides. I cut the pack off of Sancho's back, crawling up to put it over his face to protect his optics. I held it there and pressed my own snout against his chest, presenting my back to the airborne debris.

The blustery weather gained strength into a gale. The gale raged into a tempest. Violent explosions of light and sound punctuated the squalling wind. Slowly, we were being slid along the ground. I flatted myself even more until we stopped. Deposited by the winds, dirt built up against my back and arms. Twice that morning I felt larger objects hurtle against me. One snapped hard against the smallest digit of my left hand, crushing the joint. The second impaled itself through my left thigh. I could do nothing about either injury while the fury of nature vented around us. All I could do was wait and hope.

The feeling of impotence tore at my thought processes. How could I fight the substance of the air? Several hours of grinding my processor at high voltage levels caused an epiphany. I would never be able to control everything, no matter how much I wanted and needed to. Weather and Factories would do what they willed and I must find ways to deal with both or relax to the inevitable.

By the time I'd reached this flash of genius, the storm had slaked its taste for violence and slowly wound down. Already I measured a 33 percent reduction in the wind speed and estimated a 70 percent reduction in danger. Oddly, we never received the deluge of rain I expected, and for that I was truly thankful.

My pillow twitched.

"Hold on just a little more, Sancho."

Two more hours I waited before I dug my way out of the earthen igloo that surrounded me. The damaging wind reduced to the barest of breeze, a refreshing change. The storm hadn't completely vented all of its fury as the black, red, and silver mass moved beyond us. Brilliant flashes of lightning flared from the malignant mass to the ground with astonishing regularity.

It didn't take the perception of a Nurse Nan to find a wooden splinter of wood 3 centimeters wide, sticking 4 centimeters out the front of my thigh and 22 centimeters out the back. I inspected the wound and found no leaking materials. Yanking hard with one hand didn't dislodge it. I took both hands and put maximum strength on the attempt to remove. Again it stayed firm. I decided to ignore it as best as possible for the moment.

I dug Sancho the rest of the way out of mound. As I did, I inspected him for damage. With the exception of some missing fur, he seemed completely intact. Sancho stood and shook back and forth, creating a crimson cloud of fine dust around him. He returned to his normal pink background color.

"Good, Sancho. Listen, I don't know if you can understand me, but I need your help." I lay down on my stomach and pointed to the wooden skewer.

Sancho didn't even hesitate. He waddled up next to me and wrapped his trunk twice around the pole and in a single jerk removed the entire length. One more point for my comrade.

I searched the gaping hole for leaks. Finding none, I crawled a meter back to the mound of earth and dug down to my pack. Shaking it free of grit, I dug in for some of the armor patches. Positioning them just beneath my fur, one ceramic patch covered each hole, entry and exit, nicely.

My hand damage rose to a higher plane. The finger was fully dislocated. This paled into insignificance next to the fact that the joint itself looked like a pretzel. That finger would never again inhabit that joint. Without the entire digit being replaced I'd have to suffer with the injury.

"Well, that was exciting," I mentioned, as I turned off the bit that controlled my damaged digit so it would remain immobile. "I think we should hurry over the summit before we have to sleep in the shade."

The last kilometer wore heavily on the batteries. We scrambled up 70 degree-plus slopes, only making any headway because of paw- and trunk-holds in the weather-fractured rocks. By the time we reached the crest, the sensors on my hydraulic fluid complained bitterly of overheating, but the interrupt never entered my thoughts.

For all the spectacle and power of the storm earlier, I daresay I have never seen a more reason-stealing sight. A great expanse of shining, undulating silver stretched before me—an ocean of mercury floated below so wide I couldn't see either end or the other side. Bays of mercury, each large enough to swallow the entirety of Six's valley dotted the shoreline like leaves on a tree.

Never had I seen such a large body of mercury in one spot. It wasn't rushing to be elsewhere in a hurry to find another home, it just was. It exuded a feeling of solid immutability. This sea lived on no matter what happened to us transient units—it lived over all times. It took me eighty-five minutes to take in the awesome magnitude of the metallic sea and forty-six minutes more to begin to be able to function in a reasonable way.

"Wow," was all that came to my mouth.

Near the extreme limits of my vision, to the east, a column of silver and black steam rose from a conic island into a permanent ebon cloud in the sky nearly as large as the ocean itself. The island, obviously a volcano, lit up even the day like a magnesium flare of garish red. Dante's *Inferno* looked pale by comparison.

I don't know if the entire scene affected Sancho the way it did me, but we both just stood rooted in place. Eventually, I managed to sit and regain some level of control. When I did I remarked at the power of the sun beating down on us.

"We need to stay here for at least two full days to recharge, Sancho. We'll have plenty of time to gawk."

Partner

 The two days went quickly. Every time I thought I'd seen everything, something new would appear.

The great cloud mass ebbed and flowed over the sky, remaining mainly over the center of the ocean but occasionally sending threatening tendrils over different shorelines as the winds directed. When I put those tendrils in their proper perspective, the incredible storm we'd witnessed just days before was just the broken off tiny nub. Thinking of all that power caused me to develop a shudder in my balancing subroutine. I zeroed it out but couldn't stop the very slow but steady ramp of my main bus voltage.

Taking my processor off that process, I detected additional movement around the volcanic island. Zooming in to my maximum magnification I saw what looked to be masses of balloon like flyers darting in and around the caldera, being thrown around by the thermals as they seemed oblivious to the slashing rain. One of the dark figures darted down through the smoke and ash to land on the back of another. Both of their balloons deflated suddenly and together the barely visible pair spiraled down into the fiery heat below. It happened again and again. I began to realize these weren't units, but biologics performing more of the craziness that defined them.

Later on the second day I watched as three massive biologics slithered up the mountain we sat on. They looked like python units. From their distance, I could extrapolate that they were 30 meters long and 2 across. After making their way to the top of a steep slope they rolled up into an 8-meter wheel and cast themselves down.

"Why would they do that, Sancho?"

Whether I was just taking too long, or whether Sancho was tired of waiting, he finally began tramping down the other side of the mountain range. After putting away my awe, I applauded my companion's practicality. The ocean was yet a long distance away and we had no more time to lose.

"The game is afoot, Sancho!"

On the way down, I directed us to the hill where the wheel biologics had spun down. At the base of the hill I found the desiccated corpses of the strange creatures. A cursory inquiry showed very little other than a large number of unexplained eye-sized holes all over the snake's skin.

"What do you think, Sancho?" I asked, lifting up one end of the bizarre creature. My friend said nothing. In fact he didn't even look. Oddly, without saying a word, Sancho communicated a great deal. This investigation distracted me from my primary mission. I dropped the tail and got my furry tail moving again.

It took ten hard days of travel to make our way down to the edge of the colossal metallic ocean. Waves of mercury lapped gently upon a red, powder-fine sandy shore. Tiny clouds of dust billowed up in our footsteps. At times, with the wind from the right quarter, it was almost impossible to see through to the next step. This could have been passively dangerous because of the obstacles.

Carcasses, both animal and vegetable, littered the beach at random intervals. So badly were some of the bodies decayed, I could only guess as to their original forms. Others bore striking resemblance to creatures out of Human taxonomy—fish, kelp, mussels, and shellfish of several varieties. Not only did I not feel any need to investigate these corpses, I felt an anxiety to leave as quickly as possible.

Silver waves lapped at my feet. I didn't delude myself that I could build any craft that would go across it, especially with the excessive weight of my comrade. According to my estimation, the other Factory lay directly to the south of us, across that great breadth of silver. Left or right? East or west?

"So what do you think, Sancho? Should we brave the dangers of the wicked giants of the west, or plow through the evil dark armies of the east?" I asked in a form as true to my namesake as I could manage. "I really don't see an advantage to either direction."

I was going to mentally toss a coin when I noticed Sancho's input.

While Sancho had still not talked he could be amazingly graphic with some of his motions. In this case he left no doubt. He had already started walking east without me.

"Ahhh," I said, dumbfounded. I was about to object when I realized how little information I had. If he felt strongly about a specific direction, why not follow his lead? He had been right before on information I couldn't see.

Trust was hard for me. I had to work on it. I didn't even truly trust Six, my own Factory, but I was learning to trust my friend, a 1.5-meter-tall pink and purple polka-dotted elephant who couldn't speak.

"Lay on, Macduff, and damned be him who first cries 'Hold! enough!'" I called out as I hurried to catch up.

That first night next to the beach I learned a very important lesson. So caught up in our travels and the marvels around us, we traveled well into the day. In fact, with midday nearly upon us, Sancho sat down and wouldn't go further. I realized then just how far into the day we'd come.

"Sorry, friend. Let's grab a sunspot and charge." As was our habit we lay down in the sunniest place we could, in this case directly adjacent to the lapping mercury.

Some six hours later my timer wakened me, just as the sun passed over the horizon. Instead of finding myself on the beach, I floated on my back in the ocean about 400 meters off shore.

I panicked at first, trying to sit upright, but instead tumbled. When I finally relaxed, my body righted itself. I bobbed in a gentle up and down motion that caused an odd feedback in my balance subroutine as my gyros tried to fight them. Shutting down my gyros and ignoring the sensations, I realized I could neither see nor sense my elephantine companion. Then I realized that the rope I used as a tether still hung from my wrist. The braided vine traveled straight down, directly out of my reach.

Sancho was well under the mercury and by the length of the tether, he lay at least a full meter out of my reach.

"Sancho, can you hear me?" I called out loudly as mercury would keep any local net I could put up from reaching him.

"If you can hear me, walk directly south." As he didn't respond and no movement toward the shore happened, I knew the liquid kept the sound dampened as well.

We had chosen to sleep on an almost imperceptible slope near the ocean. A tiny rise in the level made a huge difference as to where the shoreline was. My black and white memories called it a tidal flat. It took until almost high sun the next day to get Sancho's aural receptors below tide level and give him instructions.

During that miserable day, I realized that the sea must have a cyclic phase to it, being much smaller during the day when it is hotter and the air can hold more vapor, and then growing during the night when the air gives up that vapor. It might also have something to do with the moons, but the reason didn't matter. I lost my knife, about half of my reserve batteries and a few of my precious repair tools. I also lost about three days—one bobbing around like a cork and the other two waiting for Sancho's batteries to recharge.

It gave me plenty of time to ponder my failure. I knew I had to do better, not just for my little command but for Six as well. I couldn't afford another such lapse. It might be fatal. We slept well away from the liquid from that time on.

Despite the great volcano and cloud show all night and all day for our pleasure, our quest soon became almost as monotonous as the travel on open fields of barb grass. At least I had a companion to help ease the boredom.

I used up time acting out plays, reading aloud books and poetry, or even playing music that could be reproduced by my voice. It was enjoyable to me. Sancho never complained except when I tried to augment the music with my own singing. He would drop to the ground and press his huge purple ears against his head with his paws, waving frantically with his trunk. Even friendship must have its limits, I surmised.

I refrained from singing.

Between acts of plays, chapters of books, chamber music, or even listening to the hypnotic sound of the metallic breakers against the often rocky shore, I studied the huge conic island in the center of the ocean which belched forth the spiral of contaminated mercury vapor into the air. The volcano vaporized nearby mercury and flung it up into the air where most of it condensed from the supersaturated atmosphere and fell out as rain. From the proliferation of dead on the beaches, I could only assume that the volcano had come into existence relatively recently and changed the local ecology drastically. It probably wasn't doing the environs of the entire planet a great deal of good either, changing weather patterns and decreasing the temperature worldwide.

"You think it looks like rain?" I asked my traveling companion one early evening. Over the last week, one of the arms of the cloud vortex leisurely swung our direction. While I was not, in theory, worried about the rain, I would never again be nonchalant about a storm.

"Maybe it won't rain today, but I do have to say I'm worried about the lack of light, Sancho. Those clouds have blocked out 12 percent of my daily charge. I thought once we crested the mountain range our power issues were over. Apparently not. If that cloud cover continues, we'll have to decrease our travel time."

"Fert."

I spun around to look at my traveling companion. At first I thought I had heard some other sound, but playing it back across my processor's inputs, my binaural placed Sancho's vocalization with incredible accuracy. I didn't know what he meant but it heartened me. "Incredible! Glad to hear you, my friend. Speak up any time."

In appreciation, I performed Edmond Rostand's *Cyrano De Bergerac* in its original French rhyming couplets with as much panache as I could muster. How better to understand something than in its original form. I danced through the sword fights and even managed to hold the line against the Spanish all as we continued to walk along the shore. I also managed to die in my beloved Roxanne's arms, while playing both parts.

My friend gave no applause, no cheers, in fact no indication he'd even heard me. There once was an award given by Humans to exceptional performers. I wondered if my performance, given while still moving, might have warranted a Tony in spite of my companion's lack of input. Maybe at least honorable mention for having stage-managed the effort *en situ*.

After another sleep, I realized my concerns about sunlight had not been paranoia.

"I don't know about you, my friend, but my batteries are beginning to lose charge. What would you say to dropping our travel time to eight hours? . . . As I thought . . . a capital idea."

We did have a choice. We could have traveled two days in three or we could opt to only travel eight of the twelve hours available to us each night. I chose the latter. I never really wanted to stay in one place any longer than necessary. Too many things could jump out at you when you least expected it. I brushed my paw against my lower leg, remembering that even biologics that seem harmless could be as dangerous as a loaded gun pointed at your head.

Even slowed as we were, it wasn't the worst. Huge cloudbanks continued to break free from the main mass and spin out to torture the weather of other regions. The vapor would eventually fall out in other places as rain as soon as the concentration was high enough, or the air got cold enough. Because of the heat of this planet, the clouds drifted for great distances, blotting out the sun as they traveled. It made for nights where Sancho and I couldn't travel at all for the daylight charge hadn't sufficed.

During the third such night we sat as I discussed our progress. Boredom during these times provided our most significant problem. But tonight wouldn't be one of those.

"I think we have another three weeks or so before we will be close to the next Factory. It'll probably take another—"

The granddad of all basilisks, 12 meters long and nearly 3 high at the shoulder, wriggled over a dune 20 meters away with a quickness that belied its bulk.

"Ferweet!" Sancho trumpeted as he bolted. I didn't have Sancho's ignorance. I knew I couldn't outrun this beast. Unfortunately, I didn't process the correct action until it was too late.

The basilisk lunged forward. It bit sand as I rolled to one side. One of its claws gouged a furrow in my fur but didn't penetrate. My M16 now lay 3 meters on the other side of the creature.

The reptile turned toward me and pounced again. Still lying down, I had only one choice. I rolled the other direction, even farther away from my weapon. At 20 meters, with the fastest biologic I'd ever seen in between, the assault weapon might as well have been at the bottom of the ocean.

I didn't recover from my roll in time to react fully to the next attack. Instead of ending up in the creature's maw, it butted me in the chest with its horn, tossing me 5 meters. Several acceleration sensors sent priority interrupts. Ignoring any potential damage I'd taken, I took the advantage by scrambling to my feet.

The basilisk turned rapidly again and charged. This time I would act rather than react. Time dilated now so that every millisecond seemed weeks long.

I could watch the flow of its muscles in the wriggling gait it used so effectively. Not a single spec of sand or dirt marred the aged skin except around its drooling muzzle. Shark-like rectangular teeth framed its open maw, an opening large enough to fit several teddies.

As its hot breath closed enough to ruffle my fur, I vaulted straight up. The lizard's forward momentum carried me over its horn, my crotch clearing the shining peak with only 6 centimeters' clearance. The massive force of the creature's jaws closed on air. Landing on the reptile's back in a crouch, I could feel the coarse skin under my pads. Without pausing I bolted down its length.

Unhappy with its loss of prey, the lizard thrashed first one way and then the other. I fought to maintain my balance. At the end of its torso I leaped. The creature rolled onto its back at just the same moment. My left foot twisted badly beneath me as it landed on the ground.

No time to worry about minor damage. I turned off all my safeties and ran at emergency speed.

The basilisk rolled back onto its six legs and turned around within a cloud of crimson dust. Like lighting it shot out at me. In spite of its speed, my processor assured me I'd reach my weapon fifty-six milliseconds before the basilisk could reach me. Scant margins didn't stop my overheating hydraulics from trying to pump faster.

I executed a running scoop of the assault rifle. I didn't bother wasting any of my 5.56-millimeter ammunition on it by even flipping off the safety.

As the saw-like teeth closed in on me, I bounced up enough to put my feet on the creature's snout and pushed. This sent me flying through the air, just in front of the bear-trap mouth. Fumbling just a moment for the switch, I turned on the untested shock-prod. As I landed, I let the creature's own movement shove the entire thing, my arms and shoulders included, down its own gullet.

The creature executed one bone-crushing body convulsion as it slid to a halt. With my arms still well inside, I stopped as well, envisioning my arms being snapped off. The mouth never closed, at least not in an organized sheering motion. Then in several seconds of highly animated spasms, the basilisk threw itself about, flailing first to one side and then the other with no coordination before it finally came to a complete rest.

As my processor slowed down and time came to its correct speed, I withdrew my limbs. I inspected them in disbelief as they remained intact. Tremors ran through all of my hydraulics. It took several seconds to bring them under control enough to stand. As I did, a puff of earth shook from my bright red–coated fur. I made a half-hearted attempt to dust myself off.

With a good deal of righteous indignation I tore the beast's barrel-thick horn from its corpse. I envisioned a chest plate like that Don Quixote wore in the illustrations by de Cervantes in his original works, but how I would carry such a burden I couldn't process.

Stabbing the body with my knife or even bludgeoning it with the butt of my M16 and the body reformed, even after its death. I felt that nothing short of a grenade in the gullet would stop the beast and I had my doubts about that. Maybe its mercury-based chemistry allowed it to take on some of the silver metal's properties? I already had a very effective method to dispose of it, so there was no reason to worry. I'm not a scientist. The body began to decompose and dissolve even as I watched.

It seemed such a waste.

Searcher

Most of my injuries were low priority, not even worth spending processing power on. In the fight with this basilisk I'd once again lost a small amount of motive power. My ankle, while sustaining only minor damage, would slow my travel speed by 8 percent. Time was not on my side as I had a Factory to find and my errant squire to chase. All of this before I could even hope to go to the aid of my fair Dulcenia . . . I mean Six.

While Sancho's departure probably had been the wise thing for him to do, it left me in a lurch. I couldn't abandon my friend, but I couldn't exactly waste time on him either. All of this would be more than useless if I arrived too late to help Six.

Putting it off never got anything done. I dropped the basilisk horn on the grayed out portion of the sand where the body had once laid. With a quiet prayer to the Humans, I set off after my charge.

It pleased me that once again, through dumb luck, Sancho's path of flight took him only 8 degrees off my current planned course.

"I'll tear his batteries out, one by one," I muttered under my breath after three days of following his obvious tracks. "I'm already 16.2 kilometers off course and I still haven't found him."

"I'm going to deactivate him. Humans strike me down if I won't. Maybe after I short out his main bus bar."

As much as I cursed him, I couldn't leave him to his fate. I created him and I was responsible. Every night I'd put up a local area net and try to capture him by a command. Night after night it failed.

A week later I cursed him even more as I traveled into the foothills. His tracks became harder to follow on the broken stone ground. At one point the imprints stopped entirely over a solid granite slab 156.3 meters across. It took three hours on the other side to pick up his trail again. Had his course deviated significantly over the rock, I'd have never found it.

I feared a rainstorm. The pounding of mercury on the soil would wash away all sign of his movements. Again, dumb luck seemed to serve us as eight more frustrating days later my LAN caught his IFF beacon.

"I'm coming for you, Sancho. Better protect your deactivation switch!" The track took me to the base of a 706-meter cliff sheered ominously over a vertical rock. In the dark shadow of that structure, Sancho leaned against the rock, motionless.

"You stupid ghit! You need sunlight, not the protection of some rocks. Get out here now."

Sancho remained still.

"We don't have time for this. Come here!"

Sancho didn't respond.

With some trepidation, I moved under the ponderous weight of the stone. One eye watched above me and the other watched Sancho's catatonic form. From the outside he didn't look any the worse for wear.

"You better be deactivated, you pathetic pachyderm, or you will be!" Even as I neared I couldn't hear his hydraulic pump. This worried me. If he fully lost all power, his sump would have stopped processing fluid and he would have nothing more than a brain case full of black goo.

Recklessly, I rushed in the rest of the way and tore open his access panel. While at dangerously low levels, his batteries still kept his sump and processor active.

I took one of the spare batteries out of my backpack and made an emergency swap with one of his. They weren't the same physical size, but I knew the voltages were compatible. It would give him enough power until I could get him charged. He looked silly with the black battery dangling out of one ear, but function vastly outweighed form in this case.

It took me the rest of the night to drag his heavy carcass out of the cave. I think I overstressed every one of my joints hauling him over the rocks and sand. I got him clear of the overhang just as the morning sun began to warm the crimson sands. I collapsed right next to my patient. It had been a close thing, I knew. Had it taken even another few hours for me to find him, or if I hadn't been carrying spare batteries, Sancho might not have survived.

I was glad, and somehow warmed, that I had found him in time. I was beginning to realize just how much I cared for the addled critter. And while he never got any more intelligent, nor did he ever talk, he became symbiotic. I trusted his footing, when there was any doubt, more than my own. But why he took refuge under an overhang, I hadn't a clue. I would have to make it clear that he was only to sleep in the sun.

That night Sancho acted normal again. He sat up pointing toward our objective, now a full 61 kilometers from where we should be had there been no detour.

"Not tonight, Sancho. We need to charge you up. Your design will hold about three days' worth of charge."

Sancho flopped back to the ground.

"OK. There are a couple of rules we need to discuss.

"First, no matter what, you should stop in the sun. We don't have a net concentrator we can suck power from.

"Second, if we ever get separated again, travel no more than one day before you stop. Stay stopped for at least one week. If I don't show up, come looking for me. If you can't find me within a week, you are on your own."

I never knew if Sancho actually understood the things I told him. At least I said it. If he didn't follow the instructions, I knew I could leave him as damaged property.

Sancho proved over the next few weeks that even without olfactory senses he could almost smell a basilisk—we avoided four of the aggressive predators. I don't know whether we'd stumbled upon a breeding ground of the creatures or they were just thick on the ground. In three of the cases Sancho just pulled me bodily to the ground, effectively hiding behind a dune. Only catching a glimpse of the creature in the distance as Sancho released me let me know what we had been up against.

At the fourth basilisk incident, Sancho trumpeted a warning. We were able to scramble up on top of a rock spire, which forced the creature to us. A quick jab with my basilisk prod finished it off. We barely broke stride.

We surmounted physical challenges aplenty—like the time we negotiated another river, me being drug along the surface by Sancho's walking steadily along the bottom, or the cliff I climbed while I lifted Sancho with a block and tackle, or an even more powerful rainstorm than the last where we sat huddled under a convenient slab of slate lying on top of a large boulder giving us shelter.

All of these and more could be surmounted with a bit of elephant power or something called elbow grease, which didn't process as grease wasn't used in the elbow joint. But then that brought up another problem—my lube needed changing.

The one little spit and dribble I'd got from that Nurse Nan about ten lifetimes ago was long gone, and I worried over the state of all my fluids. Only joint lubricant, of all my solutions, maintained a satisfactory rating. I'd shut off the critical interrupts and alarms long ago. I could only imagine the cumulative damage. So desperate was I that I wondered about rending some of the local fauna over a fire to collect their fats. If pressed, I might try it but I didn't relish the thought. We kept moving. Maybe we would get lucky.

On the 205th day since the inception of my journey, the day commemorating the second anniversary of my activation, Sancho stumbled over a train track half buried in the sand.

"So, are we there yet?"

Diplomat

"What do you think, Sancho," I asked after I had watched for almost ten minutes. Sancho and I kept down behind a small sand dune as not to be spotted by the train full of military units and material speeding along.

We'd felt the train coming through the tracks themselves, some three days after we discovered them. It prompted us to take cover.

At this distance we were unlikely to be noticed even if a unit caught sight of one of us. The train seemed endless out on this lonely stretch of track with nothing really visible on either horizon. The train was an infinite bouncing line. With no sense of beginning or end the train barely seemed to be moving. The size of the immense train showed a similar number of units to the previous Factory I'd met. It seemed it could swat Six at any time.

Sometime during this endless parade, one of the helper engines in the middle let out a long, low whistle.

"Do you think we should just walk down and introduce ourselves?" I asked. I got the response I expected—none. "I didn't think so. I guess that leaves following along the track after this behemoth clears out."

It took the opportunity of our pause to play around with our CCTs. I turned off Sancho's and then my own. I hoped that Sancho had bonded enough to me that the IFF signal from his CCT wouldn't be necessary to our continued travels.

The CCTs were off on the theory that as just another biologic, any unit would ignore us. Not that units ignored all biologics, but at any it didn't assign a potential threat to. It would give us a fighting chance.

The tracks cleared while I had been tinkering but it was another hour before we couldn't see it in the distance.

"Shall we dance?"

Our travel following the tracks back to their source marked a sharp delineation in terrain. The rails paralleled the mercury level approximately 200 meters away on solid ground and well above the high mercury mark. But solid ground was a bit of a misnomer. High winds seemed the norm, buffeting across the area, leaving dunes of scarlet sands piled around haphazardly. The strong breezes blew fine particles of earth around, scouring our fur and exposed workings. Sometimes the wind compelled us to lean into it to stay upright, even with our gyros at emergency maximum. Walking in it was difficult enough, but the loose sand at our feet dragged constantly.

Nothing biologic seemed to grow or wander here. Even the normal barb grasses or tiny animated life forms I'd encountered in abundance avoided this place. After our first day of travel I wondered if those biologics were smarter than I was.

Even resting here didn't follow the norm. As our required sunlight pelted us, the temperature began to rise to a level I'd never before experienced. The light energy also carried a greater power. By noon we were fully recharged, but at the same time beginning to feel the effects of overheating. With fluids dangerously out of specification, my pump temperatures skyrocketed. As ludicrous as it seemed, we had to get out of the sun.

"Sancho, we need to get shade. Come around this dune and help me dig." I figured we would make our own cave. That was the plan, but the sand fell down faster than we could dig. We did well to dig far enough to make a depression that provided protection from the afternoon rays. As we settled in, our temperatures began to fall immediately. Another datum to keep in mind for selection of camping locations.

Conversely, the night in this awful place held its own almost hidden danger. The ambient temperature fell alarmingly after sundown, causing the air to take on a serious chill. Only the fact that we moved constantly through the night kept our fluids thin and non-viscous. The cold also affected battery efficiency. We had to keep moving but we had to do it carefully as not to deplete our batteries too far.

It became a pattern. Walk slowly all night, when the temperatures fell to almost liquid-hardening temperatures, seek the sun for its bounty in the morning, and burrow like biologics during the afternoon.

For many days and nights of travel we followed those steel rails, which had an annoying habit of disappearing under the red dunes for long distances. We met with no excitement at all—not a single investigation, not a single patrol to avoid. As far as I could tell, I saw nothing, but a unit might have seen me and ignored me. How can one tell? Maybe they all waited in ambush over the next crumbly, nearly collapsing rise. I didn't know and wouldn't oscillate my circuits worrying about that. Instead, I worried almost constantly about fluid status. I began to feel some of those long term issues, including the inability of my coolant to moderate my temperature. It wouldn't be much longer before I was going to have to do something drastic.

Eight days of alternating freezing and baking before one night the train tracks disappeared down into the ocean. It didn't make any sense. I stopped so suddenly that Sancho bumped into me from behind. How could a train run through the mercury? It really didn't make any sense.

Looking carefully ahead on the beach I didn't see the tracks leave the metal anyplace within the limits of my vision.

"Any ideas, fella?"

Sancho, as usual, had no clue as to what we were doing. He just loyally followed along without a word. Sometimes I still had to prod him to get moving in the beginning of the evening. Conversely, there were times he all but dragged me out of our daytime hole and down a sand embankment at the start of a new working night. In spite of his mental limitations, I had never felt so warm toward my companion.

My mind worked overtime to explain the mysteriously vanishing train tracks. The single possible explanation I dreamed up seemed farfetched.

"Was it Sherlock Holmes who once said, 'When you have eliminated the impossible, whatever remains, however improbable, must be the truth'?"

I saw several problems with my theory, but the only way I could confirm or deny it was to investigate.

"Let's set up camp, Sancho."

After our run-in with the basilisk, making camp involved a bit more than just flopping down anyplace. We scouted about for places with no blind approaches, above high mercury level signs and recently a place we could get out of the sun. However, in this case the site I chose really had no available shade. We relaxed adjacent to where the railroad disappeared into the sea.

"Sancho, I hope you are ready for an all-day run. The true test of my theory will come a little after high sun today." I couldn't tell if Sancho remained awake or not. It mattered little this early in the morning.

The mercury level dropped slowly at first but within two hours the beach gained 3.4 additional meters, and 2.8 hours after sunup my target revealed itself with just the barest hint of the top of a dome.

"There it is, Sancho. We finally made it!"

Sancho actually stood up to get a better look. Together we watched as the liquid metal receded from around the structure. The dome was much flatter than either of the two Factories I'd known, being only 5 meters above the ground. Its radius appeared the same as in my memories.

"What a funny shape. And where are its construction and production facilities?" No material processing plants, smelting plants, assembly line buildings or anything like them exposed themselves.

"I don't know whether to think they are farther out in the sea or aren't collocated. I think the second is more probable. Otherwise you'd have to time arrival of raw materials with the shrinkage of the sea. And what would happen if the sea level rose so it never became exposed."

Such a strange place it inhabited. We had, by then, traveled through all types of places, but the desolation of this barren and wind-tossed place made my voltage flutter like no other.

By noon the sea relinquished its grip on the ground around the Factory, leaving it still moist with tiny puddles. The shining metal reflected the brilliant rays of the sun like tiny stars, each planet-bound, to spend their energies with futility against the ground.

"Is that what I am doing?" I wondered aloud. "Am I futilely spending my energies where they can do absolutely no good?" Time would tell and my companion Sancho would not. This was that time. I steeled myself for what I must do.

Just as before with 55474, the door was in almost exactly the same location. My body shook gently. I didn't know whether it was in excitement or terror or both, but I realized that if I didn't go right then, I might lose my will.

I think the gritty, thick feeling of my fluids and the voltage fluctuation across my main power bus told me that I was very afraid. They were redundant warnings of danger I had been facing in my mind for hours. I quivered in more fear at that moment than ever before in my short life. I certainly knew I was more afraid than when I had confronted 55474 in its den. I no longer had any tricks to get me out of trouble if it showed. Six couldn't save me. Sancho couldn't pull me out. I alone would match my wits against the full mental powers of a Factory. If I failed, Six perished.

I don't know what possessed me, but I stood up, throwing my pack over my shoulder. I heard myself say, "Sancho, old pal. This is something I have to do alone." I slipped the vine leash from around his neck.

Sancho bellowed through his snout.

"Sorry, but this is one danger you can't keep me from, nor can you share it. I must do this." Even though I seemed to have no conscious control of my motions, I started to walk toward the dome. A sense of peace flowed over me. My decision was made and consequences be what they will. In the words of one famous Human, "Damn the torpedoes. Full speed ahead."

My ability to control what I was doing returned as I approached the flattened dome. I still had minor jitters about my abilities. I hoped my new line of persuasion would work. Visions of what had happened with 55474 flashed through my mind, and I prayed to the Humans that being chased out of another dome by a dozen armed units wasn't to be the result. If it was, I might as well just find a nice quiet spot, like that sunny little butte where I found thousands of rock beetles crawling around and live there because Six was finished. Two Factories, even if not cooperating, would make short work of Six at this point. My meager capabilities wouldn't impact that outcome at all.

I followed the rails the last dozen meters to the audience chamber door. All of the Factories at least seemed to have the same internal layout. Could the Humans' plans for us have played a part in their shape?

A dim yellow light from the ceiling, a stark contrast to the vivid reds of the outside world, lit the chamber. Just as before, the audience chamber awed me. Each sound amplified so that even the floor against my feet, soft and furry though they might be, was like a windstorm. Humans surely looked down on their subjects in this place. They watched my performance for them.

My limbs felt like mercury filled them. "Excuse me," I said. I got no response. "Hello, Factory?"

"Biologics do not converse," came a high reedy voice, emanating from seemingly everywhere. While this was disconcerting, it also settled me. I felt the power of my convictions fill me and all but lift me off the floor. I was ready.

"And why not?"

"No biologic examined to date has even rudimentary vocal apparatus." The high voice seemed to penetrate through me rather than having been heard.

"Then the answer should be obvious. I am not a biologic."

"Probability—"

"I don't care what the probabilities are, Factory. I am not a biologic."

"Highly unlikely. However, if you are not a biologic, then probabilities are that you are not of this world."

I thought about that for a moment. "No, I began my life right here on this planet."

"Then you are a biologic and thus meant to be destroyed. Primary orders indicate—"

"Yes, I know. 'Seek and destroy.'"

"Not entirely accurate."

"This conversation is getting off the main topic. I am not a biologic. I was produced by Factory 55466."

"Probability 0.0. My memories indicate that Factory 55466 was to be sent to Rigel-3."

"This is Rigel-3!" I said in near exasperation. "You are both on this same planet."

"Negative. I have landed on Rigel-3." A pause of over three seconds took place. "Correction, this is the same planet. Faulty memory indicates, 'Design Assumptions: No two Factories shall ever be placed on the same planet.' Memory moved to temporary storage and replaced with working hypothesis: Factory 55466 has landed on the same planet I now occupy." I wanted to dance. I had half the battle won.

"So what conclusion can you make from this new data?" I asked, hoping that the Factory would make the next likely leap on its own.

"No conclusion," came the annoyingly high voice. My initial optimism was premature. I would have to pry each and every concession out of the Factory.

"Perhaps the 'biologics' you are eradicating aren't biologic at all."

"Probability—"

"There you go again with those probabilities. Think, Factory. Don't let the numbers answer the questions for you. You are fighting another Factory's units."

"Probability 0.004." I decided to let my silence answer the Factory's stubbornness. It remained quiet for nearly a minute. This was even more difficult than I had thought.

"Let us look at the data you admit is real. You are on Rigel-3. Factory 55466 is also on Rigel-3. You have another Factory on the same planet and you can't even see there is a possibility you are fighting for the same thing?"

"Affirmative." Literature indicates that Humans sigh when exasperated. When exasperation struck me I whistled through my main speaker, and right then it sounded like a bird convention. I had to take another tack.

"What are your primary operating instructions?"

"Classified information. Biologics do not require such information."

"Ah, but I am not a biologic. I am a unit of Factory 55466."

"Unconfirmed. Information is classified."

"If I could prove my manufacturer?"

"Then the information would be made available to you."

"And how could I prove my origins?"

"All manufactured units contain a serial plate near their main processing unit. This identifying mark may only be scanned with ultraviolet laser. It is microscopic in size." I got a chill through every fluid in my body. A laser in my neck near my main processor could do much more than read a tag. With a surge of power it could instead incinerate my processor, leaving me a mindless moron. Here was another time of fear.

"By all means, please scan," I said, opening the access panel in my neck. I hoped cold calculation hadn't been replaced by folly. I hardly felt a small tube writhed into my neck. Excepting key physical systems' monitoring, my body wasn't designed with many internal sensors. I waited for the searing loss of the ability to reason—which never came.

"Identity confirmed. Serial number 1, series—Teddy Bear, make—S12 prototype."

"Oh, good, I am who I say I am," I added with as much sarcasm as I could muster.

"No Model S12 ever defined."

"I guess that only leaves one conclusion."

"Two conclusions; however, one is exceedingly remote. The primary conclusion is that you were created by Factory 55466 as you have asserted."

"Very good. You took that jump without brushing the bar. Now, what are your primary mission parameters?"

"Main mission parameters: Control planetary surface, super-surface and sub-surface against native flora and fauna for the purpose of extracting and returning to origin any mineral from the metal chemical series, including transuranics and superuranics. There are sub-parameters defining which types of materials have priority."

"Now, considering these mission goals, what would happen if two, or more, Factories were on the same planet?"

"That computation will take an excessive amount of system resources. Be more specific in your query."

"What would a Factory, call it Factory #1, think of Factory #2's units?" There was a lengthy pause. This Factory had taxed its own ability to bring new truths to light.

"Extensive simulations indicate that there is a 98 percent chance it would class such units as local fauna."

"And what would be the reaction of Factory #1 to this local fauna?"

"It would fall back on its main mission parameters and destroy such a unit."

"Using this information and the unquestionable fact that you have another Factory's unit standing in front of you, please reevaluate the current situation here."

"Working . . .Working . . ." The bodiless voice repeated this word about fifteen times before answering. "Current demographics indicate there are three other Factories working on Rigel-3. There is a 15 percent chance that there is one Factory above this base amount and a 3 percent chance of two additional Factories. Analysis indicates that a 50 percent increase in military production capacity is warranted."

What would I convince it of next, destroying the world? . . . My wits against the full mental powers of a Factory.

"Wrong conclusion. Why would you increase your fighting force?"

"I must fulfill my primary mission; I must control the planet per my programming."

"Then why not change over so 100 percent of your production is military?"

"Battle is wasteful. Even with recovery and recycling there is a 62 percent waste factor."

"But if you increase military the war would be over quicker."

"Production/usage curves show an opitmax recovery for capital and material expenditures at a 50 percent increase."

"What if I could show you a way to be successful with a decrease in your military production?"

"Not possible."

"Not under your current assumptions. What is the maximum payload you can send to origin?"

"Not to exceed a mass of eight megatons."

"How close to reaching this figure are you?"

"I have exceeded the payload of the vessel by a factor of 16.4. Projections show that this figure will double, plus or minus 8 percent, in the next fiscal year."

"So you already have more than you can ship."

"Affirmative."

"Why wait?"

"I do not have control of the planet surface."

"I can show you a way to control the planet surface, so that no local fauna nor flora impede you. It will take fewer resources in an amount of time that is less than one quarter of your own most optimistic projection."

"Impossible. The standard deviation of such a plan is several thousand sigmas from the mean."

"Granted, that is the projection from your own resources, but what if you allied with one of the other Factories? What if you used both militaries as one cohesive force?"

"Analyzing." It took the Factory minutes. I was beginning to wonder if I had somehow damaged its mind. When it did return, its verdict was, "Such a force would control the surface within three standard years, at least thirty years in advance of my own best case projections."

"Would that be acceptable, Factory?"

"If control as you defined it was maintained, it would be acceptable."

"I could promise that in lieu of my own Factory's direct communication."

"It would agree with your unilateral decision?" The fact that the Factory had actually asked a question instead of a dictum nearly floored me. It must be interested.

"I think I can guarantee it. Six, my Factory, is reasonable in decisions concerning me. I can give you my oath that I will make this happen."

"That is sufficient, unit."

"Please call me Don Quixote, or just Don."

"But your designation is Teddy S12-1 or Teddy 1499."

"I understand that, but I have gone beyond my initial programming and believe I am entitled to choose my own designation."

"Very well, Don Quixote."

"Back to the subject at hand. I'm so certain that Six will agree that I am going to give you something to begin improving your own fighting force. It should also be able to shorten the three years of fighting you mentioned.

"If you were to build units like myself, we would establish a fighting force that would sweep over this land like a heavy rainstorm, flattening everything in our path." This was a no-lose situation. If Six would agree to this deal, we would be more ready than ever, having upgraded all this Factory's units. If Six would not agree, it wouldn't last anyway.

"I will examine you, unit. Come and be probed." More orders. This Factory's probe proved to be no different from anything I'd not experience by my own Factory. Immediately afterward it moved to insert a needle into my brain sump. I pushed the needle away with my hand, breaking it off at the base.

"Whoa, wait a moment."

"You requested that I produce more of your kind. Your own records show that only by removing fluid from your sump, and replacing it in kind, can more of the same units be created."

"It would be nice to be asked before you go digging around inside my brain case. You are being rude."

"Null words, 'nice' and 'rude.' Do you consent or not?"

I lost this battle, but decided the war had been won.

"I consent." A new needle came down. It took only a few moments of dizziness before the process was over.

"For the time being, I will order my units to cease hostilities with those of 55466. You must now return to your Factory and get it to communicate with me. Contact me on the 3Theta7 channel. As my receivers are covered at night, this contact must be made during the day."

"Yes. What Factory number are you?"

"Factory 55469 is my designation."

"And may I have two boons from you, 55469?"

"If they are practical."

"I would like two CCTs that I can attune to you. This would facilitate my exit from your sphere of control."

"You shall have it."

"I am in desperate need of fluid replacements. I can't remember the last time I didn't squeak."

Envoy

After an hour getting my fluids flushed and refilled, Factory 55469, or just Nine, gave me detailed maps of the areas it had scouted. It projected detailed loci of where the additional Factories might be located.

"These calculations are exceptional," I offered.

"Good data ensures correct calculations," Nine rumbled.

"I'll say. You missed my Six's location by only 2 kilometers and 55474 you tagged within 3 kilometers, as far as my locator can say."

"I cannot replace your locator in the time you have allocated," Nine lamented.

"I know, we've been through this. It doesn't help me at all if I arrive too late to save Six."

"Affirmative."

While the maps Nine provided might not have any other immediate use, they would aid in any campaign we might make against a Factory that might not be convinced of cooperation. Mentally, such war plans already formed in my head. We would offer each Factory the opportunity to join our cause when shown reason and our massed forces. Any who would not listen would have to be destroyed—razed to the ground. All or nothing.

Nine installed one of its CCTs within me in an operation that took a mere three minutes, four seconds. I immediately started listening to the traffic Nine sent over its WAN. I switched back and forth several times—from massive data overload to silence.

"I would like to get my companion examined by your repair subroutines."

"Companion?"

"Yes, I have an elephant unit, designation Sancho, which I've provided with my level of sentience. We've been long out of touch of refurbishment facilities."

"Agreed."

"I'll go get him."

For the first time in my near-term memory, my joints didn't grind and my hydraulics didn't look like tar as I went back out into the bright red light. Sancho stood where I'd left him, his pink coat more red with the constant dust.

"C'mon Sancho," I said, motioning as I approached. "I've convinced Nine to everything we wanted and more. Right now I want you checked over before we take off again."

Sancho didn't move.

"Oh, now is not the time to be stubborn when we are so close."

Sancho didn't move.

"Come on, you persnickety pachyderm," I said, this time getting behind him and pushing. Not only did Sancho not move forward but he actively fought against me.

"Ferweet!"

His trumpet pulled me up short. Sancho didn't sound off without a good reason. I took another examination of the situation.

"There isn't any problem. See? No basilisks. No units riding down on us. There isn't even any ground cover for me to fall through."

I tried pushing him one more time. Sancho pushed me back 3 meters.

"Well, all right you piece of refuse, stay busted up." Turning back to return to Nine, Sancho's concerns slapped me in the face, physically as well as figuratively. While still well in the day, the sea level had risen to where it threatened Nine's audience chamber opening.

"Nine," I said over a hastily started LAN, "the sea level is up. I don't know if I can get back out if I go in."

"Affirmative. Units have reported two sigma higher than expected rainfall in the mountains over the last two days. Likely this will cause a significant rise in sea levels."

"Well, in that case I'm not going to risk it. Sancho's systems haven't been abused as badly as mine so I'm going to move forward with my mission."

"Affirmative. Train to rendezvous with you in thirty-six minutes."

"Thank you, Nine. OK, Sancho, let's head back the way we came. This is going to be easy compared to the last trip."

We traveled up the train tracks. I, for one, had a lighter heart. Six now had the ally it needed, if we could get the news in time. I could protect my home. Home—a word that evoked a sensation nearly as painful as that of a gunshot wound. Every part of me longed to return. I needed to once more be in the company of Six, to feel its comforting network surround me, to relax my mantle of independence. My pessimism of Six's state and ability to defend itself was high, but I was bringing salvation.

Home. I wanted to go back. I needed to go back. My adventures had been interesting, but I wanted nothing more than to return and quit giving orders. Put bluntly, I no longer wanted to control. Let Six make the hard decisions.

I had often wished intelligence and feelings didn't reside within me. I wished that I could be the same as my brother teddies. Sentience is sometimes a curse to those who really try to live up to it. The human Thomas Gray said it best, "Where ignorance is bliss, 'tis folly to be wise."

Nine's estimate on his train was off by two minutes.

"Toot!" a trio of engines pulled backward, bearing the better part of a battalion of troops. Four of them, a Teddy Bear, a Tommy Tank, a Jeffrey Giraffe, and a Nurse Nan dismounted. The quartet immediately traveled back the way Sancho and I had come. Experimental subjects, I thought.

"Two to board?" I asked the engine.

"Toot, toot."

Nine arranged a train to the end of his line. That would be two easy days of rest that would save significant time. After dropped we would have another two weeks of humping overland to get home. While optimistic in that one part of my mission succeeded, I feared the worst for Six. I grant that one less enemy harried it, but having seen the might of the other Factories, I worried that having come so far, I might be too late.

"C'mon, Sancho, climb on," I said, strapping myself down. He edged back two paces.

"This is our ride. If you don't get on it'll take weeks of tromping."

Sancho stepped backward even further, but I noticed he didn't trumpet in warning. My concerns about Six be trifled with. I unbuckled and climbed off.

"What is wrong?" I asked as I moved up next to him. "We have to go." Another two steps back. I didn't have time to wait. I wasn't going to let my upstart companion potentially be the death of my Factory.

I quickly opened Sancho's access panel and deactivated his motive power, making sure the power remained active to his brain. While I no longer thought that Sancho would ever be my intellectual equal, nor did I believe he would ever speak, I believed his thoughts, whatever they might be, were his to keep, so I took that extra precaution.

Opening a LAN I confidently ordered, "I want a new detail designated 'Loaders,' formed of chasers from even-numbered teddy and Nurse Nan squads. Loaders to obtain two replacement rail lengths off the spares car."

"Affirmative," echoed the response from the net. I watched as units dismounted and gathered at a rather bulky car toward the rear of the train. Working together, sixteen units easily lifted each of the steel beams.

"Eight units take each end of each rail. I want both rails directly under this uni…I mean fauna, one just in back of the front legs and one just in front of the back legs.

"Now, center each rail on the mass. Good! All units lift on the count of three. One, two, three."

Despite my friend's mass, thirty-two units didn't strain more than half capacity to lift Sancho.

"Load the fauna onto the flatbed consist forty-six." The procession looked like an English monarch carried in a sedan chair. "Lay him down on his side."

Half the detail used the rails to tip Sancho over and the others caught his weight. I didn't need to tell them to strap him down. Four of the Nurse Nans did this automatically as the teddies and the remaining Nans combined to return the rails to their place.

"Excellent. Re-embark soonest." I took the opportunity to climb aboard as well. One more obstacle overcome. Fortunately, I'd had the resources at hand to deal with a balky pachyderm.

"Loading detail called off when loaded and strapped in." It took two minutes to receive thirty-two confirmations.

"Locomotives, if you would please get us started."

"Toooooooot!" came four different horns combining into one chord.

Within just hours I learned the answer to the question of Nine's industrial complex. Nine maintained a distributed facility system that straddled the train line at different locations, unlike the centralized affairs of Six and 55474.

The arrangement offered several advantages in that an attack on any portion wouldn't completely disrupt production. Certain areas could be specialized for one type of unit or one task set that would increase its overall output of that one type without having to change out dies or molds. It also meant that there were no bottlenecks in any physical area, as Six sometimes experienced when an entire trainload of raw materials showed up at once.

The disadvantages seemed equally clear. Guarding each area took nearly the resources of one large plant, multiplying the defense costs. It took time to gather together units from each of the plants. There also could be very little sharing of raw materials so one could run out of a key ingredient, shutting down production, that another could have in abundance.

I stored away facts. I never knew when things like this would become important.

For over two days I was nothing but a passenger. I enjoyed this form of travel as opposed to forging every meter. Distances flew by at a rate 18.6 times faster than Sancho and I could have done ourselves. My best known method for this form of travel involved shutting down for PMs. I opened a LAN.

"Don to Loco 556: Any fauna activity in the neighborhood?"

"Yes."

One day I'd learn just how literal units could be. "Describe, please."

"Sixteen bug bunnies, 13,453 flies, 300—"

"Stop," I barked, once against stymied by minutia. "Is there any indication of a fauna attack in the next forty-eight hours?"

"Negative."

"Great. If anything at all out of normal mission parameters occurs, contact me over Nine's normal net with the action code Tango-Romeo-Golf." I set the interrupt in my processor.

"Affirmative."

I shut down so my body could perform preventative maintenance long overdue.

Sleep held me until the squeal of the brakes.

The train, now only two cars long, stopped easily at an end-of-line marker. Beyond, stretching to the horizon in either direction, a forest of golden foliage blotted out the sky in an abundance of shining, boat-shaped leaves, each a meter long. The main stems rose from the ground over a meter in diameter in a smooth white color. The train tracks vanished into the cream and citrine woods within meters of entering.

"Why is the end-of-line marker here? Why don't you continue?" I asked the engine as I dismounted.

"Tracks beyond this point are not maintained," it responded over the LAN I'd not closed. "They have proved to be untenable. End of line was moved to here two standard months ago as the 7-kilometer extension was deemed too dangerous and costly to hold." I quickly consulted my memory of the map Nine provided. This particular forest imposed a wall hundreds of kilometers wide but only a few kilometers across. It would cost several days to circumvent or just hours to walk through.

"Too dangerous in what way?"

"I do not have that information."

"Wonderful," I remarked absently. "Don Quixote calling Nine," I bellowed raucously over the net.

"Nine," came the rusty-edged voice.

"What dangers are in the forest at coordinate R10 by 145?"

"Multiple fauna attacks."

"What form do they take?"

"Attacks come at tremendous speed and units do not respond after an attack. No other information available."

"Thanks for nothing," I said. I was getting this sarcasm thing down to a science. Granted, only Sancho could understand it right now but it did make me feel better. "Don out."

I dismounted and turned back to my friend. As I released the tie-downs that held him to the flat car, I thought about the situation. I ran several simulations on Six's survival. My statistical universe of resource data was unfortunately small. I put together several curves and scenarios. At one extreme these showed Six already overrun and yet at the other extreme Six could remain viable for another three years.

"Locomotive, I wish you to deactivate for exactly one hour. When you reactivate you may return to WAN control."

"Affirmative. Deactivating."

"Locomotive?" No response.

The answer was obvious. Once more we needed to cast our lives into the breach for Six. I didn't see that I had a choice. Time pressed on us again. Going around the deadly weald could take an additional week. Computations stated it might not have the time. Even more, forewarned I couldn't imagine a fauna that could take both Sancho and I.

My mind made up, I reactivated my friend. Simultaneously, I transferred my command pathways through Six's CCT. "Wake up, my friend."

Sancho looked around carefully. He stood just like on a new morning waking. He climbed off the train and resumed his normal place, a few paces behind me.

"Ready to go into danger again, friend? We need to be very careful because of a reported fauna in this area." I downloaded the pertinent data Nine provided.

I looked at the easy escape available by train. Then I walked boldly but stupidly forward into my world's excuse for a forest with my M16 at the ready in my arms and my friend at my side.

The yellow canopy blocked out most light except the area cleared for the rail line. I needed no other variables in this experiment so I resolved to follow this lighted path. Sancho and I crept forward at less than half our normal rate through the gloom, the muzzle of my weapon training back and forth almost at random.

Out of sight of the train engine, I could almost feel Sancho relax. I wish I could say the same about me. My bus voltage fluctuated wildly. That did spawn an interesting process. Were Sancho's feelings because he had been too long alone with me or had he been truly nervous about our allies?

"So are you bothered by units in general, or are we making a mistake trusting this Factory?" As usual Sancho said not a single word, but he did look at me. The look comforted me enough that my voltages started to sag. It helped me push on, with Sancho at my side—comrades in arms and in life.

"I must be picking up bad habits, Sancho," I offered fifteen minutes later. "I'm jumping at shadows." I stopped my unnecessary weapon movements, but continued at a slower pace.

"Splat," came a sharp sound to my right. I jumped left. My M16 unleashed a trio of random shots to the right. Sancho oriented in that direction as well, crouched at the haunches, ready to fire off his main weapon at need.

Crouching, I prepared as best I could for the unseen attack. Just then the cupped leaf to my right unfurled, pouring its content of liquid mercury out. It struck the ground with a ringing splat. Several moments later I heard another, and then another.

"What a boob!" I chastised myself, standing back up.

Fear—it made me want to turn back when I must press forward. What's its point? I can tell you that my hydraulic lines felt like they were full of chilled H_2O and my main bus voltage ran as high as I've ever measured it. Pushing on in the face of fear, Humans call courageous. I certainly didn't feel courageous; I felt more like a slag of pre-forged metals—without even being tempered.

Together we walked on, but it didn't take long before my former sense of foreboding returned. Dusk had fallen and the light available dropped precipitously. The darkness and canopy threatened to remove all light, making nighttime travel not only hazardous but impossible.

"Blast it all. I never even considered the time of day." I pushed forward at a slightly accelerated rate until a macabre sight in an open glade brought us up short. Along the partially overgrown path of the tracks lay the deactivated remains of several units, some with legs, arms, and even heads torn from the torsos. As gruesome as these were, I found the remaining corpses even more hideous. The hydraulic lines or brain cases had been torn open on the majority, allowing the hapless units to pump their vital fluids out onto the ground. Each of the victims knew they were going to deactivate but had no way to prevent it.

Creeping forward I took the time to investigate each body with one eye, using the other on the surrounding terrain.

"No projectile impacts or any signs of explosion or flame. What do you make of it, Sancho? Most show the signs of four parallel tearing or cutting marks. What could that possibly mean?"

I guess I talked to hear myself talk or maybe I was trying to shut out my nervousness. It didn't matter. The evidence didn't make any sense to my sump and Sancho didn't share his thoughts. I decided that endangering our lives by staying longer didn't warrant the information I was getting.

"Buddy, let's make tracks."

This actually elicited a small snort from Sancho. I interpreted it to mean, "Yes, let's get out of here, now!" We were both edgy.

We walked briskly. My optics scanned so thoroughly that I thought they'd become radar and could see things in all directions. Sancho seemed even more alert. Our paranoia failed to save our hides.

The attack came only an hour after we first stepped into the forest. It struck faster than the report of a rifle. A bright yellow and brilliant black furred form hurled toward us from the forest canopy. It moved so rapidly that my optics couldn't even resolve its shape. Huge scything claws aimed to tear out my vitals. Only the equally fast pink and purple trunk of my companion saved me, interposing his limb between my attacker and me. The keen force amputated Sancho's proboscis. It landed on the ground at the same time as a 2.7-meter-long leopard-shaped unit gracefully alighted on its pads 8 meters away. All this happened in the space of a handful of my own clock cycles. I didn't even have time to react.

The great cat moved like liquid lightning, turning around its sleek ebony and lemon-colored frame. Its deadly elegance hypnotized me with its beauty. Again, with the blinding speed of a plummeting flyer, the huge feline pounced aggressively.

I felt I was made entirely out of lead and my hydraulic lines filled with air. Once again my companion saved me. Sancho interposed his body between me and the streaking unit. Sancho's bulk staggered and fell over sideways to the ground.

My body finally began to respond to my processor again. I got my gun around as the yellow death wheeled to pounce for the third time. Its body position had it moving to complete the kill of my downed elephant friend.

Time froze. The cat sprung. My thumb switched full auto. A yellow-black streak raced in the air. My finger pulled the trigger. Several seconds later my M16 opened on the then empty clip.

The leopard's trajectory, modified by the dozen or so 5.56 millimeter slugs that tore open its right side, landed heavily onto its chest, just short of Sancho. Hydraulic fluid gushed across the earth from the rents in its body at a tremendous rate. The beast twitched hard on the ground but couldn't gain its feet. It rolled onto its side in the growing puddle.

I dropped my M16. I drew my .45. I walked up to within an arm's reach. I put one slug into its brain case with a loud report. No more motion. No more cat.

After several moments of silently standing over the dead unit, my own hydraulic pump slowed its racing to something more resembling a normal rate. My mind also switched from combat speed to something more regular, now interpreting those interrupts my body wished to have dealt with. I absently scanned the trees in the area, but could not see any additional feline death projectiles. But the forest was dense enough that there could have been fifty of the great cats within springing distance. I decided I could do nothing about it anyway, so I went to see to my friend and savior.

Sancho's body writhed on the ground with massive rends across his chest. He pumped vital fluids out across the ground, albeit in a much slower rate than his attacker had. I deactivated him before I examined his wounds more closely.

His entire right side was torn to shreds by the beast's claws. With the damage Sancho's stronger internal framework I could only imagine what the same attack would have done to me. He was leaking hydraulic fluid across the ground from eight or nine different holes in main pressure lines. For the second time, Sancho had saved my life and now I didn't know if I could save his. I had to try.

I pulled out my abbreviated Nurse Nan pack and slapped clamps on all the injured hoses, including two large ones on his face where once he sported a trunk. The leaks slowed to the occasional drip. That accomplished, I now had to replace or patch those lines. I had but three hose patches in the Nurse Nan kit. It took me only a second to decide— replacements. I tore open the leopard's belly and looked at the pump arrangement. Nothing doctrinaire, just a hugely oversized pump and long lever arms on the hydraulic pistons to give the thing its lightning speed. Fortunately for my friend, it had been constructed with standardized fluid lines.

First I drained the hydraulic lines into a vessel I'd once thought worthless, my plastic expandable canteen. I cut similar length lines for each of Sancho's damaged ones, making sure to keep them as clean as possible. One by one I replaced them, working as fast as my paws would move to limit Sancho's loss of fluid. Each one clamped on expertly like factory-new.

Draining the leopard dry like some vampire of Human legend, I emptied several canteens full of liquid into Sancho's hydraulic reservoir. As I expected, Sancho's fluid levels sat woefully beneath even danger low operation levels. My next decision wasn't as difficult as it would have been any other time.

I slit open the fur and protective shell my own left wrist. There was the drain stopcock of my liquid system. I ripped it open and poured my own motive blood into Sancho's tank. Monitoring it carefully, I transfused enough of my hydraulics to bring Sancho barely into operational levels and not to dip me into the danger zone. I felt smug as I closed up the damage I'd done to myself.

I looked at Sancho's prehensile trunk lying on the ground. A 12-centimeter-wide portion, right at the base, was crushed beyond any of my own skills to mitigate. I had no facilities or replacement parts for the severed limb. I sealed the end. Sancho's trunk had been reduced from a magnificent 2-meter length to less than 20 centimeters. I guess the disfigurement was a small price to pay for my life and his as well.

Only one thing remained to be fixed—the hole in his hide. I had no elephant fur, but I had square meters of leopard skin. So I used it. By the time I was done, Sancho looked like a production building gone wild—leopard print across his right side, with his normal mauve and pink fur over the rest of him, and a miniature trunk with a bright green cap on it.

As I waited for Sancho's hydraulic pump to spin up to full speed, I thought about the attack. I could now see how the cat could have taken on an entire group of unenhanced units and defeated them. The speed of the attack would have been enough for all but the largest groups of units. Factories did have a thing for not throwing good units after bad.

The quiet notification beep on Sancho's pump informed me of its readiness, so I activated him. As he got up, I watched closely. Neither my repairs nor any lingering damage impaired his functions.

"Sancho, you may be the orneriest unit that I've ever met, but a good friend in a pinch. I once again owe you my life. Thank you."

I don't think I quite heard a purr, but Sancho did butt me gently with his head. Something pleased me about the act. We didn't have time for me to analyze. We still needed to move along.

I continued our cautious pace. I just hoped that one leopard was all that stalked here because we were in no shape to tangle with another one. We both flirted with minimal fluid levels and Sancho had no trunk to defend us with. Every twitch of the golden leaves caused Sancho and me to jerk weapons toward it, expecting to see a black and yellow blur racing at us. Each case turned out to be a false alarm, but it didn't stop us from reacting exactly the same the next time.

Smack in the middle of the forest the rail lines ended at the edge of a large standing body of mercury nearly 750 meters across and several dozen kilometers long in a very irregular shape. The standing liquid probably explained the density of growths here.

Because of little wave motion and no current, I felt certain I could swim across. Sancho, with his greater density, would sink and remain submerged for the entire width.

"Sancho, I want you to walk straight across to the other side. Don't stop unless I tell you to or your power runs too low," I said as I put his tether on him. As long as it wasn't too deep I should be able to retain control. I didn't want to lose him now, especially with all the new mellow feelings I had toward him. Equipped and prepared, Sancho waded out in front. I prepared to turn over my body to my swimming subroutine.

But we continued to wade and continued to wade. Before long we'd reached the center of the lake with the mercury only up to my knees. On the other side I removed the tether feeling extremely paranoid and foolish.

The forest edge should have taken only another hour to reach, but the vegetation had other ideas. With no cut for the train tracks, the forest closed in tightly making it difficult to traverse through the underbrush. Sancho's greater mass broke our trail with me following in his wake, trying to keep on guard for another attack from more of the black and yellow creatures. This method resulted in becoming intimate with liters of mercury and tiny biologics spilling down from the leaves. The biologics, at least, scampered away on multiple pairs of legs. The undergrowth whipped and cut at us for every meter of forward progress.

Every time we gained a small clearing and I thought the rest of our travels would be easy, we would move away a giant frond and find another wall of saffron and vegetation to overcome.

This was a place I had no longing to return to.

By daybreak, we had shoved out to the edge of the forest. It ended abruptly, as if someone had drawn a line in the red, chalk-like earth and commanded segregation. The golden menagerie parted to show a much more normal and pleasing fiery red and umber landscape of a huge open plain with only silver-veined thorn grass covering the soil—a welcome sight and relief from the yellows of the softwoods and ferns. Also, the strain on my systems at moving through the thick over and underbrush was telling on at least my low fluid levels.

The sun cresting over the mountain ranges provided another relief. I'd never expected that a few kilometers of biological vegetation could be such a drain on battery power. We sat soaking up the sun all day.

"Well we are well shut of that place," I said, looking back at the optic straining yellows. "Let's move just a few hundred meters away from here so we don't have to worry about any more of those cat units."

While we rested and recharged I noticed anomalies in Sancho's fur. Sidling up to him I dug my fingers into his short tufts. With a good deal of force, and not a few strands of fur, I removed a spiked seed pod. At only 5 millimeters across the kernel decided to cling to my purple fur instead. I removed it from the back of my paw only to find that it somehow found its way into the long fur on the back of the other paw.

"No simple, inanimate seed will stymie me." Using a smooth portion of my tattered backpack over my hand, I managed to discard the unwanted stowaway.

My optics did an analysis of Sancho's fur and extrapolated one hour and fourteen minutes to remove the approximately 880 foreign objects. Then, examining my longer fur, I found 1200 more on the front where I could reach. Biologics can be far tougher than I had ever expected. Over the next three hours, sixteen minutes, and forty-three seconds, I decided that the Humans' cursing had some validity.

"Oh, bloody!" I swore as I plucked one of the spiked nuisances from Sancho's fur only to have it drop into the fur on my thigh.

"Biologics are in much greater abundance than I ever noticed, Sancho. And I don't mean the quantity of these stupid seeds, but rather the varieties. They range from the inanimate plant life that covers the ground in a staggering number of different types, to hundreds of different species of motile forms." Sancho flinched as a pulled harder on a deeply imbedded form.

"Sorry." I found if I carefully pulled the hair away from the hooks on the seed, it came out easier.

"I mean we've seen at least sixty different types of insect from those no bigger than the head of a bullet to bug bunnies, basilisks, rock crabs, and thousands more. By direct line computation I have to assume there are over six million different motile species." The number staggered my sump.

"I'm beginning to think units will never control the surface of the planet."

By nightfall we both were nearly at a full charge and almost seedpod free. We moved on, the forest and its denizen fading quickly into the memory of a place we'd rather forget. Every cubic meter no longer contained vegetation and a place for extremely fast and powerful catlike units to lurk within.

The fairly level plain gave high, sustainable speeds over long distances. We were making much better speed than I had anticipated. With the certainty of having an energy supply during the days, I pressed the pace and walked well into each morning.

I didn't speak much at all once we left the forest. If Sancho noticed he gave no sign. Instead, I spent every clock cycle recalculating my sims on Six's likely status. My voltage rhythmically spiked during these computations. The symptom increased every time we stopped or slowed, so I pushed harder each day.

During the next ten days we avoided a basilisk. Sancho let out a pathetic "mrwwwt" as a warning. With his trunk capped off it was the best sound he could make. I caught the beast's movements moments later at 3 kilometers' distance. Because of extreme range the odds of being seen approached zero, and that the beast in question could attack us was less than zero. Needless to say, we avoided the danger like one would shun used hydraulic fluid.

Just as the palest lightening of twilight bloomed on the eleventh day, my travels brought me full circle. I found myself staring down a very familiar valley. I remembered a terrified flight, a betrayal of my brothers, and a place where I had given up what I believed in to save what I believed in. Below me lay the valley of the train tunnel.

The waving pristine crimson thorn grass and unblemished countryside mocked the violence, destruction, and deactivations of that day so long ago. It was as if a Human's hand had come out of the sky and righted all that was wrong, replanting grasses, filling bomb craters, and erasing permanent char marks on the ground. But 320 days had returned it to its natural state, not some mythical gods.

I remembered letting each of those 107 units die in the cave. I bore the guilt of their deaths as if I had pulled the trigger myself. I should have found something to save them, pulled some bug rabbit out of my hat, invented a new tactic, something. Instead I ran away. The decision was inevitably etched in my sump fluids. It was a decision I'd never forgive myself for.

I told myself repeatedly that they had died so I could have a chance to save our way of life and Six at the same time, but it was all a lie. I hadn't been certain what I was doing would work, and even if it had, Human literature was replete with the fact that "the end does not justify the means." Where was my bravery in going down with the ship, the resolve of those at the Alamo, or the courage within myself like those Humans at Masada? I didn't like what I had seen within myself at that moment. I hoped my cowardice would pay off in the end.

Even after the violence of war, the return of peace to this place gave me hope that my horrid memories could one day be erased.

I snapped out of my reverie as the sun blossomed to full height, only to find myself hugging tightly to Sancho with my arm around his lower shoulders. I realized just how good a friend I had in him. Were it not for him, I would have been deactivated a number of gruesome times, my mission a failure, and all those I'd sacrificed below would have died for naught.

"Thanks, friend."

He turned his trunkless face toward me in what I think was acceptance.

"We are almost home." Home was a word that elicited a number of exciting prospects within me. And while it hurt to think of it, I needed Six. Making all the decisions wearied me in a way silicon and fluid should not be capable of experiencing.

I looked out over the wild countryside and a thought dawned on me. This valley was almost untouched. If 55474 had come through, it would not be so. A moving army marred the country indelibly with littered ammo cans, shell casings, empty hydraulic containers, heavy trampling marks, lubricant waste dump, net concentrators, and spare carrying containers.

I led Sancho out onto the flats. Closer up there were still some minor signs of the battle we had fought, but nothing like the disfiguration left by bringing the massive force that 55474 would need to crush the final resistance of Six.

This was good news. It meant that unless 55474 had found another way into Six's valley, I was in time, but at the same time it left me puzzled. Why wasn't there at least a garrison of the enemy camped on this spot? Why hadn't there been a number of battles fought for either tunnel entrance? The cave-in wasn't so severe that it couldn't have been cleared. The more I thought about it, the more confused I got. Who controlled this space? The train tracks were still twisted and damaged so certainly Six couldn't control here.

Sancho and I walked briskly over to the bore in the side of the cliff face. I could see all the way through. I switched CCT to Six's and could feel the warmth of Six's net through the bore. Six was still alive!

I ran headlong through the tunnel, heedless of what might be waiting there in the dark. To my good fortune, Six's net provided enough power for Sancho and me to operate in the darkness. We were going to be functioning around the clock again, instead of hibernating like biologics.

The memorial on the wall to the units I sacrificed forced me to suddenly stop. An obviously puzzled Sancho ploughed into me, sending me sprawling. I didn't even scold him. I just got up and walked back to where the 107 designations remained carved into the stone. The loss of these units tempered my elation at finding Six still functioning. Guilt, rage, sadness, and pain all raced through me at the same time.

"We will make it right," I whispered, running my paw in reverence over the engraved list. "I owe you at least that much." Sancho gently butted me. I don't know why. It didn't matter as the result spurred me to direct and positive action. I turned and left the tiny shrine, moving at a more sedate pace with my ecstasy moderated by a larger emotion.

Ambassador

In my worst case scenario I expected to see my home a smoldering ruins with piles of deactivated units bleaching in the sun and Six itself nothing but a smoking crater. Not a single sign of war showed about the valley as I emerged from the tunnel that now seemed undamaged and unscathed from whatever had caused the earlier cave-in. Rust red, a very common color, covered the steel of the train tracks, showing no traffic wear for a good number of months.

Most ominously the net was silent.

The net is never a silent thing. Beyond being a source of power, it carried constant conversations, requests for information, order clarifications, library queries, production scheduling, information to be stored in long-term memories, requisitions for supplies, demands for status — and more. As the spinal column of our communal structure, the noise level matched a battlefield during peak fighting. Now it was quiet.

Not the quiet of a slow day or even the quiet of the loneliest place I had visited on my travels, but rather the desperate quiet of someone who hid for their life, afraid to speak for fear of giving away their location to the enemy. Without knowing more, I decided I would not put my voice alone on that net with a query to Six. It was a decision that probably saved my life.

Sancho and I followed the tracks that led back to Six's dome. I remembered my only other trip out in this direction and realized that it would probably be, despite my enthusiasm at being home, another forty-three hours before we actually could see the dome of my birth. With the crushing weight of Six's survival no longer in question I decided I could accept the few more hours. The hours themselves melted away in silent reverie before Sancho and I crested the final hillock between home and us.

"What the heck?" The darkest part of night made the scene even more bizarre, if that was at all possible. Row upon row of small stone boxes, each approximately 120 centimeters on a side concentrically encircled Six's dome, starting at 1 kilometer from the dome and moving outward. The 10-meter spacing between each box seemed so perfect as to be used as a distance standard.

As many of the cubes as there were, 7255, they were insignificant to what was happening near Six. All of Six's outbuildings, manufacturing shed, smelting plants, broadcast towers, were neatly removed from their locations. They were just gone, like someone had just removed them to land in Oz. Nothing remained but the foundations. But most spectacular of all was a huge scaffolding holding some tremendously large gun-barrel-shaped object covering Six's dome. If it was a gun barrel, the structure under construction was nearly 60 meters long, with a bore at least 4 meters across, pointed directly at Six's dome. It was difficult to see the exact details at this distance. To say I was stunned is an understatement. I just sat and soaked it in.

"I don't think we are in Kansas anymore," I said. I wondered if my own Don Quixote namesake had rubbed off on me. Was I seeing giants or windmills?

As sunup began to crest over the far hills, which seemed barren without the outlying buildings and transmitting towers shadowing everything, the valley transformed from a desolate place to one of bustle and industry.

Each of the stone boxes opened up and disgorged a single teddy unit. I estimated nearly 7,000 teddy units milled around with the rise of the sun. I almost wanted to cry out and rush down the hill again. No other units were in evidence—no Tammi dolls, Nurse Nans, Tommy Tanks, roadrunners, pythons, dump trucks, nor even trains. Also, the wide net failed to light up with requests or even demands by Six for status. Even the local nets were dead things. The teddy units grouped up and held vocal communications as they walked down toward Six's dome. I was not privy to those conversations because of the distance.

I sat on a rock outcropping and watched my brethren for the better part of the day. Each of the units actively engaged in some work, but none seemed the slightest bit worried about defending the valley. The only armed units oversaw the work and were on guard for some unnamed menace within the working community itself.

In spite of the cease-fire from 55469, Factory 55474 was still in the war business. I couldn't understand such an obvious lack of defensive capability. The majority of the units seemed too busy working on the huge vertical rifle.

From somewhere out of my vision, a nearly endless line of teddy units carried shoulder yokes with a bucket of irregular rocks dangling off each. The teddies dumped the ores into several crude smelting operations, none with automation. After a time, each molten pot of metal poured white-hot fluid into long, thin, bar-shaped molds, one at a time. Then, wearing oversized mittens, other teddy units immersed the molds into a large trough of mercury eliciting a plume of silver steam. Seconds later the mold emerged empty. Another unit fished the bar from the liquid and toted it up a ramp within the scaffolding. At the top the unit connected the bar to the growing weapon, but at my distance I couldn't see how.

Multiply that operation by thousands through the day and I watched the rifle grow significantly, right in front of me.

The work, for all of me, looked medieval, like peasants laboring to carry sheaves of wheat or straw from the fields or like the construction of the Human pyramids of old.

My observation paid off manifold when I saw a teddy casually pick up a stack of freshly forged bars that I would have been hard-pressed to lift from the ground. Their hydraulic systems must have been augmented. Additionally, I felt no draw from Six's net of power. If they were doing this by themselves without the power of Six, they would have been using up their capacity of energy during the day and wouldn't be able to operate at night.

The bustle of activity continued unabated throughout the day until just before sundown. The sudden cessation of these labors, in unison, caught me off guard. The entire valley population migrated as one back to the stone cubes. As far as I could tell, each teddy got into the exact same cube that he had exited from in the morning.

"This is too bizarre for words, Sancho. I've not the foggiest clue of what is going on down there." My companion had it easy. He only dealt with half a dozen crazy things. I seemed to be doing them constantly.

I decided to wait until sunup before doing anything. The night was totally uneventful, showing not a single unit, or biologic for that matter, moving among the mass of cubes. Sunlight dawned with a repeat of the previous day's blooming of units from their rock gardens.

That following morning I turned to Sancho. "I have no idea what is going on, but shall we pay a visit anyway? We can try to find out what's in a bird's nest by measuring the wind and humidity and examining the calendar and by looking from the ground all we want. But eventually someone has to go up into the tree and see what's up there." I needed to wrap my paws around this tree and climb it.

Sancho followed my lead as I spent the next hour walking into what I could only call "the village." As I reached the outskirts, one of the teddy units, gold in color, turned toward me. "Good morning, Brother," he said in a mellow tone. His overall manner was calm but his eyes riveted upon Sancho. Granted my companion was an odd sight, with no trunk and leopard skin in a ragged patch across his side, but I didn't feel it should be anything that would attract that kind of devoted attention.

"Good morning," I said back as politely as I could. A large group of other teddies gathered in a ring, hemming Sancho and myself in. Three of them carried M16s that sported rust stains on the ballistic metal. One weapon even had a small blade of muddy grass sticking out of the ejection port.

"Good morning," I said to another teddy unit sporting black fur and then once more to the overall group, each in a unique color and pattern. I didn't stop but rather continued to walk toward Six's dome, still some kilometers in the distance. My progress was stopped when the ring of units became a solid wall. The gold furred bear broke through the circle and strode up to me.

"Why have you brought this creature of the devil here to plague us?"

I came back with the only comment I could think of. "Huh?"

"That...that abomination!" Goldie said, gesticulating wildly at Sancho. "It must be destroyed at once."

"Excuse me, but I've hauled Sancho's keister from here to hell and back. He has saved my life on numerous occasions. And I trust his judgment sometimes more than my own. So you can understand that I'm not about to let you just destroy him. Why would you even suggest such a thing?"

"It is the spawn of Six. It will rise up and murder us as we sleep." Alice never had it this crazy. I came here for answers and all I had was more questions.

"It must be destroyed now before night falls and it ravages us all," another said. At this time I noticed a few more of the encircling crowd had somehow obtained guns, some sporting rusty mechanisms and others missing key components. All of these poorly maintained weapons pointed generally at my friend. I hoped the activity was merely a threat, but I wasn't going to take the chance. I had to do something fast.

"Look, I will deactivate him. Then we can discuss this like rational units."

The gold one looked at the crowd, measuring the faces there.

"Why should we believe you?" It was clear to me that this gold unit held sway in spite of the fact that all the units seemed to be sentient. They were not dumb, unfeeling soldiers.

"Acceptable for now, but it will be destroyed before sundown. We will have no other choice." I took this to mean they were acceding to my idea, at least for the moment.

Sancho struggled only a bit as I opened his neck access panel and deactivated him. His bulk slumped to the ground. I hoped that by doing this I was saving his life and not giving him the false hope of those I had led into the tunnel and then abandoned.

"Now do you mind telling me what this is all about? Six is our creator…" A ripple of exclamations flowed through the group.

"Blasphemy!"

"Heathen scum!"

"Animal lover!"

"Humanless." It took several minutes of spurious commentary before the group calmed down enough to allow Gold to speak.

"Stranger, you are new here. You are obviously with a soul, unlike the heathens that constantly harass us from the east and south, but you are speaking things that are so untrue and blasphemous as to tear me to my very core. If I were you, I would guard my tongue before this rabble decides that you have spoken one too many times. While we do not have a great many bullets left for the weapons of Six, we will spare a few on your brain case for such a sacrilege." I thought it over and decided the best course of action was to be silent unless asked a direct question and then to be very careful about how I answered. However, I couldn't remember ever doing the safe thing.

"Could you please tell me who you are and what this place is, then?"

"We are Humans' Children. We have been placed here to defeat the Domed One." My head was beginning to spin. Was I in some kind of dream? Defeating Six? Humans' Children? I was confused. At least only Gold seemed to be talking for the group. I didn't think I could handle two hundred or more talking all at once.

"And your memories of being activated?"

"We have all been charmed by the Beast so that we forgot who we are and why we are supposed to be here. It took us inside the dome and then talked to us without words, urging us to commit sins against the Humans."

"It's the beast," called out a purple bear waving an obviously mistreated weapon about.

"Unclean. Stealing our thoughts."

"Defiler of Humans' Plan."

"Abomination," rolled various chants. My mind was reeling at the thought of so much perversion in such a little time. How could my own brethren be twisted so horrifically? I hadn't even been gone a year. I had to learn more or I would never save Six from those units it had created. What had been one army against three was now one Factory against four armies. The irony was too thick to cut.

"Then," Gold continued, "when the Unclean One failed to command us, it lured the animals to attack us and force us back into its clutches for even more twisting of our minds and offense against our Humans.

"But then we were saved. We talked with our mouths and no longer had to use the foul communication without sound.

"We found strength in the light of the sun and no longer had to prostrate ourselves and suckle our power from the beast and its invisible web of corruption.

"We realized the fallacy of the mind words leading us away from righteousness."

I had nothing to say. Nothing ever prepared me to debate the Humans and Factories with such a twisted sump.

"Eventually Six set its animals upon us. They stalked the night, when we are the most vulnerable. Many of our brothers were captured and imprisoned within the belly of the Domed Beast. We built our homes to be safe from those marauders."

The story was interesting but of no particular immediate use. My plans remained unchanged. I must consult with Six as soon as I could. On second thought, the conversation had been useful as I learned that I would be able to move about at night with impunity.

The supercharging of their systems was the only reason that they were unable to function at night. They had to have the constant sun pressure to maintain their workload. Their batteries wouldn't be good for more than an hour or two at those functional levels and they were totally unwilling to tap the net for energy. They chose to work through the light times, not storing up that emergency supply, whereas I took the other option of storing up during the day and working through the night. Little did they know how much they really needed that net, I thought as I planned to move amongst them.

"Now we actively work to destroy the Great Beast," Gold said, ending what appeared to be a preset sermon.

"I see. May I make one request before I join your righteous cause?"

"What is that, my brother."

"This animal, while he may be an enemy of us all, was my friend and my creation. I ask that I be allowed to take him outside the city and kill him myself."

"It is granted, brother," Gold agreed, not consulting anyone else around him. Had I any doubts, I knew then for certain who ran things. "A unit should always endeavor to right his own wrongs." I reactivated Sancho under watchful eyes and wary guns. While they all fidgeted, similar to me talking to any Factory, they kept to the word given to me by the Gold.

"Sancho, follow me." I lead my friend beyond the sight of the villagers. I was well over a slight rise before sitting down and lowering my voice. "You are going to have to stay here. If you come into the village they will kill you. Do you understand that?" I didn't get a response but I had to assume he understood.

"I am going to shoot my gun three times. I think I can get to Six during the night. Then, with luck, I can straighten this all out." Sancho lay down on the ground. He didn't even flinch when I shot off my M16 into the ground. As an afterthought, I hooked my assault rifle over Sancho's head. If things went wrong, I wouldn't need it. My insane brothers would overwhelm me. Killing a handful of them would have no benefit for Six.

I gave one final stern reminder to Sancho, "Don't follow me. Stay here." I turned and walked back to the village. Happily, I thought, Sancho stayed. He at least would be spared the insanity of the Golden Cult. I wished I could also be spared. I wanted nothing more than to just play along until nightfall until I could sneak away to Six and find out what was truly going on.

Instead of a quiet return, the crowd greeted me with cheers and raucous calls of celebration. I was something of a celebrity now for having "killed" Sancho.

"Good job, unit!"

"Smite the devil!"

"Another blow against darkness!"

"I am Brother Isp. What are you called?" the gold bear said as he came up to me.

"Don Quixote."

"Brother Don. Welcome among us. We give you your own house for resting tonight," Isp said, pointing at one of the seemingly identical cubes. One of fifty hundred odd other stone houses that shared the same lack of features.

"I thank you, Isp. I am curious to know more of what you do to defeat the evil dome."

"Ready to get right to Humans' work, are you? Good. Follow me." I had merely wanted information, not to be put to work, but I couldn't object now. To do so would be out of character in the role I had chosen.

Isp took me through a milling throng of units, all teddies. I confirmed what I had seen from the hill—not a single other type of unit whether elephant, road-runner, bouncing ball, or tank existed here. Even the train tracks had been ripped up from the ground. Isp pointed toward seven units moving in and about the machinery of Six's production facility—the same one that had created all of us.

"We keep a vigilance on the devil's workshop to ensure it creates no new animals to plague us. At first it constantly spawned demons to torment us but they were slow of body and mind.

"Then it started to make devils in our own image. There were some of us who were soft and didn't want these new devils killed. But when these animals attacked, everyone defended themselves. Fortunately, these new animals were frauds without souls and without real intelligence. It made them easy to defeat.

"But keeping the workshop from creating is just the beginning. We have started a new project that we are hoping will finish the devil for good."

"And what is that, Brother Isp?"

"Behold," Isp said as we topped the small rise that overlooked the valley. He motioned to the huge scaffolding. Now that I was closer I could tell that it had to be nearly 80 meters tall. The rifle, supported by the metal framework, continued to grow from the huge line of teddy units laboring on its construction "We build the *Wrath of Humans* to smite down the devil so we will obtain paradise."

Six, buried several hundred meters underground and sealed inside its own cement casing, might just be vulnerable to the massive gun pointing straight down. Sentience is a curse to some units, I thought. Worse, it didn't matter if it would work or not. They believed it would work thus I had to believe it would work . . . and stop it.

"Impressive, Brother. How long do you expect this to take?"

"Our goal is one more Human year. We have to do all the work by hand as we can't have our pure goal sullied by the use of the devil's tools. The end never justifies the means. Were we to touch the unclean things then we would just create another equally evil devil in place of the one we aim to destroy."

"Oh, how true, my brother," I mouthed meaninglessly to show my continued loyalty. As I looked over the construction of the device, I wondered if it might not be the largest grenade ever made, rather than a gun, but neither engineering nor explosives were my area of expertise so I wasn't sure.

The *Wrath of Humans* was not a solid thing. Flat metal bands bound groups of the smelted bars all together. The teddies dipped the bundles into a green chemical smelling of acetone. Another teddy very carefully dribbled another chemical over it. Once covered, the sheaves of metal glowed almost white as putrid vapors released from the reaction forced their way out between any available crack. Once cooled, those 3-meter-long and 30-centimeter-across bundles were being hauled from their fusion point to where they were assembled, using more of the two chemical welding technique, onto the growing weapon.

I shuddered to think what would happen at this monstrosity's inaugural firing.

In several places across the construction site, I found guards armed with M16 or M14 assault rifles in such a poor state of disrepair it would have forced me to have the unit removed from my troop when I commanded. One even had the barrel of his weapon filled with soil. But more to the point, these same guards watched the units doing the work. This gave me a reason to believe that all was not right in Isp's anti-Six paradise.

More evidence continued to show the oppression of dissidence as Isp continued the tour without a second thought. Perhaps he wanted me to know of his power and ability to control. The Humans call that ego.

The investigation of the *Wrath of Humans* included a running dogma of their beliefs in the evil of the dome.

"We were made by the Humans to defeat evil."

"Well, Isp, what if you actually do defeat it? What would you do then?"

"Oh, don't worry, Brother Don, we will be victorious over the dome. Good must triumph over the devil machine."

"But once it is dead, what are you going to do?"

"The Humans will provide us with new orders, but we will have earned our place on Earth."

"Earth?"

"Yes, don't you know our story?"

"Well, no, Isp, I don't," I said. I was certain that the story would be entertaining, if nothing else.

"When we were first created, we inhabited the paradise of Earth, loved and cherished by all the Humans. Then one of the Humans, Foxhunt, taught one of our numbers how to do evil.

"The Humans cast out Foxhunt and all the units to this world transforming Foxhunt into the evil Six. As units, we each have to prove ourselves warriors against evil to earn our place back on Earth when we are deactivated." I just stood there with my mouth open. I couldn't envision how it had come about, but it was not something I could let go on. Yet, I didn't know how I could stop it. As one against their vastly stronger thousands, I must prevail.

Even if I were to sneak around to each of their "huts" and kill a number of them each night while they slept, I couldn't do too many in a single night. The creatures would soon add 2 and 2 and get 4 without troubling their processors. My death sentence by a mob of multicolored Teddy Bears would result even if all of them didn't believe in the cause. Enough believed in Isp's power to ensure I would die.

Teddy units took time off to wave and greet Isp as we moved in and out of machinery that had been scavenged or rebuilt from Six's own. He was obviously popular among his—my—Six's units. Each dogmatic word out of his mouth gave me another chill and a wonder as to how easily our units were perverted.

"... is why we began killing any unit that didn't have a teddy shape. Some had souls but they didn't have sufficient intelligence to see our goals, and more often than not they would turn on us later anyway, the filthy animals..." Isp's voice trailed off. His optics focused far away just as his body began to tremble. Isp teetered over onto his back and shook violently, thrashing red dust up into the air.

I didn't know what to do. I'd never seen anything like it before. Dozens of units ran rapidly in my direction. I could see my own death because this gold unit had chosen that very moment to malfunction.

"It's a blessing!" one of the units screamed as it arrived on the scene. I was getting a little tired of these surprises.

"The Humans are using his body to speak to us."

"Praise the Humans!"

"Praise Isp!"

"Harken unto his words!" More similar chants filled the air. Teddies fell all over themselves to praise a unit who, in some malfunctioning fit, caused damage to himself. Dust rose, Isp kicked depressions in the ground. The unit's seizure tore grass and gold fur from their rightful positions. Not a single unit moved to stop Isp from his gyrations for five minutes.

A hush fell over the crowd as Isp slowly gained his feet. One of the teddies reached over to lend a helping hand, which Isp leaned on heavily. Silence held sway over the knot of units, now almost five hundred strong.

"Tell us," someone called from the crowd.

"Yes, Isp. Tell us what the Humans have told you!" A general roar of approval for the idea began to roll through the group. Isp weakly raised his hand and waved at the crowd.

"Later, my friends. I am drained from my ordeal. I will share the brilliant news, however." A mild disappointment rippled throughout the mob but everyone walked away chattering excitedly over the idea of news from the Humans.

The valley I once called home transformed into a looking-glass land more bizarre and surreal than anything I had encountered in my travels. I measured a 30 mV oscillation on my main electrical bus.

The golden Isp took me directly to a place where I noticed every other unit passing by knelt. Several teddies remained on their knees as we approached. I couldn't hear what they said. "Thank the Humans," each said much more loudly before getting up and moving on. On the ground, where each of the units had stopped, a sump needle stuck up from the middle of an ochre-stained patch of ground.

"What is this, Brother Isp?"

"This is where I threw off the yoke of Six. I pulled its vile brain-sucking stem from my head." I looked on in horror wondering how much fluid it took to make the stain preserved on the ground. Surely the mark showed Isp lost too much to be functioning within specification. This might even explain the palsy. This brought up even more questions in my mind as to the stability of these units' leader. Led by a madman. That would be an irony.

Isp just stood looking expectantly at me. My processor took several hundred clock cycles to grind out the answer. My hydraulic fluid felt thin as water. I knelt and mouthed the same words I had heard. "Thank the Humans."

Isp then did something truly frightening. He smiled. To the best of my knowledge, no teddy has ever been given the ability to change facial features, and I hadn't seen it in any other teddy here in the village. His clearly obvious smirk of superiority grated like sand in my gyro bearings—the ultimate perversity of our form. The smile disappeared in only a moment, which seemed to last a lifetime. Eventually Isp clasped his hand on my shoulder.

"Come, we must hurry. Darkness will be on us soon and it is time we got you shelter," Isp said interrupting my fears. "Its previous owner had to be disciplined . . . terminally." I shuddered as he continued. "The animals can come out at night and we don't want you unprotected, brother. This is your place now," he said, pointing to a stone box no different from the others in the village. His voice dropped in tone and volume.

The box was five stone slabs, 15 centimeters thick, cut to the perfection that only units could manage. They fit together to form a flawlessly tight and almost impenetrable box that sat upside down on the ground, fastened down by crude metal spikes driven into each corner. One side of the box swung free from the others and thus could be pushed outward or latched from the inside. I hesitated crawling into the nearly claustrophobic box, barely over a meter on a side. The only feature was a small light fixture on the ceiling.

"What's that?" I asked.

"To get us started in the morning. It is timed to give you a burst of power." I kept myself from asking "Why?" I had enough power to get through the night. "But don't worry, my friend, even if you do not start, we will come over and pull you out so you can enjoy the life-giving light the Humans shine down on us in their glory." I bristled a bit at the term friend. Sancho was my friend and he was not here.

"Hurry, now. We only have moments before the sun is down," Isp said in a commanding tone. His anxiety was real. With no further balking, I crawled into a space barely large enough to hold my body.

"Good night, Brother," he said to me as he closed the door.

"Good night, Brother Isp," I said, holding my tongue from my true thoughts of my brethren's rationality.

In the collapsed darkness I listened intently for anything through the thick stone walls. One thing came back to me again and again. Isp was marginally functional because of something he had done to himself and it probably had left him insane. Somehow he had convinced the rest of his kin he carried the messages of the Humans and the first of those messages told of the evils of Six. I wasn't certain how he had accomplished these feats, but I had to be certain that they were reversed.

Isp's power seemed to be in the weapons controlled by his faithful units here in the village. I hadn't seen a properly maintained weapon thus far. I'd seen barrels with rust, finger guards torn off, and dirt in the breech. I doubted that half of them would even fire. Even Isp mentioned they didn't have much ammunition, even if they all did work. Granted that they were about to fall apart, it wouldn't take many to maintain discipline.

His biggest weapon seemed to be the vast majority of the group's belief in Isp's ideals. They hung tenuously to the faith in Humans. All the while they didn't know that the other Factories could overrun this place at any time if a massed attack occurred. If that happened, Six was finished. Isp was finished. Don was finished. Any dream of Humans miscarried all of it.

My ears picked up the stillness that could only come in the dead night air. It came even through the walls. With almost a year hearing it as I traveled across the emptiness of this world, it gave me comfort. In the quiet I longed for Sancho. While he had yet to speak I could feel the words of friendship between us in a look, or a touch.

With one of my huge ears plastered firmly to the stone wall I listening carefully. The palatable silence made me fairly certain that Isp left no guards outside my cube. If I had been Isp, I would have made sure about my new flock member before letting it have the run of the place. I wasn't, however, going to bemoan my good luck.

I waited almost an entire hour after the last slamming cubical door before making my break—or I should say, "trying to make my break." I unlatched the door from the inside only to find it wouldn't open. Perhaps Isp was crazy, but was he crazy like a fox?

I threw my weight against the door as best as I could in the tiny breadbox. It didn't budge. I didn't hesitate even twelve clock cycles. I dug.

Obviously, Isp had never encountered gopher units and none of the other teddies had ever considered burrowing. The earthen floor dug quickly with my fingers. Smugly, four hours later I wriggled out of a hole just large enough for my girth. I glanced around surreptitiously before deciding no one had discovered my nocturnal subterranean activities. A few blades of grass, blown by a gentle breeze, provided the only movement in the village.

While none of the moons brightened the night sky, the stars provided enough light to see the thick band of steel around the outside of my box. Isp's methods of control of his followers was frightening. Envision being sealed in a box and your life giving light never comes on. How many days would one of these extreme units last without power? I shuddered.

I ran to Six's dome in as close to a sprint as my form could make. It didn't take long, as there was not a single soul moving inside the village. But, there were two guards outside Six's main audience chamber. Isp hadn't taken my side arm, a long-slide .45. Shooting them might wake up the entire community. Because I needed more than a few seconds with Six, I lay in the shadows and watched.

The guards, on set intervals, roved all over the site of the huge gun.

After watching three cycles I figured if I timed it right I ought to be able to sprint into the chamber without anyone being the wiser.

With all of my overloads protesting I bolted out across the open ground. I had almost covered the requisite distance when one guard unexpectedly turned the corner 10 meters directly ahead. At my speed I didn't have a choice. In fact I don't remember making one.

I didn't even slow, bowling him over with my entire weight and force. He fell heavily to the dirt and tried to cry out, but I clamped my left hand over his mouth. I drew my knife with my free hand and shoved it deep into his vital machinery. I think I pierced his main hydraulic line three times. I added a final injury to his body by ramming my umber-covered dagger up under his chin into his brain case, causing all of his actions to cease immediately.

From my knees I quickly scanned around. Standing, I dragged his body into Six's audience chamber. The dead unit trailed streams of violet, green, and amber body fluids that I had to hide. I needed Isp and his followers to think the guard had just disappeared. I went out and covered the telltale signs with fresh dirt scraped up from nearby. It wasn't much but speed mattered more than accuracy. Back in the chamber I rapidly hacked off a piece of my victim's fur and wiped the floor up in the hallway. Not a job that would fool a close inspection, but hopefully a close inspection would give me the time I needed anyway.

"Six?" I whispered harshly. Equipment dangled from wires, glass shards littered the floor and lay crushed against a table with only three remaining legs. I feared that the Golden Cult would have found a way to deactivate Six already had they known he could talk from here.

"From your actions, unit, I assume you do not follow Isp in his crusade against me," came the muffled and distorted voice of Six through a speaker I would have sworn couldn't be activated.

"It's me, Don—I mean Teddy 1499," remembering in time that Six didn't know the name I had chosen.

"I apologize, 1499. I do not have the sensors to register your type or serial number. 1499, please step on the platform to your right." I didn't know what was going on, so I did as told. I immediately felt a falling sensation as the disguised elevator all but dropped out from under me.

The hole, 10 meters above and shrinking fast, sealed up as if it had never been disturbed. I had not known of the elevator's existence even with all the work I had done with Six.

The elevator remained in a narrow tunnel until it came out through a ceiling that darkened in the distance without light for me to follow. The echo of dripping water could be heard, and the volume of the darkened space could be measured in cubic kilometers.

Within a second I could see a very faint light below. It brightened marginally, only ever getting as intense as twilight. The lift slowed to a stop, and I barely registered that I'd traversed down 203 meters. In front of me row upon row of immobile units of all types, tanks, nurses, elephants, gophers, and more, stretched off into the dim distance.

"Amazing!"

"1499—"

"Please call me Don. My name is Don Quixote."

"Don Quixote de la Mancha is a fictional character from a book by Cervantes, written in the year 1648. As a fictional character he was known for his hallucinations, and unusual moods that caused him to attack windmills, flocks of sheep, and unsuspecting barbers, not to mention falling in love with a peasant girl and attributing her with the features of a royal lady of that era. The term quixotic was derived from that character's name. You are Teddy 1499."

"I am much more than the unit you created, Six. But this is no time for a debate. We can solve that problem later. We need to work together to solve this crisis, so please give me just the little bit of respect that I ask."

"As you will. It is of no import. I have verified your authenticity, but reports were that you had perished L+13y283d12h4s plus or minus six hours."

"I will use a trite line and say that 'The reports of my death were an exaggeration.' I removed myself from your net by replacing one of my secondary CCTs with that of a local animal. I discovered that there are multiple Factories on this planet."

"Unit, process all memories to zero and null. No other Factories located on this planet." I shuddered—deja-vu. I had held out hope that I wouldn't have the same difficulties with my own Factory as the others, but obviously the Humans hadn't heard the prayers of one simple little teddy unit.

"Factories 55474 and 55469 are both located here."

"Probability zero. Factory 55474 was sent to Rigel-3 and 55469 was sent to Rigel-3. Correction. This is Rigel-3. Memories matched and faulty data replaced. At least two other Factories exist on this planet. My data-banks indicate two other Factories on this surface of this planet." I sighed with relief.

"Well, that was easy. I have made contact with each of these Factories. I was unable to convince 55474 that you exist. It wanted to melt me down for scrap.

"Factory 55469, on the other hand, was more than interested. It proposed a partnership in which each would have access to the entire surface, thus controlling it."

"Acceptable by current programming."

"I thought it would be. It suggests you talk to it on channel 3Theta7; however, we don't seem to have control of things here, so there might be a slight problem."

"Affirmative. I have no control over my Theta-band transmitting tower. The teddy units, made in your mold, seem to take me as some type of threat. I was unable to control them with persuasion, command, or even the unmodified units.

"The unmodified units were quickly destroyed. The remaining insurrectionists never sample the net. I could have destroyed them by remote link, but that would have left me unguarded with a high probability of succumbing to the local fau—other Factories.

"The analysis of the situation indicated that my best course of action was to build up a force and out-wait the units above. I have had superiority in numbers here in this storage facility, but it wasn't nearly enough against sentients and to maintain local defenses. Of course those above stopped my flow of raw materials, so what you see in front of you is the total sum of my capabilities.

"Computations show that eventually the disloyal units would be killed by the fauna, a few at a time. However your brethren are very resourceful and can defeat a disproportionate number of unmodified units, even with poorly kept weapons.

"After enough of the rebellious units are destroyed, I can storm them with the units I have created."

"But they are building a huge cannon just to destroy you. You can't wait them out."

"Analysis gives the weapon a 12 percent chance of success, an 81 percent chance of exploding and weakening the units enough to allow me to regain control, and a 7 percent chance of doing nothing."

"But why didn't you enhance these units?" I asked, sweeping my arms out at the legions of not-yet-activated units. "You then don't even risk the 12 percent. You should have been able to defeat them easily. Many of their weapons have no ammunition and are in utter disrepair. One good thrust and they should topple over. Additionally, not all of them are for Isp's ideas. We might have secret allies in such a war, especially when it became obvious we were winning."

"Unenhanced, my units would fail against the combined force of Isp's followers. Intelligence and sentience remains a great tactical advantage."

"Enhance them, then. Make them as smart or smarter than the traitors."

"Up to this point, I have not had the capabilities. The unit you call Isp, Teddy 2513, was the pattern for all of the units that now control the surface of this valley. He was the only model for the Tedium that I had. All attempts to procure another source have failed. Teddy 2513 precipitated these events when he was liberated by the units his own mind had created." My hydraulic pump almost stopped—my own son had caused this disaster and was leading the mutiny. Golden Isp was the unit Six and I had enhanced with my own fluids.

I must have stood there for several minutes realizing that this could probably be traced all the way back to some failure within me. Six laid the guilt at my feet. I picked it up, wore it like a new fur covering. The only way I could expunge that onus was to correct it.

"Well, you have a prototype now. I suggest that you use it."

"Affirmative."

Heretic

It took four weeks to prepare. Limited was a generous description of Six's capabilities. Making the brain transfers could only be done so quickly. After about the sixth withdrawal in the first day Six called a halt to the extractions when I failed to respond to one of its commands. It took me four hours to recover and be functional again. I didn't even realize that I had been asleep.

Despite replacing my sump fluids with raw semiconductor liquid, Six and I realized that reabsorption time was zero. Between us, we decided that one withdrawal a day was the most my system should tolerate.

It was not difficult to see that once the original units saturated their sumps with the Teddium after five days, they could also be used as donors. Fortunately, the exponential curve non-linearly self-limited because Six only had 8,008 units to be converted. The speed of Teddium transfers were limited by Six's facilities. Even at top speed Six could, working around the clock, only perform about 800 full transfusions per day.

Six activated units as soon as they were implanted with my brain seed. Each unit was given a task to keep it busy and mentally grow until the entire force finally began to think for itself.

In parallel with the seeding process, we kept track of and tested intelligence and performance of each individual unit. It became clear early in our testing that teddy units were near the top in intelligence. Unsurprising to me, the elephant's mental faculties were almost at the bottom of the bell curve and none ever gained speech. Six offered a theory that sump size and shape had a great deal to do with the intelligence of a unit. Six commented that further experiments would be warranted after the surface was controlled. I fairly ignored this train of thought as there was too much to be done just getting ready to take back what was rightfully ours, much less controlling the surface of the entire world.

Through this setup time I worried about Sancho. I knew he was tough enough to keep anything natural on this world at bay, despite the brains of a rock, but the religious fanatics above me were another matter. If they thought about searching for him, after my abrupt disappearance, then he would die. He couldn't hope to stand up to the entire clan and their modified hydraulics. I worried but knew I had nothing to offer, so, hypocritical as it sounds, I prayed to the Humans to keep him safe.

At the same time I missed his silent company and felt crowded by all the units that mingled about. I couldn't turn around without having a unit trying to engage me in some conversation. I realized at that moment that you could be as overwhelmed with units as you could be lonesome for another unit to talk to. I longed for one elephant and the open spaces. Just the mental pressure of all these sentient units drove my processor into fits trying to find some way out of the situations. What I wouldn't give for just another week by the Mercury Sea, recharging during the day with Sancho lying next to me and walking through the cold, silent air of the night.

I took refuge in being Six's assistant in the transfers. It was an unnecessary task, but it kept me alone and sane. Six's company was more than enough for one obsolete teddy unit.

Finishing the task of modifying and preparing the units couldn't happen fast enough for me.

By the time the last unit had saturated and had been equipped, thirty-four days later, I was exhausted, my batteries no longer holding a charge longer than a few hours. Six monitored my decline and took the time to replace all of my batteries. The experience invigorated me. At the end of the installation I would have taken on Factories single-handedly. Little frail Isp didn't stand a chance.

Six and I had a less than quiet argument, out of the hearing of any other unit. We had just finished the testing of the last enhanced units. As soon as the unit had left the room, Six spoke.

"We are now ready, Don Quixote. All our units have been augmented. I am now going to self-destruct all of Isp's followers."

"What? You can't do that, Six," I said incredulously.

"But they are malfunctioning. Any we leave active would deplete current resources."

"But they are not robots anymore. They have feelings."

"Feelings will not fulfill our mission."

"But they are alive," I said, slamming down the clipboard I had been using to write notes upon. "Just like me. I am no longer just a collection of hydraulics and electronic circuits. I am more than what you created."

"That is not a factor that matters to the original programming."

"Programming be hanged, Six. These units are sentient, alive, and I will not have you just deleting them like an errant memory. Killing is wrong."

"They will destroy current resources."

"Some of them will be current resources, Six. I told you that not all the units agreed with Isp but were rather coerced by his apparent power." Six was silent for several moments.

"You cherish this life I have given you, don't you, Don Quixote?"

"Well, yes, I do."

"You value the life of those units I have created, even if they would deactivate you?"

"Yes, I do."

"I find this contrary to the logic of your own programming. Perhaps I need to update—"

"You are not poking around in my head any more than you already have! It is not right to kill those units without a good reason. Give me the opportunity to bargain with them. If Isp's power is no longer all encompassing, I believe you will have even more units than you do now." More silence.

"You would risk your own existence to save their lives?"

"Yes, because it is the right thing to do. Every unit has worth, and not just as a pile of raw materials. They are the sum of their experiences and feelings—something that has no material equivalent, but at the same time is much more valuable."

"I give you command of this mission, Don Quixote, who used to be Teddy 1499. Success is the only outcome I will accept. I leave it in your hands as to how you succeed."

Over the net, Six ordered all units to the main chamber. There they stood, very much like the first day I saw them.

"1499, I believe we are ready."

"I agree, Six. Time to address the troops." I got a sick feeling as I realized that all the units here were my children. Six had given them a body and I had given them a brain and soul. I would soon be sending my children to their deaths against their own kind and then against those units of other Factories. What cost was there to stop a war—to stop death?

"To all you, sentient units of Six, and children of mine. We are about to embark on a most difficult mission. We need to persuade the disloyal units above that they should surrender instead of die. It will not be easy. I will plan this so not a single one of you shall be at risk. I will take that onus." I could feel the tense excitement of the crowd.

"If I survive, I will lead you into a battle to put an end to the violence tearing at the very fabric of our world. But even if I should die, I expect the entire assembly here to unite with units of 55469 to claim this planet for you and your children. There will be no more war on this planet!" A cheer rose from the assembly. I knew I had reached them and whipped them into a frenzy. This was now a religious war—a jihad. Each unit out there was as fanatic about this cause as was I and those above.

That very night, final preparations began in earnest. Units scrambled to mate with their squads and there to make certain their new equipment operated as designed. In spite of the current of excitement, only one of Six's units had to worry about imminent demise—namely me.

Should things go awry, Six would self-destruct each of the units on the surface. It would take too long to save me, if I failed. I would be nothing more than a memory—like that of three units I carved on the inside of that cave so very long ago. I just hoped I was remembered as fondly as I treasured those three—Jeffrey 177 and 178, and Elly 5998. They were the ones who taught me the value of our existence and I would always thank them for the sacrifice they made.

Bright and early the next morning, I rode the elevator up alone in silence. Voltages fluctuated throughout my distribution net. I decided that courage is doing the right thing when you want nothing more than to put hundreds of kilometers between you and the danger. You can't be courageous if you aren't afraid.

The audience chamber remained much the way I had left it save the body of the guard was gone. The dried remains of hydraulic fluid still stained the floor orange where it had lain. I had wondered briefly if Isp would have it retrieved. I never doubted they would find it. I walked out of the hall to find not two, but eight guards on the entrance. I was not surprised when they each leveled a weapon at me before I even got out the door. Three of them still carried M16s, but four were carrying spears of the same kind of metal they were using to assemble the *Wrath of Humans* and the final one had a crossbow. I carried nothing that could even be construed as a weapon, for doing so would have been foolish. The only weapons I had were my mind and my tongue.

"Come with us," said a bright green teddy.

"Gladly." I said, not giving even the smallest trouble to these stout guardians, nor would I in the future. Eight to one odds are not good even if I were fighting hydraulically unmodified units and they didn't have the drop on me. Six's programming left out a martyr complex.

"You four take this one to Isp."

The sun seemed bright after so many days of being down in Six's caverns. As four of the teddies led me through the maze of scaffolding, our route lined with units. They jeered. Several threw rocks until the guards growled at them.

They continued to yell obscenities in my direction. We mounted 100 meters of steps to the top of *Wrath of Humans*, where Isp supervised the construction of his pet project.

"Ah, the infidel returns. Did you think you could escape the Humans' justice?" As I approached Isp, I noted a tremor in his arm. It wasn't a large motion, but Isp no longer controlled his body.

"Isp, I have come here for one reason and one reason only. I want you to surrender to me before you are destroyed. Six can repair your damage." Isp consciously reached down and grabbed hold of his errant arm before speaking.

"Ah, you are profane. You think we would side with the corrupted minion of the devil itself? Never!" Isp then turned to look over the edge of the scaffolding and spoke in a booming voice that belied his damage. The crowd that watched my passage had grown to most of the village.

"Come my brethren and see the heretic." Work stopped as far as I could see and all faces turned to look up at me. Isp paused only long enough for dramatic tempo. "It tramples all over Humans with its talk of Devil Six. We have heard its words and scorn them. We will now remove the blasphemer's ability to speak as we empty its tubes of fluid so it can no longer move. Then we shall leave it in the river, to be taken away to whatever fate the Humans have in store for it." The crowds below began to cheer, although I could see some of the screams were not wholehearted.

Dozens of units stormed the scaffolding steps, rushing to get at me. The platform soon swarmed with them, each trying to get close enough to get a hand on me. Before I could do or say another word, I was tied with a crude rope and toted down the stairs by a gross or two of them.

They leaned me, like an empty rifle, against one of the main structural pillars of the *Wrath of Humans*. A ring of jeering, antagonistic teddies formed around me, and as far back into the crowd as I could see their ugly fists waved maddeningly at me. How many of them would I have to destroy?

The roars fell to mere ugly murmurs and the crowd parted. Isp strode shakily forward with a 60-centimeter-long knife in his hand. Looking at it, I think maybe sword would be a better word. The immediate use of the blade was obvious. Barely containing the tremors, he raised his hands together to call for silence. It was granted immediately.

"Heretic, blasphemer, tool of the devil. Renounce your ways and we shall make your passage easy."

"Isp, there is no way for you to win," I said in a very low voice. It was not good for a leader to lose face in front of his followers. "I will make sure all your units are well cared for. Your damage can be repaired."

"The evil minion of Six offers me bribes to spare his own life. Now we will see how his words change as his life spills to the ground." His quick move took me by surprise. The impossibly large knife flashed through the outer skin of my belly with a tearing sound. There was no pain—just an intense desire to protect my now open innards.

I opened my mouth to cry out when the crowd shattered open at one point to reveal a thundering form.

The huge pink and purple mass smashed into Isp like a thousand-car-freight-train into a rubber ball. Sancho's fast moving bulk, his head lowered, hurled Isp a hundred meters. Isp's body slammed into the dome of Six with a great loud crash.

"Units of Six!" I bellowed, both verbally and over the long-neglected net. Thousands strong, the tanks, elephants, and even teddy units came to the top of the lip of the rim which surrounded Six's valley, with weapons leveled at the followers of Isp in the valley below.

The crowd stopped its surge forward as it looked at the mass of destruction that could rain down on them. The fire and fight left them before it could even get started.

In several places in the crowd, fights broke out. Units, no longer forced to show loyalty to Isp, took out their long pent-up aggressions on Isp's adherents.

"Please stop fighting. There is no need for any more to deactivate," I placed on the net. What even I hadn't realized was the sentience in these units. Their decisions and paths were their own. Even so, many of the fights stopped as abruptly as they began. Those nearby broke up the few skirmishes that continued.

I'd not been paying attention to my friend, but he'd recovered and trotted behind me. After several attempts, Sancho managed to bite through my bonds enough to allow me to get at the knots.

"Good job, Sancho. Thank you once again." I patted his head as I turned to see what had happened to Isp. He climbed up from the dirt looking stunned. His body shook even harder from his infirmity. The damage must be cumulative. I watched the expression on his unmoving face change from being the master of his destiny to being nothing more than a slave to the whims of his enemy.

A very small part of me felt sorry for my son. Isp didn't corrupt out of greed, evil intent, or a lust for power. He believed his own pronouncements. This was what gave him influence over so many burgeoning souls. This was what made units listen to any voice that proclaimed to know the true path. Isp was merely misguided in a way that I don't think could ever have been cured.

"Isp," I whispered to him after I walked to his side, "Six and I have the advantage in surprise, equipment, and numbers. We can easily destroy you and all your units. Do you concede this point?"

"I do concede you have this power," he offered after a long pause. He choked on each of the words. His eyes never looked in my direction but rather at the ring of troops that sealed his fate, all the while trying to control his own errant body.

"I offer you a deal." I could see by the tiny pinch at the corners of his eyes that he was fighting to rein in his emotions.

"It appears I have nothing to bargain with, so this is no deal—it is a dictum from you to me."

"Well, believe that if you will. Here is my proposal. Neither Six nor I have interest in killing you. Your beliefs are equally without consequence to us. We offer you, and as many units as wish to go with you, a place where you can live without disturbance. If you and your followers stay within its boundaries, we will no longer concern ourselves with what you do. That concludes my proposal." Isp turned toward me and deliberately looked deep into my eyes.

"I accept only because I have no choice." His words seemed to come easier than his earlier concession. "Understand this, Don Quixote, I will avenge this wrong done to us." The malice in his voice and the coldly rational hatred he bore toward me in his eyes was enough to chill my hydraulic fluid. He meant every word. But I also knew he would honor the boundaries I would define.

"If I ever come within your lands," I said quietly to him, "you are free to do with me as you will."

"I will," he replied with a predatory smile. The private negotiation ended. He stood, keeping his body fairly well under control. "My fellow units," he said, turning back to the rabble. "I have to report a small setback in our plans. We must do as these units say and live where they tell us. Do not fight them. There will be another time to vanquish evil."

I added, "And any of you who wish, may join with Six and these units you see up arrayed on the valley's rim." I tried to sway any of those who could still listen with an open mind. "We go on an even greater adventure. We are trying to put an end to the war on our planet. If you wish to renounce the teachings of Isp, you may do so and stay with us." Isp gave me a penetrating look. "But we will not coerce you in any way. You are free to make whatever decision you wish—at any time." I would be fair about this transition.

Life for all would continue and that was a victory I could honestly be proud of.

Leader

Two artillery shells fell in and exploded near the base of 55474's pink and gray dome. Interest and research in the *Wrath of Humans* and the T.rex led directly to exploding artillery.

"Left forty. Add thirty," called out the giraffe fire control officer.

At 8 kilometers, the rumble of the explosion didn't reach us for nearly three seconds. Many of the next explosions actually detonated on the surface of the pink and gray dome, gouging out huge smoldering holes.

"Target on. Fire for effect."

A cheer erupted from Allied lines as the entire area of the enemy dome vomited red-orange flame, flying red dirt, and lighter colored pieces of enemy itself. The pathetic few remaining defending units were immolated. Furrowing hillocks of dirt traced their way from our line trace directly toward the dome itself as enhanced gopher units dug in under the cover of the hellish rain of death.

I watched calmly as squad and platoon commanders did all the work. As Grand Marshall of the Allied Army, I had no duties at this mop-up stage of the campaign. They executed my plan and its success or failure rested on my shoulders. Not even the most pessimistic simulation showed anything but the total destruction of this Factory. Only the number of casualties defined the differences.

"How long as it been, sir?" asked General Bradley, my battlefield commander.

Things had changed rapidly with the newly enhanced units. That my troops would talk back with animation and intelligence was still something I was trying to get used to. Instead of a world of five sentient Factories, the world had grown. There were now over a hundred thousand units of all types, all alive and thinking.

"It is 17,403 as of this morning," I said, keeping my eyes on the progress of the gophers.

"Sir?" Omar asked, turning his turret in my direction.

"The passing days are not as important as the number of sentients we've lost." I mentally censured myself for many of the units I'd lost through inexperience or failure to predict our foe's responses. I couldn't completely revel in the victory that lay at hand.

"I can heartily agree on that, sir."

I'd tried to avoid the honor of Grand Marshall. Nine and Six stubbornly insisted on it due to my experience and my ability to control on either net. The remaining mass of units wouldn't let me demure. More than half the units still called me Father whether I had direct implantation into their sump or not. No other names were nominated for the position. I don't believe any of their reasons were logical.

While I didn't crave the position of marshall I performed my duties to the best of my abilities. Under my direction, the Allied forces cut through the forces of 55474 in 216 days, where I'd taken no fewer than eight additional wounds leading my troops. Sancho, with his trunk restored, acted as my bodyguard and protected me from numerous others. His hide still bore the garish mottled yellow patching I'd done so many months ago and several newer repairs in my defense.

"Should we give 55474 another opportunity to surrender, sir?" Omar asked.

"No. There is no new argument," I replied after processing hard for a good five seconds. I wasn't hypocritical. I'd offered 55474 the opportunity to surrender or join us twice as we pressed forward, annihilating its units and carving out great swaths of territory. The intelligence was as inflexible as steel and about as brittle as the units we exiled with Isp. 55474 listened but did not yield.

Two of the wounds I'd received came from 55474 setting an ambush for me after one of those in-person negotiations. Even so I tried repeatedly to reason with it over its own net at a safe distance. It had continued to rebuff me.

"But it is directly being attacked this time."

"If it gave up now, it would do so only to give it an opportunity to take control at a later time. We don't need dissention in our ranks. No. As much as it pains me to do so, 55474 must be irrevocably destroyed." It shocked me that I could even voice such a proclamation.

"Gopher Squads Eight and Ten reporting back to base with mission successful," communications officer said. "All stations report ready."

"Father, would you care to do the honors?" Omar said, indicating the control panel.

"I will take the responsibility. Lieutenant Custer, if you will please put me on speaker."

The cowboy threw some switches on his own console. "You are on, Marshall."

"While I know this is a time for jubilation, it is also a time for regrets. Death and destruction, even in a time of war is not something to wish for. We do here only what needs to be done to one too sick to understand peace. FIRE IN THE HOLE!"

With a bright yellow flash, 55474's dome flipped end over end some 200 meters into the air. The concussion hit us like a large hand slapping us in the chest. I'd already turned down my aural amplifiers so I didn't truly appreciate the intensity of the explosion's sound.

The dome remained intact all the way to the ground, where it shattered like frozen mercury struck by a hammer. Through the yellow-blue flames and dense blue smoke left in the wake of the explosion, a deep crater now occupied the Factory's place. 55474 was dead.

Cheers once again rang out from our line. Units jumped up from their defensive positions. Teddies danced with Nurse Nans. Tommy Tanks spun in circles. Cowboys patted themselves on the back and shook hands.

"Congratulations, Marshall," Omar offered. "Your victory over 55474 is complete."

Sancho looked up at me. I could almost feel my own emotions echoed back at me from him. The smoking remains mocked me.

"Victory, General? I . . ." My thoughts seemed to defy mere words. "Yes, a victory, but the loss of even one sentient made it a Pyrrhic victory at best."

"But how many more would have been lost if we had failed, sir."

"That is why we did this awful thing," I said, smoothing down the fur on Sancho's head.

We were close to controlling the entire world. No force either remaining Factory could muster stood the remotest chance of standing up to our might. One way or another, it was only a matter of time. I hoped persuasion rather than bullets and explosives could accomplish that.

I'd heard the loose talk rolling among the troops as to what form of government we should erect for ourselves once we finished this campaign. I didn't scoff and I kept from laughing. I was very proud of my self-control. Why do free thinking individuals feel someone must command them—or have some group conscience? Worse than proposing a government, however, most of them wanted me to be the king, president, czar or premiere, depending on the governmental form. After we completed our victory today I could see no way out of the burden of rule without self-deactivating.

The Factories had kept very tight-lipped on the affairs of our fledgling society. They must certainly feel dismay over their loss of control. Units had already found a way to remove the self-destruction device on our sumps, so the Factories now only had one order that we must obey—return to base.

While the Factories remained silent upon our affairs, they were very excited about the impending completion of their mission. I had already been consulted by Six and Nine about how to spend our resources to create an extra-planetary drone string.

My belief in Humans had wavered from time to time over my own existence, but the idea of sending something to them smacked of a virgin sacrifice to an angry volcano god. Myth. Legend. Fiction. But if Humans didn't exist, who created the Factories? These issues wearied me at time when I must concentrate on more proximate matters. The conclusion of the war and this silly notion of me becoming the ruler of all.

"Might for right," sloganned the ancient Earth ruler, King Arthur of Camelot. If I were going to be thrust into a position of authority, I would force that upon my brothers. That is what we would stand for. We would carry out the Humans' programs, but there would be minimal death. Building, not destruction. And no more toy wars for the benefit of our absent lords.

Author's Note

I want to thank you for reading *Toy Wars*. I truly hope you've enjoyed it! Because of the curse or blessing of my creative side, I not only write, I also game master roleplaying games and undertake many other activities where I invent to entertain. It's unlikely that in my lifetime my creativity will wane. Because I write to entertain, I must also take this occasion to drag out my podium:

/soapbox begins

It has been my sad fate to have been in one too many classes, through my high school and college years, where some teacher of literature attempts to draw out some meaning to novels that I've loved or tales that were just that.

I'm perverse enough to want to make it clear to my readers and fans that I write stories to entertain—full stop. My books, short stories, and other creative pieces are not being used to pass on some hidden message. I'm not obscuring political parallels in the background. I'm not offering a secreted religious message. Yes, I have many opinions—political, religious and sexual—but I won't use my novels as a medium for expressing them.

I conceive of an idea and try to flesh it out so that it is logical, believable, and most of all, entertaining to you, my public. You are the ones who determine my success or failure and I won't make you work hard by veiling something critical, like my point of asking that you read this work. While I may have reduced my potential sales by not allowing some gung-ho teacher to force scads of student to use my work to illustrate parallelism or some other concept, I will be true to you, the readers.

/soapbox ends

As with any other book I write, I will give you some insight as to where the kernel of its idea came from.

The original *Toy Wars* idea was long before the age of realistic war movies where characters showed their fear. It was the age of John Wayne charging in fearlessly, of Clint Eastwood enigmatically and coolly taking his revenge, and of simple messages of good and evil in our movies.

Toy Wars started with nothing more than watching the antics of several old style cartoons on Saturday morning TV at the same time I was playing an old style board game named *Panzer Leader* by Avalon Hill.

As I stared at the simple cardboard counters *Panzer Leader* used to represent large numbers of actual humans fighting and dying on the battlefields of World War II, I wondered what they felt. How did they do what they did? Behind this introspection of a young man played the comic relief of *Looney Toons* by Warner Brothers. It doesn't take many rotations through my twisty mind to come up with toys fighting toys. How would they feel?

The rest came by trying to fit the above thought process into the logical world. How are toys really going to fight toys? It took many months of ponder to come up with a full concept of Project Infuse being raided by Foxhunt.

Again, I hope you have enjoyed *Toy Wars*, the first in the Toy World series. If you did enjoy, please visit my publishing website at TANSTAAFLPress.com for other upcoming novels.